– EARLY READER REVIEWS –

'Ominous, slick and unnerving'

'Riveting'

'The ending had me page turning like a woman possessed... I am usually pretty spot on at working out what is going on, but not this time'

'Excellent'

'This is a brilliantly written book and I couldn't wait another day to see the end... a fascinating psychological thriller that I would highly recommend to anyone'

'An excellent thriller... five stars'

'Genuinely gripping... this is a definite page-turner'

'I thoroughly enjoyed this book'

'Put some time away for this book... a terrific psychological thriller with lots of lies, deception, tragedy and twists'

'Fantastic'

'A thriller full of twists and turns, secrets and lies'

'What an amazing book. Loved it from beginning to end'

'An exceptional read... I was sucked in from the very beginning'

'A solid five star psychological thriller about obsession and friendship'

'Full of twists and turns... completely spell-binding and addictive. The writing style is fabulous, the characters are all intriguing and interesting and the plot will keep you guessing and racing through to find out all the answers'

'An intense thriller about friendship and jealousy'

'It had me gripped from the beginning to the end... full of suspense and twists'

THE GOOD FRIEND

JO BALDWIN

RedDoor

Published by RedDoor
www.reddoorpublishing.com

© 2019 Jo Baldwin

The right of Jo Baldwin to be identified as author of this Work has been asserted by her in accordance with sections 77 and 78 of the Copyright, Designs and Patents Act 1988

ISBN 978-1-910453-66-7

A CIP catalogue record for this book is available from the British Library

Cover design: Clare Connie Shepherd
www.clareconnieshepherd.com

Typeset by Fuzzy Flamingo
www.fuzzyflamingo.co.uk

Printed and bound in Denmark by Nørhaven

For my four Kenchies

– CHAPTER 1 –

June 2013. Gare de Lyon, Paris

A shoal of colour darts to and fro, weaves in and out. People pressed for time. Pushing, pulling, like the ebb and flow of a tide. Among them a young couple, laden with luggage, grasp hold of two small children, faces tense as they try to locate their train. On the platform, the guard peers at his watch, taps it three times and raises a whistle to his mouth. He catches sight of the family and hesitates, his pointed nose and chin jerking up and down like a grub-hungry woodpecker. He points them towards their carriage, slams the door shut behind them and blows on his whistle.

Inside the carriage, the mother babbles away in Gallic relief and points her children towards four reserved seats while the father takes on the task of rearranging the near-full luggage rack to accommodate two big bags. Triumphant, he rejoins his family, his sweaty sandals squeaking through the carriage like mice.

My gaze drops. I am aware that I have been staring at strangers for too long, have been seduced by this new tableau of togetherness. However, it is not mine to share. A wave of loneliness washes over me, but I force it away and turn back to look out of the window, towards the station's canvas of bustling anonymity.

The train starts to advance forward, tentative at first like a toddler's first steps, then gradually gathers momentum as it grows in confidence. A murmur of calm descends over the carriage. Soon we reach the edge of the city and move into the suburbs, where the scenery changes. Modern tower blocks stand tall and foreboding. Lines of brightly coloured clothing hang like forgotten bunting from balconies. A bright-blue sky forms the backdrop to a toy town of rooftops, service stations and out-of-town shopping centres.

We scoot through a tunnel. A ghostly white face blinks back at me from the darkness and it takes me a moment to realise I'm staring at myself. I pinch the bare flesh on the back of my thigh. *Stay strong. You've got to do this. Finish what you've started.* Something my mother advised me to do when I was introduced to a new routine: a new term at school or having to read out loud in class.

'If you pinch yourself, it will hurt, but only a little. Just focus on the pain and you'll forget about the rest.'

I close my eyes and picture her gentle face. If only she were here now.

As the train nudges through a trajectory of silent landscapes, I catch sight of a meandering river making its own journey south alongside my own. Its presence provides comfort, in the same way that a flock of wild geese might for someone out hiking alone in the wilderness.

The wilderness. That's where I feel I am right now: in an emotional wilderness. I know that I have to draw on my full mental strength in order to see this through. And I will. I have to. There's no going back.

***

The train jerks forward, jostles me awake and throws my pillow – a rolled-up cardigan – to the floor. My head is thumping. I reach above me to try and twist some cold air into my face, but the aircon's already on maximum. Where's the refreshments trolley when you need it? I lean over the empty seat next to me to check down the gangway but apart from the odd foot tapping up and down, it's empty. The rows of heads remind me of bottles in crates, all chinking along to the same gentle rhythm. That old Police song 'Message in a Bottle' jumps into my head and I wonder what message each of us is taking to our destination – a marriage proposal perhaps, or some sad news? I haven't decided what my message is going to be. A lot will depend on the answers to the questions I need to ask first.

The song carries me back to that summer when Kath and I, bored with the monotonous day-to-day of living in the Somerset countryside, took ourselves to the river with a bagful of empty glass bottles we'd found at the local tip. We decided that if we were going to change the course of our destinies, we needed to get to work straightaway. So, perched on the riverbank, we wrote a heap of SOS messages, with our names and addresses printed on each, making an appeal for someone to come and rescue us from our life of drudgery and hardship, which of course wasn't the case, but like any pre-pubescent teenager we liked to live in a semi-imaginary world of swashbuckling pirates, armour-clad knights and ermine-cloaked princes. In ceremonious style, we dropped the bottles one by one into the fast-flowing river, ran along the bank, watching them bob up and down in the rippling ribbons of water, until they disappeared out of sight.

Three years later, Tom knocked on my door, a sludgy bottle in his hand, my message in the other, and changed my world forever.

The pain still lies deep within me. I've learnt to manage it over the years, but today it feels stronger, throbbing like a toothache, yet in the pit of my stomach. Without thinking, I reach out to sketch a heart and arrow on the breath-misted window. I'm poised to fill it with initials, when my companion opposite moves in her seat to cross her legs.

'*Pardon!*' she murmurs, as one high-heeled foot brushes my calf. She glances at my artwork and smiles in conspiratorial recognition.

Quickly, I wipe it away and pick up my magazine to cover my pink embarrassment. *You're not supposed to look back. Only forward. The future. Remember?*

The train continues to hum and whistle its way forward, speeding intermittently through long narrow tunnels. The sky gradually empties of sun-bursting clouds the further south we go, becoming silver-grey. My eyes follow a carpet of tufted green into the distance. A lone caravan sits in a field, a battered old car parked alongside it. Perhaps an elderly couple live there, penniless but filled with love and laughter watching a game show on their small TV; or a lonesome man of the south who's travelled north for work, sitting behind a pile of empty beer cans, staring at nothing and missing his wife and children; or perhaps it's a large family squeezed into the tiny living space like sardines in a tin, arguing and goading each other, until one of them jumps up and leaves, slamming the door shut, never to return. Alone for the first time, like me. Each and every one of us is cocooned in a separate bubble. We bounce along in our own worlds, sometimes colliding, but rarely stopping to look around until our bubble bursts and we are alone. And only then do we notice copies of ourselves everywhere.

'*Désirez-vous boire ou manger quelque chose, Mademoiselle?*'

An efficient-looking woman wearing a dark-blue dress nods at me from behind her refreshments trolley. Stumbling over my limited French, I point at a bottle of still water. Her nimble fingers count out the change in my outstretched palm.

'*Merci.*' I unscrew the lid and stretch out more freely across the unoccupied seat next to me, briefly catching the eye of the French woman opposite. She leans across the table that separates us.

'Excuse me, but do I know you? Somehow you look familiar.' Her English is fluent with the faintest accent.

'No, I don't think so.' I shrug my shoulders stiffly. 'This is only my second time in France.'

She shakes her head in a puzzled manner. '*Excusez-moi*, I am mistaken. It must be that you look like someone I know.'

She is striking, probably in her early fifties, immaculate in a pinstripe suit, with brown, glossy hair pulled back into a neat chignon. Her red lipstick stands out against her olive skin.

'No worries. It happens to me a lot.' I bury my face in my magazine once more.

'*Billets, s'il vous plaît!*'

Now what? Passengers are reaching for their tickets. The inspector moves slowly down the carriage, the impatient clip-clip of his ticket punch heralding his arrival. *But where is my ticket?* I was holding it when I sat down. My hands rummage deep in my bag, the punching sound gets closer. The woman is watching me. I reach for my coat on the shelf above, but the pockets contain nothing but a lipstick-smeared tissue. Now frantic, I can feel my face reddening. The inspector stands waiting patiently, tacitly refusing to offer support or assistance. He reminds me of my father.

'Excuse me, *Mademoiselle*, but I think this is your passport, *n'est-ce pas*?'

The woman bends down and retrieves the burgundy booklet from under the table. It's open on the page that shows my identity photo. I spot the ticket squeezed between the pages as she passes it to me.

'*Merci.*'

I hastily pass the ticket to the inspector, who clips it before moving on.

'Ah, so it is you!' The woman still holds my passport and looks openly at my details. I take it from her and push it away into my bag.

'I know you now – *la fille en or* – the golden girl of the swimming pool.' She claps her hands, delighted by her discovery.

'Please, don't speak too loudly. I have come for a quiet break, for some time alone.' I look around to check no one has heard or understood. Fortunately, the man next to her has been asleep since Paris.

'Of course. But don't worry. I don't think French people will recognise you. I do because I was in London last year when you won your medals. Those images of your father crying because you'd just won gold. So moving.'

A snort threatens to burst out of my nostrils. I feign a

cough and put my hand over my mouth. What she doesn't realise is that he was crying because I hadn't broken the world record.

I need to be alone, to refocus. *Don't ask me about myself or you'll draw a blank.* That's how I've managed to survive all of these years.

'Excuse me.'

Abruptly I get up and walk to the space between the carriages. Here it feels less oppressive. The gentle rattling is reassuring and confirms that I am moving forward. South. Towards the sun. Isn't that where people always head when they're looking for a better life? I look out at the moving countryside but can't shake away the image of my father's face, staring back at me.

***

'What do you mean you're going back to the UK? Your home is here in Perth now. What about me? What about Scott? All the time we've dedicated to your success.'

My father moved around Aunt Muriel's dusty backyard like a boxer, high on his toes. His face was puffy and red. He jabbed at the air in frustration.

'That's the problem, Dad. It's always been about you. What about *me*?' He tried to say something but I raised my hand to cut him off. 'Listen, I need to get away. I'm burnt out. I haven't had a break from this in eight years. Just give me some time please.'

Last time I caved in to him and I've lived to regret it ever since, so I knew I had to stay calm and strong for my own sake but never had I seen my father work himself up into such a state before. He spluttered saliva as he spoke

– as he yelled. There was even a whole chain of expletives.

'You're not going back home to look up that ex-boyfriend, are you?'

'If you mean Tom, no, of course I'm not.' I tried to remain passive, my arms at my sides with fingers crossed for comfort.

My father gave me a pointed look. He moved away towards the house. I thought that was it, but he swung round and lashed at the air, his face now contorted into a sneer. 'Good thing I listened to that friend of yours and moved us out here. She had her head screwed on. Knew what was what. Enlightened me about a few things.'

'What do you mean by that, Dad? What did Kath say?'

I reached for his arm but my father shrugged it off and refused to answer. So I let it go. Maybe he was regretting his words already. I needed time to reflect, to revisit the past in my head and work out what he meant. The sooner I got away from him the better.

At that point in the argument Scott had arrived. He took in the situation, pulled my father to one side and tried to reason with him. For my sake.

'Let her go just for a while – a couple of weeks for Jenny to think things through.'

I felt such relief – finally it was over between us. My father nodded. He looked at me, so exasperated that his eyebrows seemed to be touching in the middle. His remark about Kath, though, was assuming centre-stage in my thoughts. What had Kath really said to my father? What had she enlightened him about?

***

The woman looks up from her laptop when I return to my seat, closes the lid and smiles. She holds out a small, rectangular box. Inside are a dozen or so brightly coloured macaroons nestled in tissue paper. Thanking her, I select what I hope is pistachio. The smooth shell crumbles as soon as it enters my mouth and the subtle nutty flavour gently dissolves on my tongue.

Slowly, I start to unwind. We chat about my stay in Paris and the sites I visited in three days: the Musée d'Orsay (her favourite place in the city), the Eiffel Tower, the Père Lachaise Cemetery and more. However, I don't tell her about the blisters on my feet from my night-time walks along the banks of the Seine, the bridges I stood on for several hours, staring down at the grey, unforgiving water and wondering if I'd made the right decision to come to France. She tells me she is returning home to Provence from Paris, where she works during the week as a lawyer.

'And what about you? May I call you Jenny?'

I nod. Now it doesn't seem so bad to have been recognised by this stranger. If anything, it's good to be taken away from my worries.

'So, where are you going next, Jenny?'

Gripping my water bottle, I glance out of the window to take a moment, struggling to release memories that have been hidden away for so long.

'I'm visiting a childhood friend. She lives in the Languedoc.' My voice stammers over the last word. I'm not even sure how to pronounce it.

'She is married to a Frenchman?'

'No, he's British. They moved out here a couple of years ago.' A shudder threatens to break out of me, so I hold it in by tensing my spine. It doesn't go unnoticed. The woman – Florence, I think she said – moves forward, with a look of concern. I can tell that she wants to reach out and touch my hand, so I quickly pull it back to avoid any contact. I don't need sympathy. I have to stay strong.

Fortunately, I'm saved by the train's horn heralding its arrival at a station an hour or so north-east of my own destination. Florence retreats and starts to get her things together. The sleeping man next to her opens his eyes, blinks twice, checks the time on his wristwatch, reaches for his raincoat and briefcase and, in true White Rabbit style, gets up and hurries down the carriage without so much as a glance at either of us. Florence shrugs and laughs.

'So, little golden girl, it was very nice to talk to you.'

I shake her outstretched hand.

'The Languedoc is very beautiful. Enjoy. And you must visit the lavender harvest in Provence, if you can. It's glorious.'

I watch her walk away and a small feeling of regret spreads through me. I realise I felt drawn towards this woman who exuded a mix of both strength and concern, traits that my mother and my old neighbour Mrs Holt embodied. How I miss them both.

Florence passes a tortoiseshell cat, which sits cleaning itself on the platform, nonchalantly licking its paws before pushing them behind each ear. Mrs Holt lived around the corner from us and was a great source of comfort to me after the untimely death of my mother from cancer. She took in a host of stray cats over the years, and that's probably how she saw me – a stray – or rather a heartbroken child sitting on her wall, hoping to be invited in for some maternal comfort. Her death, only a few years after my mother's, cut deep. I couldn't understand how two people that I cared about could be taken from me in such a short space of time. I remember telling Kath that I was a hoodoo and she'd be better off avoiding me. Kath convinced me that it was just bad luck and no one's fault.

'You and I can stick together and ward off any evil spirits,' she'd said. 'Friendship is the most powerful spell of all.'

Now I wonder if that's true. Ours is just about to be put to the test.

– CHAPTER 2 –

The platform is deserted. That's my first thought when I arrive at my destination and lean out of the window to open the carriage door. My second is that the air is different here. There's a strong scent of something sweet – a herb – basil or mint perhaps. Maybe from hanging baskets or the countryside beyond the train station. My stomach rumbles as I hoist my rucksack onto my back and walk towards the exit. A dishevelled guard who looks as though he's been dozing rushes past me to shut my door properly and blow the whistle for the train to depart. There's no sign of Kath in the near-empty car park out front, so I return to buy a croissant from the small kiosk. It's stale but I don't care. I push the entire pastry into my mouth and chew on it slowly, enjoying the fact that no one is paying any attention to me. My father disapproved if I rushed my food and liked to draw attention to it in company. If he could see me now, he wouldn't be impressed. My small act of rebellion brings a smile to my face.

I take my pack outside and sit on it in the shade, wondering if, true to form, Kath will be very late. The number of times I had to cover up for her at school when she missed the register. Two teenage boys, wearing only shorts and trainers, kick a ball around in the car park. Their tanned, skinny bodies gleam like polished oak as they take it in turns to gracefully kick the ball into the motionless air.

Kath and I used to go and watch the boys in the year above us play football after school – until the incident with Mr Brown put a stop to it. That day, we were sitting on the railings sharing a hotdog from the chip van. One of the players caught Kath's eye and she boldly shouted out to him – something about his nice legs. After the match, the referee, our PE teacher Mr Brown, came over to tick us off for putting off his players. Kath smiled graciously at him and apologised. He nodded curtly and went into the changing rooms. Kath disappeared for a few minutes. I assumed she'd gone to pee in the bushes, which she sometimes did, and it wasn't until later that I realised what she'd been up to. We'd gone back to her house to watch some TV, when there was a knock at her front door. No one was in except the two of us. Kath threw me a look, which told me she knew who our visitor was. Mr Brown did not look happy when she opened the door to him. Someone had scratched the word 'faggot' on the door of his green vintage Morris Minor and he wanted to know if we had seen anything. Kath didn't bat an eyelid as she denied all knowledge. After he'd gone, Kath showed me her house key with the flakes of green paint still clinging to it. I was mortified that she'd made me complicit in her crime.

'If you ever do that again, Kath, you can find yourself another best friend,' I told her. It took a lot to make me angry and she knew it.

'Oh come on, Jenny, it was just a laugh. Sometimes you can be such a moral do-gooder.'

13

Car tyres crunch over gravel, like corn popping in a saucepan. My stomach leaps upwards. She's sure to have changed after all this time, but how different will Kath be? As I stand up to check if the small truck pulling into the car park is hers, the afternoon sunshine glares into my eyes.

'Jenny, you look great!' The truck door slams shut.

Still expecting the chubby eighteen-year-old I remember from eight years ago, I'm stunned to find a petite woman with short dark hair coming towards me, casually dressed in cropped combats and a close-fitting T-shirt. We hug, and a moment later we're like dancing figures turning round and round on top of a music box, our arms entwined. I pull back to scrutinise my childhood friend. She looks good. Her skin is lightly tanned and radiates a healthy glow. Her features are the same: the pale mouth with the thin top lip and pouty bottom lip. The long, slender nose, with larger-than-average nostrils. The high chiselled cheekbones and those dark eyes, which give nothing away.

'You look amazing, Kath. This French lifestyle obviously suits you.'

She puts a hand to her hair. I register that the ringlets I remember are gone.

'It's great, but hard work,' she says, and I wonder what she means. 'How was the train journey?'

'Good. I met a nice woman called Florence – a lawyer. She shared her macaroons with me.'

She picks up my pack. 'Oh Jenny, you haven't changed at all, have you? Still drawn to lonely women.'

My shoulders tense, but I let the comment pass. 'How far are you from here, Kath?'

'Half an hour or so. We're in the middle of nowhere. Who'd have imagined that I'd be happy to live in the sticks again?' She laughs and throws my pack onto the back seat.

Soon we're on our way and I sit back and try to relax as Kath weaves in and out of the dual carriageway without indicating. How I loved watching her when she played for the school hockey team. She'd bulldoze up and down the muddy field, head down, ruthlessly knocking the opposing team aside before cracking her stick to the ball and sending it flying into the corner of the net. She was the best player we had. But then, around the same time that I met Tom, she dropped hockey, for no reason except to say she'd had enough and preferred to support me at my swimming galas instead. As she chatters away merrily, I feel a renewed warmth for the schooldays we shared together, and realise how lonely I've been in Australia with no close female friend to confide in. She tells me about her reasons for moving to France two years ago. Just before I left the UK, she'd enrolled on a catering course at the local college. Then she got a job in one of Bristol's prestigious hotels.

'The irregular hotel hours got to me after a few years. I was at the end of my tether. Then one day a guest left behind a magazine about property in France. I started flicking through it and realised that with my catering qualifications and experience, there was an opportunity for us here. A business, good weather and hopefully a better quality of life.'

They found an old farmhouse, situated in the littoral, the low-lying area between the Black Mountain – la Montagne Noire – and the coast.

15

'It was all we could afford and after all the conversion work is complete, we'll be up to our eyes in debt.' She rolls her eyes at me and puckers her lips. That comical expression is one I remember well. 'What about you, Jenny? Are you serious about retiring? I couldn't believe it when I got your email out of the blue. Why would you want to give up on your success?' She shakes her head incredulously.

I shrug and look out at the flat scenery stretching out on either side of us. 'I'm burnt out, Kath. I'm thinking about doing a Masters in sports management. There's a couple of programmes in the UK that start in the autumn. I haven't told my father yet, mind you.'

'Good luck with that! And what about your love life? Is that Aussie guy still around?'

'Scott? Yes.'

'So why isn't he here, with you? The invite was for both of you.'

'I know that, but he's too busy coaching.'

'Is he like Tom?'

I grip the door handle tightly.

'I mean does he look like Tom?' she presses me.

'Not at all. The complete opposite in fact. Bondi Beach-blond, tanned and muscular.'

She glances quickly at me and laughs. 'Yes, well, Tom was always one of a kind looks-wise wasn't he, with all that long hair hanging over his eyes?'

Before I can respond, the car jerks sharply as we pull off the main road and join up with a smaller country road. Vines dominate the scenery. Row after row of tufted green-leaved bushes line up in fields of bright-orange soil. Each vine stands upright on a thin, twisted branch. They look like pink flamingos gathered at a watering hole.

Streaks of poppies shimmer along the edge of the fields. Kath points out the tiny white stone huts dotted around.

'Shepherd shelters,' she explains. 'Originally built as an easy way of clearing a field of its stones.'

'So when do your first guests arrive?'

'In roughly three weeks. And there's still so much to do. Mainly to the garden.'

We turn off onto a small track and Kath points out *La Miellerie*, the nearby honey farm and vineyard where she works part-time. The farm's main building is a *maison de maître*, the former manor house in the village, which is hidden away behind a tall wrought-iron gate.

'Bernard and Sylvie run the farm. They're lovely. Middle-aged, but very lively. Always holding parties to celebrate one thing or another. They've just got a deal to sell their royal jelly to a skincare firm so we're all very excited about that.'

A blanket of shade envelops us as we climb a narrow lane with tall cypress trees on either side. After several minutes Kath turns sharply into an open gateway. The bright sunlight dazzles the windscreen and the tyres on the gravel throw up dust.

The main house has been carefully reconverted in a pale grey stone, which sets off the light-blue shutters and wooden window-frames beautifully. Outbuildings peep from behind the main house. These must be the holiday lets that Kath told me about in her email. The front garden still needs to be landscaped. Large terracotta pots stand empty. A green hosepipe snakes along the ground beside them. A cement mixer stands quietly in front of the main door, a torn bag of cement spilling out onto the ground. A spade sticks out of it.

'Oh, for goodness' sake, that was supposed to have been cleared away by now,' grumbles Kath. 'Hopeless!' She slaps the steering wheel before pulling up alongside the mixer and turning the engine off. 'Anyway, welcome to *Les Olivades*!'

A dog barks close by.

'Kath, it's beautiful!'

Out of nowhere a black Labrador appears and rushes over to greet us. I open the door and it jumps up at me, so I reach down and stroke its silky head.

'Hello, you! You're friendly, aren't you?'

'Pilot, get down!' shouts a deep voice.

My legs feel hot and stiff from the drive. As soon as I step onto solid ground, they start to quake. I hold onto the roof for a moment and shake out the tingling sensation in my fingertips.

He makes no move to come and greet me, so I shut the door and turn slowly towards him. Pilot continues to jump up and down energetically as I struggle to pull myself together. There's a ringing in my ears. I move my tongue around to stop it sticking to the roof of my mouth. *Stay calm. Focus.*

I prepare to greet Kath's husband. Lift my head to gaze into those familiar hazel eyes. Eyes that used to melt me.

'Hello, Tom.'

− CHAPTER 3 −

His hair has greyed prematurely. He combs it back with his fingers, unsettling the grey and then I realise that it's powdered cement.

'Hello, Jen. It's good to see you.' His eyes travel steadily between me and Kath who has moved to stand between us. They settle on me. 'I'd give you a hug, but...' He slaps the powder on his whitened shorts. They make his legs look even more tanned.

'Tom, why don't you go and take a shower? You look like a ghost with that muck all over you.'

Tom. The way she says his name.

He walks towards the house, his lean body even more muscular than I remember. He is still beautiful.

A small black shadow darts out of nowhere, stirring up dust around us. It disappears behind Kath.

'Hey, Jenny, let me introduce you to our little treasure, Rosa.'

With her gaze also on me, Kath reaches behind her for the shadow − her daughter. *Their* daughter. I take in a small mouth, long eyelashes, dark hair knotted into two rope-like plaits. Her head is bowed. She kicks at the gravel under her canvas shoes.

19

'Rosa, this is Jenny – Mummy and Daddy's best friend who I told you about. Don't be shy!'

Slowly, Rosa lifts her chin and... oh, those eyes.

Kath looks at me triumphantly. 'Yes, she's the spitting image of Tom, isn't she? There's no doubt who this one's father is.'

I bend down to Rosa's five-year-old level. 'Hello, Rosa. It's lovely to meet you at last.' I catch her small hand and hold it gently. She responds by wiggling her fingers.

'Are you going to stay with us?' She looks straight at me with those eyes.

'If that's OK with you, I'd love to stay for a short while.'

She smiles and takes my hand.

'Rosa, why don't you show Jenny around and I'll get us something to eat?' says Kath.

Still holding onto my hand, Rosa skips us around the back of the house, where the outbuildings have been converted into holiday lets or *gîtes* as she calls them in perfect French. She jumps onto a swing in the small play area, leans back and kicks out her slender brown legs to gain height. I cup my hands to peer through the windows of the two *gîtes*. They've been decorated tastefully in a neutral palette, with splashes of colour here and there. Rosa continues to swing while I stand and watch her. It gives me some time to gather my thoughts, to take a few calming breaths.

'Mummy says we're going to have a pool next year,' she says eventually.

'Wow, that'll be great, won't it? Can you swim?'

'Yes, but not as good as you. Daddy said that you won gold *metals*.'

'I'm very lucky. I won three gold medals.'

'Perhaps Jenny can help you to swim without your armbands, Rosa.'

Tom has joined us fresh from a lightning-quick shower. His hair is damp and, although shorter than before, still hangs down over his ears in maypole-ribbon strands.

'Now I can say hello properly,' he says, and bends down to give me a hug. The musky odour that invades my senses is so familiar. He picks me up, swings me about and for a small moment I allow myself to be transported back to a time when it was just us – him and me. Round and round on a carousel of dreamy distraction. That's until he bends down close and I feel his breath in my hair.

'Hello Mouse,' he whispers.

I pull away from this long-ago nickname and he puts me down. In an attempt to hide my annoying blush, I take my time to retrieve my flip-flops, which have dropped off.

'Swing me, Daddy, swing me,' Rosa pleads.

He obliges by spinning her round and round, high and low. Her giggles are infectious and when Tom puts her down, she wobbles around dizzily for a few moments. The pair look at each other, laughter in their eyes, and I sense the deep bond between them.

'Lunch is ready!' Kath waves at us from the kitchen door.

We sit outside the back of the house at a distressed wooden table surrounded by an assortment of different chairs, most of which look as though Kath has picked them up from the side of the road to save them from the local tip. The late afternoon sun has shed some of its intensity and starts to play peekaboo through the gaps between the tall cypress trees in the distance. Tom points out the craggy Black Mountain to the north. Overhanging grey clouds make it appear foreboding.

Kath sets out a delicious-looking quiche and salad, which we quickly demolish. She always made wonderful tarts and cakes. It was just the mess she left afterwards that used to rile her mum.

'How is your family, Kath? Do you see them very much?'

Her knife clatters onto her plate.

'Not at all. Mum and I fell out a while ago.'

'Really? That's a shame. I'm sure she's tried to patch things up though, hasn't she?'

'Not really. But then, I'm not interested. We're better off without them, aren't we?'

She ruffles Rosa's hair and looks at Tom. He doesn't look up and continues to eat.

'So, are you and Scott going to settle down and have children?' she asks.

This time he glances at me.

'Scott is Jenny's *boyfriend*,' says Kath, leaning towards Rosa, who responds by cupping her face and giggling coquettishly into her hands.

'Who knows? This break will be the decider I think. We've both been tied up with the Games.' I look down and pick at the pastry crumbs on my lap.

'You've had a fantastic career, Jenny. We've tried to follow your races. I'm so glad you got in touch. I was beginning to lose hope that I'd ever hear from you again – let alone see you,' says Kath. She chinks her glass against mine and takes a slurp of water.

'I'm sorry. I've been terrible at keeping in touch with

people. I keep saying I'll get into social media but I haven't done anything about it yet.'

Tom continues to say nothing. He reaches over the table for another piece of quiche, pushing it into his mouth inelegantly. Kath tuts. Rosa giggles again.

'What about you, Tom? Are you still a journalist?'

He leans forward to refill my glass. The water dances and sparkles.

'Yes, but no longer covering the Middle East. I'm mainly writing about life out here – news, travel pieces, even the odd restaurant review.' He pauses and looks about him, as though he's considering whether to say any more. 'I've also secured a book deal to write a novel.'

'That's great. What's it about?'

'A murder mystery set in deepest France.' He winks at me, unsmiling. I haven't a clue whether he's joking or not.

'Well, I look forward to getting a signed copy when it's published.'

An image of Tom lying on the rock by the river where we grew up comes to me. We called it 'our rock'. He would sit for hours scribbling away in his notepad, biting on the end of his pencil when the words weren't flowing. He used to enthuse endlessly about this mammoth epic novel he planned to write one day. He had already plotted out the entire story in his head: the characters, the setting, the ending. The protagonist was a French girl called Jeanne. I want to remind him of it, but am aware that I have to tread very carefully around this unfamiliar domestic set up. And, of course, Rosa will know nothing about Tom's and my past.

As if on cue, she jumps up from her chair, knocking it to the ground. I reach to pick it up.

'Calm down, Rosa,' says Tom.

'Can I show Jenny her room, Mummy?'

'Of course, you can, sweetheart. But wait to see if Jenny's finished eating.'

'Now, Jenny, please say now!' She jumps up and down like a yo-yo on an invisible string.

'I'd love to see my room, Rosa. Let's clear the table first, shall we?'

'I'll clear up this time – you go.' Kath waves us away.

Tom gets up too, to do a few hours' work at the farm. He bends down to kiss Rosa, then departs. I force myself not to watch him go before following a skipping Rosa into a large farmhouse kitchen, through a doorway and up a wooden staircase. She points out two bedrooms, 'Daddy's study' and a bathroom before reaching the last door at the back of the house.

'Ta-dah!' She swings the door open to reveal a display that stops me in my tracks.

It seems that Kath has gone to a lot of trouble to make me feel at home. There is a counterpane on the bed, handmade by the looks of it, in blues, greys and a smattering of scarlet, similar to my favourite duvet cover, which now lies forgotten in Aunt Muriel's cupboard in Perth. Small ornaments, which I'd packed in a box and handed to Kath for safekeeping the day I left the UK eight years ago, are laid out carefully on the dressing-table, along with a framed photograph of Tom, Kath and I, taken at Lyme Regis. We look so young, so carefree. The wind was blowing hard that day. Multiple strands of hair fly above our heads and over our laughing faces. We dared to walk along the top of the narrow Cobb, the harbour wall, as the sea lashed out at us. Kath tripped and almost fell, but Tom pulled her to safety just in time. She wept hysterically in his arms afterwards and refused to swim ever again.

I pick up the small fossil that I found on the beach the same day, and gently caress it, spiralling my finger around its warm ridges.

'Jenny, look at this!'

Rosa has pulled a red chiffon scarf away from the wall to reveal a huge framed collage. It's a detailed showcase of all my successes. Newspaper articles in both English and French, magazine images, even old photos of me in my swimming gear. I move closer to study this work of art. It's glorious. I can only imagine the huge amount of effort that must have gone into creating this.

'Mummy and I made it. It took us a very long time.'

'Rosa, it's wonderful!' I fight back tears and stroke her hair.

Now I am angry with myself. How could I ever have doubted Kath? It doesn't make sense that a manipulative character would go to such lengths to do this for me. Surely I must have misinterpreted my father's words. It's more than likely that Kath tried to persuade him against moving us to Australia. She was my best friend and always looked out for me.

I rush downstairs to find her. 'Oh, Kath, that's the best gift anyone has ever given me.' I hug her close. 'How can I ever repay you?'

She pulls back to study me, a strangely haunted look on her face. Our eyes lock.

'You've done that already by coming here. You've come back to me, haven't you?'

I nod, unsure what she means exactly. However, I don't want to unsettle this moment by asking.

'I care so much for you, Jenny, which is why I've always looked out for you. And this is a token to prove that. We go back a long way, you and I. Before you and Tom, before me and Tom. Best friends forever, remember?'

'I do, Kath.'

Her shoulders visibly relax and she gives me a wide smile. 'Come on. Let's have a glass of wine.'

– CHAPTER 4 –

Boxing Day. Two lone figures struggle against the elements on the same stretch of wet pavement, one heading north, the other south. Eyes are cast down: one pair pays close attention to where she's walking, superstitiously trying to avoid stepping on the pavement cracks, before realising with horror that her white socks look like used teabags and her father is sure to notice when she gets home; the other, in wellington boots, jumps noisily in the ink-well puddles, trying to force out the anger that has built up inside her. She doesn't care what her mum will say when she gets home. A gust of wind sends a plastic bag streaking across their field of vision. Both girls stop to stare. Like a weightless balloon, it rises higher and higher into the sky, until finally it merges into the pale grey mist above their heads.

At that moment, I turned back to continue my journey of no real purpose. Having been cooped up in a house alone with my father for the past week, I needed to get out, stretch my legs and breathe in some fresh air. And that's when I came properly face to face with Kath. She was standing very still looking at me, nose running, face pink and blotchy. At first I thought she had chicken pox or some other skin complaint, but the wild look in her eyes told me she was angry. We stood staring at each other for what seemed like five minutes but was probably only a second or two. I didn't know what to say. My eleven-year-old self was always lost for words at moments like this. Kath wasn't a new face, of course. She'd recently moved to my town and had been put in a different class to me. As the new girl, she had received a lot of attention and seemed quite happy to be tagging along with the Simpson twins and their raucous crowd.

So there we stood, metres apart, a gusty wind blowing in our faces and a drizzly rain dripping from our hoods. I'd been pushing some boiled sweets round and round in the pocket of my mum's old raincoat, which I'd grabbed from the hook on my way out. It swamped me, but at least it kept me dry. I didn't have a tissue for Kath, so I offered her a sweet instead. She looked down at my hand as if I'd just offered her a dead beetle. Well, the sweet was probably several months old and the sticky wrapper had a hair or two clinging to it, so I can't say I blamed her. Then she touched my palm, ignoring the sweet, and squeezed my fingers gently before letting go. Something happened in that brief moment – a connection passed between us like an electric current – which marked the start of our best friendship.

I tossed the sweet aside and giggled nervously, my sodden feet creaking up and down in my wet patent-leather shoes. Kath broke into a deep-throated peal of laughter. I stood and watched her, unsure if I was the object of her merriment.

'You look like a drowned rat in that,' she commented.

I gazed down at myself, the hemline of my coat hanging just above my purple kneecaps. For some reason, it looked hilarious. I joined in with her laughter, until my stomach was aching so much I had to bend over and hold it tight.

'Where are you going?' I asked her, finally. 'I'm Jenny.'

'I know who you are. I've seen you in town with your dad. Your mum died.'

It wasn't a question, but I answered her as though it was. 'She did. Four months ago.'

Kath didn't say anything. She just carried on looking at me, so I added: 'My dad will probably yell at me when I get home looking like this.'

'At least he'll notice you.' Kath chewed on her lips.

I watched with fascination as they slowly deepened into the colour of strawberry jam. 'Are you OK? Did someone upset you?'

'Not really. The same old thing. My brothers get to play, I have to help at home. You wouldn't believe the presents they got this year – football boots, games, blah blah – and all I got was a vile pink jumper with multi-coloured pom-poms on it. It's disgusting, looks as though a cat has puked down the front. I asked my mum if I could swap it and she said that it wasn't from a shop – she'd bought it from someone who'd knitted it, so that's that, the end of my Christmas. I've just come out 'cos if I stay in there any longer I'm going to have to put a pan on the cooker and set the house on fire.'

She didn't stop for a single breath during this little speech. It was exhausting listening to her talk so fast, but also exhilarating.

'What about you?' she added. 'Why are you out in this disgusting weather?'

'Oh, I've been stuck indoors for too long with Dad and

needed to get out. Hey, why don't you come round and I'll do your hair or something?'

It turned out that Kath had moved to the same new estate as me with her parents and two younger brothers. Her dad had taken over the local garage and her mum, a trained hairdresser, cut people's hair in her kitchen. It wasn't a very sophisticated set-up. You had to lean over the kitchen sink while she washed, shampooed and rinsed your hair, using a spray attached to the taps. Usually, the water was too hot or too cold so you'd be wriggling around in discomfort until she got it right. Then you'd sit on a chair with newspaper underneath as she snipped away. I always reached out to catch the falling locks, fascinated by the idea of slugs that have just been sprinkled with salt.

'You'll have to sit still, Jenny,' her mum always told me, 'or I'll snip one of your ears off by mistake like that artist, Van whatisname.'

'You mean Gogh,' I replied one day. That impressed her. She'd said that line so many times that curiosity had finally got the better of me and I went into the school library to look through one of the few art books in its collection. I'd enjoyed flicking through the pages of Impressionist art: Picasso, Monet and there he was, Van Gogh, with his bandaged ear self-portrait, his sunflowers and his starry night, which was my favourite.

'Well, well Jennifer, that is very impressive. You have been doing your homework, haven't you?' she laughed. 'Kathleen, you'd better take note of your friend here. Jenny's going to go far one day. Not just a talented swimmer, but a brainy one at that!'

Kath glowered and turned away. I sensed she resented all the attention her mum paid to her brothers and the last thing she needed was her mum cosying up to me. I did feel sorry for Kath and if what she said was true – and I never doubted her – it didn't seem right that she had to help with all the chores, while her brothers ran around causing mayhem. Kath said they were always stealing things from her room – CDs, pens, books, even her clothes. Her mum refused to step in and wouldn't let her put a lock on the door. So whenever Kath had something special that she didn't want her brothers to take, she kept it round my house. I emptied one of my drawers for her and told her to think of it as hers.

We were different in most respects. I was more easy-going than her. A 'do-gooder', as she put it. She was headstrong, more impetuous and very bossy, which I'd often tease her about. The good thing about Kath was that I could say anything to her, be blunt and tell her to shut up if she was being too ridiculous or petty. But most of the time we had a lot of fun together, took long walks into the woods, played make-believe games and pretended we were the only people alive on the planet. Of course, there were times when she could be intense and overly protective about our friendship, but she was fiercely loyal and would take on anyone with that sharp tongue of hers if they dared tease us about our closeness.

'They're just jealous.' Kath said once, after a gang of older teenagers shouted and swore at us when we were walking home from school holding hands. 'Can't bear to see friends having a good time.' She held my hand tighter and pulled me along until we were both skipping and laughing, oblivious to the whistles following us down the road.

Everything we did, we did together, except swimming,

of course. Shortly after my mother's death, Mr Brown phoned my father. He told him that I had the potential to be good, so I went along with it to please Dad and hoped it would give us both something positive to focus on. He and Kath were my biggest fans. The two of them seemed to get along well. She knew what to say to him, would compliment him on a new tie or a nicely made cup of tea, and she always managed to work her charm on him when I needed an excuse to go to a party or the cinema.

I guess the first small chink in our friendship was over my neighbour Mrs Holt, who had horrible-looking bunions and was forced to wear slippers whatever the weather. I used to go to the shop for her and one day when I'd taken Kath along with me to get some cat food, Mrs Holt invited us both in. I'd become used to the acrid smell of boiled milk, but Kath had to rush out after five minutes, saying it made her gag. She refused to come with me after that. I, on the other hand, really enjoyed the old lady's company and would regularly pop in after school to feed an ever-growing number of stray cats for her.

'Sometimes I think you love that woman and her cats more than you love anything else,' Kath said one day, elbowing me in the ribs slightly more than just playfully.

'Of course I don't, silly,' I reassured her. 'Best friends forever, remember?'

I could feel the ghost of her elbow in my side for several days afterwards, a reminder that Kath had insecurities and I needed to pay her extra attention to scare them off.

Now, as I catch a glimpse of that intense – almost worried – look on her face, before she turns away to grab a bottle of Sauvignon Blanc from the fridge, I realise that nothing has changed: Kath is still insecure – and she still has this ability to make me feel like the young girl I used to be.

***

The late-afternoon light slowly dims and dusk takes over, casting pixelated shadows over this postcard setting. Kath and I have moved to the front of the house with our glasses of wine, our laughter breaking up the monotonous sound of the cicadas, which buzz all around us like an electric fence. It's time to seize this moment and delve a bit deeper.

'So remind me how you met up with Tom, Kath?'

She's about to take a sip of wine, but instead pauses, puts down her glass and leans forward, elbows on the table, hands clasped under her chin. Her spider-leg eyelashes blink several times. They were always longer than mine, even before we discovered mascara.

'I bumped into him when I was working in that hotel in Bristol, a year or so after you left. He was over from the Middle East to help his mum and sister pack up the house for Canada. You know they emigrated, don't you?'

'No, I didn't. Tom and I were no longer in touch by that point.' I sit up straight. 'That must have been hard for him. They were so close.'

'You're telling me. He'd never have moved out here if they were still in the UK. Do you remember how he said he turned down Oxford University just to be near his mum?' She smirks.

'I guess he was always worried that his dad might turn up unannounced and force his way back into the house. He was really violent, apparently. Anyway, Tom loved it at Bristol University, so it worked out for him, didn't it?'

I don't add that he and I wouldn't have got together if he'd gone to Oxford. He had a weekend job working behind the bar at my swimming club, which sealed our fates – his and mine.

'So, anyway, his mum married this Canadian bloke, Stanley. Tom came back to Bristol, found out I was working close by and dropped in to say hi. We hung out and it sort of clicked for us both.'

She leans forward and pats my arm. I want to snatch it away but leave it there, trying my hardest to give her the benefit of the doubt. I can't stop two people from falling in love, can I?

'You've been so understanding, Jenny.'

I swallow hard and look away, not sure I can trust myself to say anything. Rosa is playing with her dolls on the swings. She coos at them softly, lost in her make-believe game.

'You've got a beautiful daughter,' I say to put us on safer ground.

Kath watches Rosa too. 'Loves his girls does our Tom. Yep, it wasn't easy for him losing his mum and sister, after everything else that had happened. Things were pretty dark for him. Fortunately, I was there to pick up the pieces.'

Just as I'm about to ask her what she means, the truck swings into the driveway, its headlights shining our way.

Kath raises her hand to her eyes. Her voice hardens. 'Why does he always do that? He should turn them off when he comes through the gate. I've told him so many times.' Clearly exasperated, she jumps up. 'Better get some supper together now he's back.'

I follow her into the house, confused by her tone. Why would such a small thing bother anyone so much?

Thankfully, supper is a relaxed affair and I drink too much wine. I've only had the odd glass over the years due to the rigorous training demanded by a world-class swimming career, so after a second glass I'm feeling giggly. Rosa is bemused by our merry behaviour. She sits back on her chair swinging her legs, beaming round at each of us as she chews on countless pieces of bread.

After dinner, Tom takes a tired yet reluctant daughter up to bed. Kath and I clear the table and sing along to some favourite tunes playing out on the speaker. I'm dancing around the room, drying a pan, when I almost collide with Tom, who has stopped in the doorway to observe us both. He squeezes my hand quickly and heads to the table to pour himself a glass of wine. Even he can't resist the impulse to move his body fluidly around the room in time to the music. That familiar expression of rapture on his face. *My Tom.* I shake away the difficult thought.

We settle back down at the table, still high from the dancing. Tom knocks back his wine freely and starts to tell us a funny story about an encounter with a sheikh and his many wives in Qatar several years ago. He impersonates each and every character with the humour I remember so well. For a moment, I allow myself to relax fully and throw my head back with laughter, and Kath joins in with the wisecracks.

Something's not quite right. Kath has stopped mid-sentence. I rock forward, a tear of laughter skimming my face. *What's up? Shit! I'm patting his thigh.* I pull my hand away as though it has touched burning coals. Kath, glass in hand, looks bemused.

'Oh shit!' I look at my lap, unsure whether I should be apologising for my drunkenness to Kath, Tom or both of them. My face is burning. 'I've had way too much to drink. Time for me to go to bed.'

There's a long silence when all I want is to be swallowed up by the floor. Then Kath starts to laugh.

'Oh, Jenny that was so funny. If you could have seen your face!' Kath dabs her eyes with a tissue, and for a second I'm unsure if she is sad or happy. 'It was as if you'd opened the door on the bogey man! We'd better make sure you get to the right bedroom tonight, hadn't we Tom?'

Tom says nothing, simply raises a sardonic eyebrow to reassure me.

'This is why I don't drink alcohol these days,' I tell them. 'Can't take me anywhere.'

How could you be so stupid? I grab a magazine and start fanning my face. My abdomen still hurts from all the laughter, but now I feel as sober as a judge.

'Actually.' Kath's voice takes a more serious tone as she sits down again with a fresh glass of wine in front of her. 'I know I haven't checked this with you yet, Tom, but what do you say about Jenny staying to help us out here over the summer? We could really do with an extra pair of hands.'

Tom looks at Kath's brimming glass sternly for a moment. 'I'm sure Jenny has other plans, haven't you?'

His eyes meet mine. They are challenging me. I look away, back at Kath for reassurance.

'I haven't got any firm plans, although my father thinks I'm only away from Perth for a couple of weeks. But listen, I really don't think–'

'Come on, Tom,' pleads Kath. 'Don't be proud. You know we could do with a bit more help to get everything ready and to keep things moving along. There's Rosa to take care of, the guests, the wine harvest, the honey contract.'

Tom reaches into the cupboard for a jug. He lets the cold tap run before filling it, then returns to the table with three glasses, pours water into each of them and hands one to me. Kath and I glance at each other and smile. It feels like we're schoolgirls who've just asked if they can have a sleepover.

Tom studies his long fingers wrapped around his glass as if he's about to crush it into splinters. Unexpectedly, he puts it down hard on the table, making us both jump.

'Jen, are you really sure you want to be cleaning bathrooms and bedrooms for the next couple of months?'

I take a sip of my own water to mull over his words. It doesn't sound as if he wants me here at all, but maybe that's the way I'm reading it. I really don't know if this is a good idea, but the thought of a summer away from my father, away from pressure, away from my rigid training schedule, all those huge expectations, is bliss. This way I won't be eating up my savings either. Two months, Tom said. That will go fast. After that, I can return to my other life knowing that I haven't any unfinished business.

'Listen, I'd be delighted to stay and help out if you guys won't mind having me for a short–'

Kath doesn't let me finish and instead comes over to hug me. She turns the music up and dances around with glee. Tom and I raise our water glasses at each other, perhaps each trying to read the other's mind. At this point, mine is fuzzy. I need to lie down.

Pecking each of them on the cheek, I stumble up to bed, throwing myself fully dressed on top of my duvet. I close my eyes and immediately the room starts spinning round. I open them again and try to concentrate on the darkness above me. A wave of nausea suddenly swoops, so I rush to the window to take some gulps of air. A gentle breeze tugs at my hair. I turn my face towards it for a few moments before returning to bed.

When I wake again it's unclear how much time has passed. The world is still moving and I groan. I get up to use the bathroom and on my way back to bed am drawn towards the cool air coming along the landing. I can hear whispering voices, or is it just the sound of the wind in the pines? It gets louder, more urgent. Kath and Tom are arguing. They must be standing by an open window downstairs. 'But that's what you...' He sounds angry, forceful. 'But Jenny doesn't...'

Kath is trying to win him round. I recognise that tone so well: the long drawn-out syllables, the persuasive note. I wish I could hear their words, but I'm too far away. However, one thing I know is that I was right. Tom isn't happy about me staying. He doesn't want me around. This was a bad decision. Tomorrow I will talk to him. Tell him that I'll go away. But why did he have to call me 'Mouse'? That was 'our' word.

Back in bed I mull over the letter I received just as I was making plans to return home after the 2007 World Championships. They say you can die of a broken heart.

'I'm sure you'll be as surprised as I was when Tom declared his undying love for me... I sincerely hope you can understand and forgive us for

falling in love. I didn't plan it... the baby will be
the icing on the cake. I am so excited.'

Words scribbled on a dirty-white page and posted in an airmail envelope to break such devastating news.

I refused to swim for a month afterwards. Both my father's and Scott's assumption was that I was exhausted after a long season and needed a break. Scott came to see me every day. He didn't ask any questions, but suggested I take two weeks to rest fully at a yoga retreat in Bali. He said yoga had helped him as a teenager when he'd started to develop anxiety attacks. Scott was right. The emotional pain had fastened itself around my chest like a tight elastic band, and although daily yoga practice helped to ease it, there were still times when I could feel it sitting in the pit of my stomach, like a heavy stone. A reminder of what I'd lost. I picked myself up and carried on for years, cutting myself off from my friends and winning every race with ruthless intensity. Until one day I realised that in my desire to prove that I could survive, I'd become someone I didn't recognise. I had no friends. I was an empty shell. I was nothing. Most of all, I wanted out.

Now, I lie back down on my bed and wrap the pillow around my ears as if it's a Jane Austen bonnet. My silent tears soak into the cotton cloth to form grey clouds on a pale background.

– CHAPTER 5 –

I look around in the dark. The sheet is twisted around my legs and the quilt lies discarded on the floor. I pull it back over me and lie back on my pillow, slowly coming to and realising that my head hurts. I reach over for my watch on the bedside table: 9 a.m. A squinting light is trying to break through the closed shutters. I get up to open them and am dazzled by the brilliant blue sky. If only my head wasn't throbbing so much. I close them again, leaving a pencil-thin gap to let in a gentle breeze which carries in those intoxicating scents of the Languedoc once more, this time tinged with the dampness of the morning dew, soon to be burnt away by the sun.

A dog (Pilot?) barks in the distance and birds chatter in the pines, completely oblivious to the unwritten rule of silence which a hangover demands. Last night's wine has made me groggy and thirsty. Hearing footsteps and voices outside, I peep through the half-closed shutters to see who is already up and moving about. Kath and Rosa are getting into the truck. Maybe they're heading over to *La Miellerie* to help pack the royal jelly orders that have come in this week. It's the weekend, so Rosa won't have school today.

Sensing that I am alone in the house, I go downstairs

to the kitchen in my nightie. I let the tap run until it is the coldest it can be, then stick my head under it and drink noisily until I have quenched my thirst. The view out of the window is murky. Particles of dust thrown up by the departing truck remain fixed in the air, taking time to settle. There's an empty box of pills on the worktop. Painkillers? A name is typed on the side: Kathleen Hargreaves. Of course, she shares Tom's name. I hold onto the worktop to let the dizziness pass. I really didn't think this through properly at all. *I never should have come.*

It had all played out so simply in my head when I decided to drop in on my way from Perth to the UK. I'd stay for a few days (a week at most), spend some quality time with Kath, and during my stay ask her if she could explain why my father had said she wanted me to emigrate to Australia. I'd then leave, content in the knowledge that my father had made it up because he wanted me in Perth making great sponsorship money and trying to break that world record, which still alluded me. At the same time, I hoped that Tom would have gone to pot and I'd no longer have any feelings for him.

How wrong could I be?

On my way back upstairs, I hover on the threshold of Kath and Tom's bedroom. There are clothes strewn all over the floor and the bed is unmade. A half-filled bottle of Chanel No.19 stands on the dressing-table. I walk towards it, bending down to pick up its discarded top lying on the floor. I inhale the floral scent and immediately think of Kath's mum who used to wear it. I always got on well with Julie. She was kind to me after Mrs Holt's death. I secretly hoped that she'd become my new 'substitute' mother, but it was obvious straightaway that Kath wasn't going to let that happen. I belonged to her, not her mum.

A few dog-eared photographs have been slotted between the dressing-table mirror and its wooden frame. Cobwebs tremble in the corners of the glass as I move closer to study the images. There's a picture of Tom lying on the grass with a baby Rosa. The doting father. I look closer at a photo of Kath and Tom, his arm around her waist. She's wearing a fascinator. I know it isn't their wedding photo because she sent me that with the letter. No, this must be someone else's wedding. I peer closer. There's something familiar about those earrings. They look like–

I swing round at a creak behind me, hands behind my back to hide the photo. Tom is standing in the doorway, arms folded loosely, his head inclined slightly. He's dressed casually in a T-shirt and shorts. His feet are bare. I wait for him to say something. He makes me feel so uncomfortable, so awkward. It's the first time we've been alone together since our break-up. I try to appear relaxed as I turn to put the photo back in its place.

'I'm sorry. I love looking at old photos.' I fold my arms in front of my nightie, conscious that it might be see-through from this angle.

Tom smiles gently and comes towards me. 'Listen, Jen, I think we need to talk. I want to understand you better. I need to know why you're here.'

I push a strand of hair behind my ear. 'To be honest, I don't really know why I came. Probably because I've decided to make some changes, retire from competition, move on with my life. I suppose I had this sudden urge to see Kath. You too, of course.' I pause but he doesn't

42

respond. 'I heard the two of you arguing last night. I hope it wasn't about me.'

He grimaces and flicks away a non-existent fly. 'Sorry about that. To be frank, Jen, it's strange seeing you again in these circumstances. I'm not convinced it was a great idea.'

'I understand. It's just – I still feel frustrated about the way things were left between us all those years ago. Recently my father said something to me about how he was glad he'd listened to Kath and moved us to Australia, how she'd been right all along. I didn't understand what he meant. That's partly what brought me here really, to get some answers, to put my mind at rest. You and Kath were such a big part of my life.'

'But didn't you think about how I might feel about seeing you again?' He rubs his cheek, almost as if he's trying to erase the memories of us. His expression is close to frustration.

'To be honest – no. I suppose I thought it might be painful for me, but I wasn't sure how you'd feel. Not after the way you ended things between us.' My tone is sharper than I intended it to be.

He blinks hard and turns away to wipe a mark on the doorframe. Abruptly he swings his head back to look at me. 'Let's go for a drive and talk some more. Bring your swimming gear. There's a lake near here.'

'OK. Just give me a moment.'

Tom nods. 'I'll see you downstairs in ten minutes.'

Once back in my room, I get ready with a beating heart, resorting to some visualisation techniques to try and bring it back to a normal pace.

Outside the house we step into a battered old Renault,

which I'd noticed last night. It's just as untidy as Kath and Tom's bedroom. Empty water bottles, biscuit and crisp packets are scattered all over the back seat.

'Sorry about the mess. Kath and Rosa are one of a kind when it comes to snacking and untidiness.' He puts a packet of cigarettes and a lighter on the dashboard.

'When did you take up smoking?' I try to sound nonchalant.

'On the day when I realised I'd made the wrong decision.' He looks wistfully ahead of him, then at me. He attempts a smile, but there's pain behind his eyes. Is he talking about me? All I want to do is reach out and stroke his hair. His smile disappears and he stares deep into my mind as though he's trying to work something out. I keep my hands in my lap. The tension is palpable. He reaches over, as if to touch my cheek. It's the most delicate of gestures.

At that moment, there's the sound of an engine. Tom puts his hand down. Kath swings through the gate in the truck, draws up alongside us and leans out of the window.

'Hi! I was expecting to see you at the farm, Tom. What's up?' Her smile is strained.

'Nothing. I had a headache, so came back to get some painkillers. I'm just about to give Jen a tour of the area – show her where the local swimming lake is.'

Kath opens the car door. 'Hang on a mo' and we'll come with you, won't we Rosa?'

Rosa is sitting quietly observing us from the passenger seat. I wave at her, she waves back, opens her door and runs round to us.

'Yes, I want to see Jenny swim like she did in the Olympics!' she shouts gleefully, jumping up and down.

'OK,' replies Tom, 'but hurry up as I have to get back to the farm in an hour or so.'

He gets out of the car, lights a cigarette and grabs a plastic bag from the back seat. Soon the discarded cans and empty wrappers are collected up. I observe him in the wing mirror as he walks to the dustbin, the cigarette hanging loosely from his lip. His butt is compact, just as I remember. An unexpected wave of heat – desire? – washes over me, forcing me to get out of the car and focus on picking the dirt out of my nails.

'Here we are!' says Kath, as she and Rosa reappear.

Kath throws a large striped beach bag at Tom's chest. The impact forces him to take a couple of steps backwards. He doesn't flinch, and turns calmly to place the bag in the boot. Kath doesn't look too happy as she opens the front passenger door, lifts up the front seat and holds it forward for Rosa and I to climb in the back.

– CHAPTER 6 –

A week passes by quickly here. Kath and I work tirelessly to get the *gîtes* and garden in order for *Les Olivades*'s first guests. There's so much to do. Tom hasn't been around as much as I was expecting. He spends a lot of time at *La Miellerie* during the summer, Kath explains. There is an abundance of fruit and vegetables to be harvested, including cherries, garlic, courgettes and strawberries. However, something tells me that he's avoiding me, secretly hoping I won't be here when he returns at the end of the day.

I haven't asked Kath about my father yet, but I know I have to for my own sanity. It's so difficult to judge when's the right time. It has to feel right – a softness in the air when we're fully relaxed and easy with each other, like we always used to be. After school, we'd often lie sprawled out on one of our bedroom carpets or outside on the grass if it was warm. We'd share our secret thoughts, our wishes, tell each other made-up stories, often late into the evening as we watched the sun go down. Here, I don't know if it's the oppressive heat that's affecting us, but there is always a slight tension between us. Kath seems wary and watchful of me now. From the moment I'm up and getting dressed, she is hovering in my doorway with a cup of tea, eager to discuss the day ahead or the plans she's made for the entire summer. She wants me to stay for as long as I can, at least until the wine harvest is over at the end of September. I am to discover and fall in love with everything the Languedoc has to offer: a boat trip along the Canal du Midi, a visit to Carcassonne with its Cathar castle, a climb up the Pyrénées mountains on the Spanish border, not to mention all of the summer festivals at villages within a twenty-kilometre radius. So my plans to ask her what my father really meant are put on hold. If I'm here all summer there will surely come a right time.

Her enthusiasm is contagious and I am drawn in once again by her appetite for life. We work on the garden in the scorching heat, planting hardy flowers and shrubs, laying down turf and enlarging the fruit and vegetable patch, so more produce can be grown in the future to achieve a year-round kitchen harvest. The work is backbreaking, but I enjoy listening to Kath chattering away to me about nothing in particular. I sense that, like me, she has been lonely and needs to make up for lost time with her endless stories, mostly about people who work at the farm who I've yet to meet. Rosa joins us after school and the work quickly turns to horseplay when she turns on the hosepipe and sprays us, with shrieking delight.

In sharp contrast, dinner is more subdued. Kath and I are so exhausted from gardening that we struggle to keep our eyes open. Tom doesn't return until late. He makes small talk before taking a glass of wine up to his study to write. Kath resents his secrecy. He has password-protected his computer, she tells me with a hard look in her eyes. I reassure her that he probably doesn't want to share his writing until he's 100 per cent happy with it.

My biggest source of frustration is my inability to sleep in. Having spent half my life getting up at dawn to swim almost every day, my body clock still refuses to adjust to a normal schedule. Every morning, I lie awake, listening to the creaks of the house, silently willing the sun to come up, so that I can creep outside to cycle to the nearby lake. It's a beautiful, tranquil spot and no one else seems to use it for most of the year, although Kath says it can get busy in high summer. Swimming is only permitted at one end and the rest is roped off. There's a bright-red sign warning people of the dangers.

'Sylvie told us that it's exceptionally deep and people have drowned in it, their bodies only recovered weeks, sometimes months, later,' says Kath. 'So be careful, Jenny, as I won't be diving in to save you,' she laughs.

Kath has also taken me to the beach at the seaside town of Valras, half an hour's drive away. I'm not a big fan of saltwater, but it's shallow enough to teach Rosa to swim more confidently, even if the water temperature is bracing. I drive us there in the late afternoon so that Kath can run some errands on her bike. Despite Kath's protests, I've promised Rosa one of my gold medals if she manages to swim twenty-five metres by the end of the summer.

'For all that support you gave me over the years, Kath, no one deserves it more than you and yours. Besides, if I'm to move on with my life, I need to stop looking back at my past achievements and look to the future, don't I?'

***

Today is Sunday and although there's still work to be done before the first guests arrive, we've agreed on a day of repose and recreation. After a rapid breakfast of coffee and croissants, Kath and I start to prepare a picnic. Heading to the garden, we pull up a rabbit's idea of heaven: fresh lettuces, herbs and huge radishes. Meanwhile, Tom phones a few of their friends to invite them along to the 'usual place', which I'm told is a short drive away.

Rosa has already changed into her swimming costume and put on her armbands. She jumps up and down in eager anticipation. Paradoxically, her efforts to drive us out of the house as quickly as possible are counterproductive as she keeps getting in our way. Kath sends her outside with the challenge of completing 100 skips in a row. She grabs her rope and charges onto the terrace with relish. She is such a joyful child – inquisitive, bold and bright. I can't help but be captivated by her.

Kath turns away from the sink, where she's washing the vegetables, and sees me studying her daughter. 'What are you thinking, Jenny; how different she is from me?'

'No, Kath, not at all. I'm thinking how lucky you are to have brought such a joyous bundle into this world.'

'She's a real madam, that one. She knows how to play to you, to turn on the charm when it's needed.'

'Ah, then she is her mother's daughter, isn't she?'

Kath looks at me hard, before a big smile spreads across her face. A tomato comes hurtling across the room towards me. I duck and it splats on the cupboard door.

'Hey!'

I try to grab a tomato to splat her back, and soon we've degenerated into a childish game of 'It', chasing each

49

other around the room and laughing like over-excited kids. This is the Kath I miss. Those times we had when we first knew each other – when we were still children. I try to make an escape into the hallway but am blocked by Tom who's just finished on the phone.

He catches hold of me. 'Now, now, *little* girls, what's going on here?'

'Out the way Tom,' shrieks Kath, 'you're spoiling our game. It!' She taps me on the shoulder and darts away.

Tom grabs her too and looks down at us with mock severity. Rosa has paused her world-breaking skipping challenge to come and see what the fuss is all about. She looks delighted.

'Rosa, get the fly swatter. I think these two need a good ticking off, don't you?'

Kath and I collapse in giggles at Tom's feet as Rosa flicks at us with the swatter. Kath waves her daughter away.

'Oh, please stop, Rosa. I'm going to explode in a minute.'

Tom gives each of us a hand and pulls us up. I fall against his chest and feel his jaw clip my head. All I have to do is look up and my nose will be buried in the warm crook of his neck – and I'll be lost to him once more. It really is that simple. And that's what scares me. We briefly make eye contact as I disengage, turning away to push the hair behind my ears. I take the hairband off my wrist to make a ponytail and return to the worktop to prepare the picnic. I can sense him standing in the doorway and I know he's still watching me. It's as if he and I are in our own bubble, oblivious to Kath and Rosa who continue to run round us in cat and mouse style. Head down, I focus on chopping every raw vegetable in sight into tiny pieces until I hear his footsteps fade away upstairs.

***

Laden with blankets, towels and enough food to feed an army, we set off for the river Orb. Majestic plane trees stand tall on either side of the straight road, giving the impression of a grand boulevard lined with soldiers.

We enter the local market town. It's deserted. Most shop fronts are shuttered up. Even the *boulangerie* has closed early today. A few skinny dogs roam the main street, tongues hanging out as they struggle to find a segment of shade to lie down in. The church bells are ringing but there's no evidence of a congregation coming or going.

'I hate Sundays in France,' whines Kath, fanning herself with a magazine. 'In winter, it's dire. You can drive around the whole region and not see a soul all day.'

'The French see it as a day to relax and have long lunches with their families. Something we Brits have forgotten about,' says Tom, catching my eye in his rear-view mirror.

'What are Sundays like in Australia?' asks Kath.

'Fun, actually. For a start it's my only day off to relax. Normally we head to the beach or have barbecues.' I pause for a moment. 'A shame you've never been out to visit.'

I hold Tom's stare until he's forced to concentrate on his driving. He swerves slightly to avoid a cat, which appears out of nowhere to streak across the road.

'I want to come and visit you, Jenny!' shouts Rosa with her usual glee. I pull her towards me and hug her.

'Wouldn't that be nice.' I look out of the window, wondering what my father's been up to since I left. I realise it's the first time I've given him any real consideration since I arrived.

After twenty minutes or so we drive across a narrow bridge, stretching high over the river. Tom parks the car close to a shady bush on the side of the road. I feel damp patches of perspiration on my dress, so I flap it up and down, willing it to dry quickly in this hairdryer-hot heat.

We descend a steep path to the river's edge. There's a pebble beach and very little shade here, so I'm glad we remembered to pack the parasols. I look keenly at the clear, crystalline water. A gang of teenagers jump and dive off rocks in the deeper part of the river opposite us. From their screams, I'm sure the water must be refreshingly cold. Tiny fish stream along in silvery streaks, darting away as soon as Rosa bounds into the shallows with her net.

'Tom!' A deep voice shouts from the path we have just left.

Tom looks up and waves. '*Salut,* Luc!'

I look up to see a stream of people descending towards us like an army of ants.

'You haven't invited Luc and Armelle have you, Tom?' The angry note in Kath's voice is jarring.

'Of course I have. Why, what's the problem?' He turns his back on Kath to help himself to a bottle of beer from the icebox. 'Jenny?'

'No thanks.'

'Nothing. I thought it was just Pierre and Marc coming.' Kath starts to scratch her arm, a nervous habit of hers that I remember well from school. She gets out a blanket and settles on it, her mouth in a pout as she watches Rosa in the water.

The arriving adults and children cross the dirt track in an assortment of impractical summer footwear. They are armed with chairs, parasols, fishing nets and picnic bags. One of the men is even carrying a barbecue.

'The French certainly do picnics in style,' I remark.

'Yes,' says Kath, who has started to throw tiny pebbles into the water. Rosa waves at the children, clearly delighted to have some playmates her own age.

By the time I have been introduced to everyone and done the customary three kisses – or *bisous* – on the cheeks, my head is spinning round, trying to remember the unfamiliar names. Luc and Armelle, Pierre and Sandrine with daughter Clara, Marc and Françoise with twins Freddie and Daniel, and Edouard the barbecue carrier.

Tom moves with ease between French and English as he settles everyone in and explains to me that he and Kath know these people from their work at *La Miellerie*, the honey farm. I can see by the way the men interact with him, touching his arm lightly when they talk and laugh, that they have a deep respect for Tom. He has always had this ability to put people at ease, including small children and old ladies in supermarkets. Even Kath when she almost fell into the sea at Lyme Regis all those years ago. Tom had sprung forward and caught her just in time, pulling her off the rocks before she was swept away in the strong waves. She was sopping wet, so he'd wrapped my blanket around her and carried her back to the beach, where she clung to him and wept for probably longer than was really necessary.

I realise that Tom is talking to me, so shake away the memory and concentrate on the blond grizzly-bearded man before me. We shake hands.

'Luc manages the honey farm for Bernard and Sylvie Girardot,' says Tom.

'Hello, Luc!'

'Pleased to meet you, Jenny.'

'And the rest of us pretend to take orders from him.'

Luc laughs and bends down to greet Kath. She raises her face to him, but is unsmiling. *What is up with her today?*

'Yes, he tries to boss us all about, even his wife,' laughs Armelle, an unusually pretty woman with caramel-coloured skin and long dark hair shrouding a graceful neck. She sits herself down next to me.

'Your English is very good,' I say. 'That's an interesting accent.'

'It's Liverpudlian. I used to visit my English pen pal every summer, so my accent is nothing like the Queen's I am told.'

'Don't worry, not many people's are.'

We sit and watch the men throwing a tennis ball to one another in the water. That's until Pilot catches it in his mouth and swims off with it, chased by a laughing Tom. I realise it's the first time I've seen Tom looking truly relaxed since I arrived a week ago. I'd put his apparently more serious nature down to maturity with age, but now I realise it's not that. Something else has been holding him back.

Armelle edges closer to me and studies my face. 'So, you are the famous swimmer who has come from Australia to visit her friends. Your ex-boyfriend and your best girlfriend.'

I am taken aback by her directness.

'They told you.'

'Kath told Luc. She said it was a long time ago and you were fine about them being together now.'

I shrug and pick up a pebble, weigh and caress its smoothness in my hand, gathering my thoughts, then turn to face her, forcing a smile. 'Yes it's all forgotten now. My career had to come first.' I search to change the subject. 'How about you and Luc? How long have you two been together?'

'Since we were eighteen. So ten years.' Now it is her turn to look thoughtful. She stares across the water at the rocks, but I can tell that she is revisiting a memory. I wonder what it is. The pebble drops out of my hand to merge with the multitude of different coloured stones beneath us. Armelle blinks out of her reverie. 'Why don't you come and help me at the market next week? I sell honey and nougat there every Thursday morning.'

We smile at each other.

'I'd like that. I'll need to check with Kath first in case she needs me for anything.'

'Good. I'll come and pick you up at 5.30 in the morning. Too early?'

I laugh. 'My body still wakes up at 5 a.m. to go swimming, so it's a perfect time for me.'

'Of course.' She smiles and gets up to join Sandrine and Françoise who are already preparing the picnic.

***

Several hours later we are all sprawled out on the blankets, having indulged in far too much to eat. The barbecue has worked flat out, cooking sausages and chicken, and now smokes gently, turning the charcoal into a pale grey ash.

The sun has moved behind us but continues to beat down strongly. I reach for my straw hat, ensuring that its shade covers my shoulders. Rosa is filling a bucket with water.

'Daddy, can I go and jump from the rocks with the twins? I'll keep my armbands on.'

'That's fine, Rosa. Just jump from the lowest one, OK?'

'She's already asked me, Tom, and I said no,' says Kath.

I look over at the rocks in question. They look safe enough to me.

'Don't worry, I'll go too and watch her.'

Kath's hands are on her hips. 'Tom, I've said no, so please support me on this.'

'It's not fair, Mum. You never let me do anything fun!' Angrily, Rosa kicks her flip-flops into the river and they start moving slowly away from her.

Kath stands up and points. 'Go and get those this minute!' she shouts at her daughter.

'No.' Petulant shake of the head.

Her mother's face clouds over. 'Rosa, if you don't fetch those now, you'll get a smack.'

I wince at Kath's overreaction. Surely she can't be serious. Looking round, it's obvious the others can see there's a battle of wills going on.

'Let go of me!'

Now Kath has hold of Rosa's arm and is trying to propel her towards the water.

'Kath!'

'No, Tom, stay out of this.'

'But you're hurting me!' Rosa starts to cry. Her face crumples. I spot a red patch on her arm where Kath is holding her tightly.

'Kath!' I am at her side and whisper into her ear. 'Let Tom get the flip-flops. It won't take a moment. I was just thinking about that time Mr Brown was mean to you and what you did to his lovely green car. Do you remember the look on his face?'

The memory works. Rosa is released and crashes over the pebbles to Tom, who hugs her. The tension in Kath dissipates and her shoulders shake up and down.

'Oh Lord, I'd forgotten about that,' she says.

'His face was a picture, right?'

She hugs me, laughing. Over her shoulders my eyes lock with Tom's. His send mine a silent thank you.

'Oh shit, what about the flip-flops?' asks Kath. She looks helplessly at the river.

Tom races into the water and launches into an impressive crawl. *He's worked on that*, I think to myself, admiring his muscular arms pulling swiftly through the flow. Pilot follows barking, wanting to join in the fun. Kath has taken Rosa aside, trying to coax her daughter round. She strokes her arm and pretends to tickle her, which amuses Rosa, even if she stubbornly refuses to laugh out loud.

Tom returns and drops the flip-flops at Kath's feet without a word. I throw him a towel. He nods thanks and rubs his face and arms. Before he can finish, Pilot sprints out of the water and launches himself into the air at Tom, who jumps back onto the pebbles to have a roll around with his pet. Rosa decides to join in and the rest of us sit around laughing at the yelps coming from the three of them, even Kath. After a while, a dishevelled-looking Tom runs into the river with Rosa on his back. Together, father and daughter glide under the water, bobbing up for the occasional breath, before diving below the surface once more. How I envy their closeness. I watch them with a dreamy regret that my father and I didn't share a similar bond. Maybe things would have turned out differently had we been able to talk to each other more easily. Maybe I'd still be with Tom now.

– CHAPTER 7 –

Although my father was a good man, I knew his expectations for me far exceeded my abilities. I could get to the top of my game and it would not be enough for him. There was always another hurdle or challenge to take on. He took my mother's death badly. We both did. It happened so suddenly. At first, he struggled to speak to me. He'd get home from work and robotically set about preparing dinner, in most instances burning a part of it. He showed virtually no interest in me. We'd sit at the table eating, me telling him about my day at school, the lessons I'd had, anecdotes about different teachers. I made some of it up just to fill the void.

Ironically, it was Mr Brown, owner of a certain green Morris Minor, who first noticed a spark of ability in me and suggested to my father that I join the swimming club. That was it. My father had found a new purpose in life. I became his main point of focus and he decided that I was going to train to be a champion, whatever it took. Six mornings a week, at 5 a.m., all the alarms in the house would sound and my father would be up preparing my sustenance before driving me to the club. Looking back, I admire his resilience, the fact that he never showed any let up in all those years he inexhaustibly invested his energies into my own success. But he refused to take my opinions into account and, not wanting to rock the boat, I played out my life as he wanted it to be played.

Of course, like any teenager, I struggled to get up most mornings, especially during those harsh English winters when icicles formed on the insides of the windows and it was pitch-black outside. But I wasn't ever allowed to be sick or even off colour.

'Take an extra vitamin tablet,' he would say. 'That'll pep you up.'

I might have shown more willingness, had my father displayed some demonstrative love. Just a cuddle, a kiss, a pat on the head would have done it, then I'm sure I would have jumped out of those covers, whooping with delight. Instead, he opted to bark military-style orders at me from the bottom of the stairs: 'Come on Jenny – up you get!'; 'Jenny your cereal's ready!'; 'Jennifer where are you – up now!'; 'This is your last chance Jennifer Parker or it's a bucket of cold water over you!' His final ultimatums always worked in shaking off any thoughts of rebellion against this regime.

The first time I won a freestyle race, I climbed out of the pool and threw my arms around him, pleased for us both. Even then he soon pulled away and patted me on the arm instead. My father had been brought up 'when times were hard and what with mouths to feed, and work to be done there was no time for any of that touchy-cuddly nonsense.'

He always insisted that he and his sister, my aunt, were created to add two extra pairs of hands to the household. And if either of them deviated from their chores, they'd receive a belt to the backside or a slap to the face. 'We knew our place,' he used to say.

Little wonder Aunt Muriel got away as quickly as she could. She set sail for Australia before I was born and settled in Perth, where she set up a chain of bakeries. She only came back twice. The first time was for my grandmother's funeral when I was nine. I don't think her visit went down too well. I remember hearing raised voices in the night. Angry voices filled with blame and bitterness. Doors slammed, cupboards shook. Then silence.

After the funeral, she kissed me and held me tight, did the same to Mum, nodded solemnly at my father and at Grandpa, then left for Perth. Those two men were like peas in a pod. I'm sure they had probably ordered Aunt Muriel to return home and care for Grandpa, but she wasn't having any of it. Good for her.

She didn't bother returning for Grandpa's funeral a few years later. My father said it was because money was tight, but I wasn't so sure.

Then Mum died and Aunt Muriel came back for me, so she said. She hadn't married or had a family, but she was keen to finish raising me, and I was very aware that discussions were taking place behind closed doors. First, Aunt Muriel tried to persuade my father to let me go and live with her for a few years. When he flatly refused to give me up, she tried to encourage him to emigrate.

'They need skilled electricians out there, Pat,' I heard her say on several occasions as I sat on the sixth stair in the hallway, ready to take flight back to my bedroom if I heard a chair scrape across the floor. Again, my father wouldn't even consider the idea. He still thought of Australia as a place filled with convicts and deadly wildlife.

Aunt Muriel stayed on a few weeks to check we were

coping all right. She and I had a polite chat about 'the birds and the bees', then off she went, armed with bags filled with PG Tips and jars of Branston Pickle and Marmite. We waved her off at the train station and I wondered if I'd ever see her again.

Seven years later, my father and I were living with her on the other side of the world.

***

Several days after our river trip, I leave the house to pick up Rosa from school for a late-afternoon swimming lesson at the beach. She walks slowly towards the school gate, scraping the toes of her pumps, deep in conversation with one of her friends, their two nut-brown heads almost touching. They remind me of Kath and I, always reluctant to leave each other, wrapped up tightly in our laughter and togetherness. 'Thick as thieves,' my father used to scoff, when he returned home most evenings to find us upstairs in my bedroom.

As soon as Rosa sees me, a smile breaks onto her face. She waves, kisses her friend goodbye, waits for her teacher to open the gate and runs eagerly to the car.

'Jenny!' She climbs in and wraps her skinny arms around my neck. My nose is immersed in the scent of her hair. The warmth and comfort you get from a person's touch is such a wonderful sensory feeling. It's been so long since I've had that. Too long. 'I love having you stay with us. It's such fun. Will you live with us for a year?'

That little snub nose and those laughing eyes are irresistible. I tickle her under the chin.

'I won't be able to do that I'm afraid, Rosa, and I'm

sure you'd get fed up with me after a while. But I'm here at the moment, so let's enjoy what's happening now, shall we?'

I pull out onto the main road and concentrate on having to drive on the right-hand side of the road, leaving Rosa to consider my response. She sits picking at her fingernails thoughtfully, her head bowed down. Out of the corner of my eye, I see her shrug her shoulders as she lets out a long sigh and reaches forward to turn on the radio. It's a familiar English pop song that I don't know the words to, so I make some up, sing them out loud, hoping she'll join in. And before long the two of us are screeching at the top of our voices, carefree and completely out of tune.

At the beach, we bolt across the sand before it can burn the soles of our bare feet. Rosa yelps as she gets changed and makes her way into the sparkling sea, her arms raised high in an attempt to put off that moment when she will have to submerge her entire body into the briny chill. Man-made rock promontories stretch across the water to create a sheltered lagoon for us. The shelf of sand under my feet slopes away from us gradually, making this the perfect place for a child to swim. The water is so clear that I can see my toes wriggling for warmth beneath me.

The cold drives us out of the water after twenty minutes, but not before Rosa has shown me how much she's already improved. I run out fast so I can grab a towel and wrap it round her small shaking body. She bounces up and down, shivering noisily. A shadow appears in front of our sun, stealing our warmth. I turn round to confront its owner.

'Daddy!' Rosa rushes to hug her father like an eager pup.

'Hello, girls. Thought I'd drive down to take a look at your progress, Rosa. Very impressive.'

'I can do crawl and breaststroke and back stroke and butterfly.'

'You and I are going to have to have a race soon aren't we, to see who deserves Jenny's gold medal?' He ruffles her hair and digs his hand into his pocket, pulling out a €20 note. 'Why don't you grab us some ice-creams? What do you fancy, Jen?'

'A vanilla cone would be nice. Thanks.'

Rosa runs off to the ice-cream van parked on the sand a few metres away. Tom sits down next to me on the spare towel. I'm conscious that if I move my thigh a centimetre or two it will come into contact with him. His fingers seek mine out in the sand and he squeezes them gently. An electrical charge shoots through me.

'Oh, Jen, how am I going to get you out of here?' He taps his head. 'It took long enough last time.'

'Don't worry, Tom, I'll be leaving soon. This wasn't a good idea. I can see that now.' I pull my hand away.

'I'm not letting you go anywhere – at least not until we've had a proper talk.'

I look up at him, leaning on my elbow, my emotions in fresh turmoil. 'About what? Not once in eight years did you ring me to see how I was.' I keep my gaze steady. My teeth bite into my bottom lip, absorbing the pain.

Tom leans back and laughs, although it's hard to read him through his sunglasses.

'Ouch. I deserved that. I know it might not have appeared that way to you at the time, but it nearly broke

64

me having to finish with you. I went through some difficult times after you left for Australia. Got into all sorts of trouble with booze and pills.'

'Really?' So that's what Kath meant when she said that she was there to pick up the pieces.

'Yes, I did.'

His leg leans into mine. Flesh on flesh. I let it stay there.

'And now, all these years later, thinking about what your father meant when he told you he was glad he'd listened to Kath.' He exhales slowly, shakes his head. 'The thing is, I listened to her as well.'

'What do you mean?' I turn round to check that Rosa isn't watching us. She's too busy studying the pictures of all the different ice-creams on offer. 'Go on.'

'Of course, looking back now, I can't believe that I was so easily convinced by the words of an eighteen-year-old, but I was. She'd come round to my house when I was home from uni for the weekend and you were at the pool training. She told me I was destroying your chance of a great future, I was holding you back from reaching your Olympic potential.'

I look around the beach, briefly distracted by a small dog that rushes past us into the sea, pursued by a young girl in a pink bikini. I avert my gaze to stop sand getting kicked up into my eyes.

'I didn't know Kath went over to your mum's so often. Why didn't you tell me? I remember seeing her there once, but I thought she'd come to see me.'

Tom winces at the blue sky. 'I assumed your father had put her up to it, which is why I never said anything. But now I'm wondering whether it was for the right reasons that she told me I needed to *release* you.'

I put my chin between my knees trying to process this new information. 'I had told her that my father didn't approve of us and that he thought a spell in Australia would increase my chances of winning, but I never for one moment thought she'd back him up – especially when she knew I loved being in the UK.'

'Although you could argue that she was right, Jen. We did need a break. You did need to focus on the Games. You were only eighteen.'

'But it wasn't for Kath to decide, Tom. Nor you, for that matter!' I bash my heels on top of the sand and turn to him, my voice rising. 'She just wanted me out of the way so that she could have you for herself! Isn't that the truth?'

Now Tom turns to check up on Rosa. She's still in the queue. I can see her shuffling about impatiently. I rub the corner of my towel over my legs to absorb the glistening drops of seawater, trying to get a grip. This is crazy.

He turns back to look at me. 'To be honest, I don't think that is what she wanted. She looked pretty upset when I bumped into her just after you'd gone. Then I didn't see her for ages.'

'Who knows! It's too late now anyway.' I start biting my lip again, willing myself not to cry. Something small lands at our feet. Tom reaches into the sand and picks up a red ball. He hands it back to a young guy who has run out of the sea to retrieve it. He smiles sheepishly at us.

'*Merci!*' He returns to the sea to continue playing beach tennis with a young woman. He throws himself across the water to try and reach her badly placed balls, while she laughs flirtatiously at him.

'So, what about your boyfriend? You've been together quite a while now. Is it serious?' Tom raises an eyebrow. The cupid bow of his mouth pulls in slightly.

I consider his words carefully for a moment, shake my head and rake at the powdery sand with my nails.

'It's complicated.' A beat. 'Why do you ask?' I raise my head. Now I'm curious.

He starts to speak but nothing comes out of his mouth. There's an intensity to his gaze that I remember so well. I rub my arms to make him think it's the chill from the sea that's giving me the shivers.

'You're happy here though, aren't you, Tom? It's such a lovely way of life and Rosa is totally adorable.'

We throw a glance her way. She's handing over the note to the woman in the van.

'If you look closely, Jen, you'll see the cracks. Kath and I have been struggling for a while. I think we married for the wrong reasons and now we're both paying the price.'

I look around at this idyllic beach setting trying to absorb Tom's bombshell. Two windsurfers billow past on the buoyant sea beyond the rocks. A seagull swoops low, scanning the beach for discarded snacks.

'And since you've been here, she's barely uttered a word to me. It seems she's got her best friend back and I'm no longer needed.'

'I'm sorry, Tom. For *all* your sakes. I didn't realise. It must be so hard on Rosa as well.' I glance at him. My thoughts are racing, and I have the strongest desire to run away from this beach, from *Les Olivades*, and return to the life, to the success, I know. He scans the horizon tacitly. I'm not sure what more to say, but feel I should carry on rambling. 'Kath hasn't confided in me, if you were wondering. And anyway, I'm not going to be here forever, am I?'

'I don't think she's thought that far ahead. But, she'll come up with something, I'm sure, to try to keep you here. Just tread carefully, Jen.'

'Why do you say that?'

Tom absent-mindedly pats his muscular stomach. To think that I assumed he would have gone to seed! 'You saw her at the river last Sunday. She has a short fuse. When we first got here, she was fine, happy even. But over the past year – I can't put my finger on it – she's been different. Her moods go up and down, she shouts at Rosa. Mind you, in the time you've been here, she's definitely more stable.'

I turn to Tom, trying to read him. 'What do you mean "more stable"?'

His eyes dart over to his daughter who's on her way back. 'I guess you could say that a darkness had descended to cover her mind. But, as I said, you seem to have lifted it off just like *that*.' He clicks his fingers.

'Quick, Daddy, they're melting!' Rosa runs over to give Tom our ice-creams and plonks down between us on the towel.

After a few moments, father and daughter get up and walk to the shore, licking away at the melting streaks of vanilla running down their hands. He drapes an arm around her shoulder. She leans in towards him.

Married for the wrong reasons. Because Kath was pregnant with Rosa? But that's not what Kath told me. She said they'd fallen head over heels in love. Perhaps she thought they had. Perhaps they were mad about each other once, and Tom is not being entirely honest with me.

Now I'm confused. I should leave this place. Before I get in too deep. Before I get hurt – again. But, there's a side to me that's curious – curious to watch, wait and see where it's all going to lead. *Unfinished business.*

– CHAPTER 8 –

My alarm bleeps at 5 a.m. and I race to switch it off before the entire household is rudely awakened. For a moment, I'm back in Perth and it's time to get up and train in the pool. The familiar feeling of dread, which I started to experience during those last six months, quickly evaporates. It's market day.

Pilot jumps up to greet me when I enter the kitchen, hopeful that he might get a walk out of me. I pat him back down into his basket and rub his velvety ears, whispering at him to wait for his master. Most days, he accompanies Tom to work at the farm. He makes an adorable picture sitting in the back of the departing truck, pink tongue hanging out of a drooling mouth.

The early morning sun rises slowly out of the horizon like a rose-tinted fortune-teller's ball just as I step outside. Soon it will cast a majestic glow over the surrounding vineyards, teasing them to life row by row, only to pound them later in the day. As I approach the car, I can see Armelle drumming lightly on the steering wheel, lost in her thoughts. She turns sharply when I tap on the passenger window, and opens the door for me.

'*Bonjour,* Jenny!' Her cheeks lean in to give me the customary *bisous*. Her face is drawn. There are dark circles under her eyes. She seems to reads my concern and lowers her sunglasses. None of my business.

The back seat is stacked high with boxes containing jars of *La Miellerie* honey. They chink and rattle as we drive along the pot-holed lane and provide the perfect accompaniment to the tune playing on the radio. I click my fingers to add another element to our skiffle sound and Armelle joins in with laughter, her naturally sunny demeanour emerging. She tells me that she works part-time at the local *lycée* as a lab technician and she views the market as her day off.

'You will see, Jenny, there is such a nice *ambiance* there. I adore it!'

The market is already buzzing when we arrive. Vans and lorries jostle impatiently for a parking space, so they can quickly discharge their loads. Stallholders shout out greetings to one another, racing to set up their stalls before the morning rush begins. Market smells waft through the air: the sweetness of succulent strawberries, the dampness of new potatoes and other vegetables that have been plucked out of the dirt. I'm eager to walk around and sample some of the produce. But first I need to help Armelle get our own stall set up. She looks about smiling and within seconds it seems she has cast a spell. Friendly male traders offer to unpack her car and stack all the boxes on our pitch. I wonder if they treasure these brief moments when they can pretend that she belongs to them.

We place a waxed tablecloth adorned with sunflowers over two long tables and unpack the jars of honey. By 7 a.m., both sides of the bustling street are filled with market stalls as far as the eye can see. Armelle explains that we are situated in the area allocated to the *produits du terroir*, a good place to be in summer when tourist numbers are at their highest.

'Often in July and August I have sold out by ten o'clock,' she explains to illustrate the demand.

'So what do you do after that?' I ask. 'Do you have to phone Luc to bring more honey?'

'Oh no, that would be too much like hard work. I pack up and go and sit in a café. Perfect!' Her childlike giggles are beguiling. She leans towards me, her slanting cat eyes bewitchingly playful.

She's right. By mid-morning we sell our final jar of lavender-infused honey. It's satisfying to note the pile of empty boxes folded up in the back of the car. My armpits are damp from the sweltering heat and I am gasping for a cool drink. We leave our empty stall and find a table outside *Le Petit Zinc* café, which is busy and chattering with people. Little old ladies pull shopping trolleys filled to the brim with fruit and vegetables. I covet fresh melons bursting with honey-dew ripeness and dark-red cherries. Tourists empty their money belts, seduced by the freshness of the produce. The fishmonger has already done a roaring trade and is hosing down his shop front. A slinky cat lingers, hopeful that a morsel might be thrown its way.

I notice a couple of tourists are looking at me, one of them even pointing. Time for a new look, perhaps. 'Armelle, I need to get my hair cut.' I turn away from their intruding eyes. 'Do you know anywhere?'

'I have a friend Marie who runs a hair salon in Pézenas.' Armelle glances past me at the people staring. 'You don't like being recognised, do you, Jenny?'

72

'No, I don't.' I pull my cotton headscarf out of my bag, tie it securely around my head and pop to the bathroom.

When I return, the tourists have gone and Armelle is in deep conversation with one of the waiters who has stopped by our table. I hover in the doorway, reluctant to intrude. The waiter notices me and says something quietly, nodding his head in my direction. Armelle looks up and waves me over to join them.

'Jenny, come and meet my brother, Franck.'

Of course, the resemblance is obvious. Franck is the spitting image of Armelle, with equally delicate features and a slight slender body. I offer him my hand. He pats it away and kisses me on both cheeks. A tourist on the next table calls over to him, impatient to order some drinks, so he shrugs apologetically and leaves us. I watch him taking the order, placating the tourist with a charming smile.

'He's just like you, Armelle. Are you twins?'

'No, Franck is three years younger than me, but we tell each other everything. He lives in Pézenas with his partner Louis who runs an art gallery.' She plays with the straw in her glass. I notice that her pretty pink-varnished toes are twitching.

'Armelle, is everything all right? You seem a bit tense.'

Her feet scrape back and forth across the dusty pavement. 'It's nothing. I hate this time of year. Not the summer, of course. It's just that Luc has to work so hard at the farm. He comes home late, tired and we don't have any time to talk properly. *Bof*, I'm sure it must be the same for everyone.' She throws her hands up in frustration.

'Tom gets in late, too. So when will it end?'

'After the *vendange*, the grape-picking harvest at

the end of September. That's why October is the perfect month for me. It can still be warm here and we can both relax. Enjoy our time together.' She leans towards me and whispers conspiratorially. 'In fact, I plan to make a baby this year.'

'Good for you.'

I smile at her candour and incline my head to encourage her to tell me more. She is re-energised as she tells me how desperately wants a child and that she and Luc have agreed to wait until they have enough money saved to buy their own property.

'I just hope the baby happens straightaway as I am an impatient person,' she laughs.

Armelle phones her hairdresser friend. She can fit me in for a haircut, so we drive over there. Two hours later, we leave the salon. I turn to glance at my reflection in the window. My curtain of hair has been cut and coloured into a shoulder-length honey-blonde bob. It's been long forever and my back feels naked. Still, I can't help feeling a frisson of excitement.

'*Très chic*,' affirms Armelle.

'I hope so. *Merci*.'

I wonder what Kath and Tom will think. Let's hope Kath doesn't mind that I've been gone so long. I promised I'd be back by lunchtime to help her finish off preparing the *gîtes*.

'I'll drop you off at the bottom of the lane.'

'Thanks Armelle. Would you like to come in and say hello to Kath?'

She hesitates before shaking her head, gives me a sidelong look as if she is weighing up whether to speak her mind. 'I don't think Kath likes me very much.'

'I'm sure that's not true. She's just not very good at showing her feelings sometimes.' I grimace, remembering that Kath could turn off the charm just as easily as she could switch it on.

'We used to be friends, then maybe eight months ago she changed towards me. Stopped helping me at the market.' She shrugs. 'I don't know why. Maybe she is too busy. I can see that she is close to you, Jenny. With Tom, I'm not so sure. She can be difficult with him, I think. But everyone is different. Look at what Luc does to me!' She lifts her sunglasses to show me her tired eyes again. It's so tragic that it's funny and we both start to laugh.

I wave Armelle off and head up the lane on foot. Kath is pacing outside the front of the house with a can of Coke in her hand. Her arms are pink from too much sun, the shadow from her cap hides her face. She stops suddenly when she sees me and my new haircut.

'Well hello, stranger, do I know you?' she drawls in a faux-American accent.

I twirl round playfully. 'Sorry I'm late. I panicked. Got gawped at by one too many British tourists. Two, that is. Still, I felt a change was long overdue. What do you think?'

'I like it, Jenny. Suits you. Makes you more of a woman. But you know me. A bit sad for your old hair.' She walks round me and pats the now empty space on my back.

'You don't need to worry about that.' I reach into my bag and pull out a bunch of hair, which I've tied at both ends. I hand to her. 'Look, a keepsake! How silly am I!'

She holds it close to her nose. Then she embraces me and rests her head on my shoulder. 'I missed you today.

It's funny how you've only been here such a short time and you're already a huge part of my life again. God I wish you'd never left.'

We stand like that for a few moments. Does she mean eight years ago, when Dad and I moved to Perth, or this morning? The uncertainty makes me feel tense. Before I can ask, Rosa rushes outside to join in a group hug and persuades me to go for a bike ride with her while Kath cooks dinner.

We cycle along the small bumpy tracks that cut through the local vineyards, surprising the odd rabbit or lizard lounging on the dry soil, sending them into a rapid retreat. Rosa chats happily to me and helpfully teaches me the French words of the different things we see along the way. At times like this I can't imagine a better way of life and wish for one small moment that it could be mine. Then I remember what Tom told me at the beach and wonder what trouble lies ahead.

That evening, Tom gets home early enough for us all to sit down and eat together. He whistles when he sees my new hairstyle, which makes me blush. Why can't I ever control my feelings? I feel so nineteenth century sometimes.

The wind is blowing strongly, so we're forced to eat inside for the first time since I arrived. As he twists the corkscrew into the bottle of red wine between his feet, Tom explains that this region regularly gets battered from all directions by many different winds, including the well-known *mistral*.

'They can have a devastating effect, which is why there are so many cypress trees in the region. The French plant them as barriers.'

My eyes admire the skilful way he pulls out the cork with an easy pop, the muscles on his tanned arms flexed. There's a shadow of stubble running across his jawline. How I used to love rubbing my nose across its sandpapery texture. He let me shave him once. That was a disaster. In fact, that was the day I called round to his house after training only to find Kath sitting alone with him in his kitchen. His mum had gone out shopping with his sister.

'Hey, what are you doing here?'

Kath was the last person I had expected to see. Normally she didn't get up until midday at the weekend.

Tom looked embarrassed at my question. He pecked me on the cheek and just left the room.

Kath moved towards me, her hands reaching for mine. 'I dropped by to ask you about that homework we've got for history.'

'We haven't got any homework. Remember, Miss Darlington said she'd let us off this week.' I patted her hands away and moved past her to help myself to a glass of water.

'Oh, that's right. OK, might see you later?' She charged out of the door before I even had a chance to respond.

Upstairs, I found Tom preparing to shave. 'Has she gone?' he said.

'Yes, you can relax. Your *other* girlfriend has left the building.' I tried to make light of the situation but it niggled me slightly.

'Ha-ha. I have neither the energy nor the desire to manage two girlfriends, thank you very much.' He winked at me in the mirror and dipped his razor into the basin of water.

'Can I have a go?'

77

Tom nodded. I moved next to him and he let me take the razor. He perched on the laundry basket to allow me to reach his foamy face. My first stroke was perfectly smooth and left a neat line of stubble-free skin. The next one was a disaster, as I accidentally pressed too hard and nicked Tom's jaw. He laughed it off, despite the stream of blood, and I had to stick about five plasters on the cut to stem the flow.

I wonder if the scar's still there. If only I could reach out and rub my finger along his jaw to locate it, perhaps cover it with gentle kisses. My hand starts to twitch.

'Jenny?' He's looking at me questioningly, the now uncorked bottle in his hand poised to pour.

'Sorry. Yes please.' I push my glass forward and he pauses for what feels like a lifetime. Perhaps he wants me to look at him, but I can't. *He'll see how I really feel. What am I even doing here?* Instead, I jump up to help Kath serve dinner.

After we've eaten, Kath takes Rosa up to bed, leaving Tom and I alone again. The hairs on my arm start to prickle. I'm lost for words and the long silence stretches out. I gather up the empty plates and clatter them into a pile. He stretches out his foot and it nudges my own. He withdraws it quickly.

'Sorry,' we both say in unison. I laugh uncomfortably, trying hard not to blush again. He sits up straight, puts a hand on top of mine, his eyes burning into me. I feel my breath quickening, try to slow it down.

'We need to talk. Alone.'

'Yes, but not now, please Tom.' I pull my hand away and put it in my lap. I'm very aware of Kath and Rosa moving around upstairs.

I can sense his frustration as he stands up abruptly and picks up the pile of plates. 'How was the market today?'

'Really good. In fact I'd like to help out every week. It'll be good for my French.' I rise and move towards the sink. 'She's a nice person, Armelle. Very open. What's Luc like to work with?'

Tom comes over with the plates and starts filling the dishwasher while I tackle the saucepans with a scourer. 'He's great. Really easygoing. He seems a bit preoccupied at the moment, though. Not sure what that's about.'

'Who's that?' Kath re-enters the room. She picks up a cloth and wets it in my soapy water.

'I was just saying to Jen that Luc hasn't been himself lately. Perhaps it's the stress of starting a family. I know he'd love to have a child soon.'

'Having a baby isn't going to help their marriage, is it?' snaps Kath.

The silence forces me to turn round. Tom and Kath stand a few centimetres apart, facing each other as though poised for a duel.

Tom continues to hold Kath's gaze. 'As far as I'm aware their marriage is fine. Why, what have you heard?'

Kath shrugs and turns back to the table. She wipes it steadily from side to side, holding her hand at the edge to catch the crumbs.

'Oh nothing, just general tittle-tattle. You know.' She rubs hard at a mark on the waxed cloth. 'Anyway, tomorrow we've got to see the bank manager, Tom. Can you take Rosa to school, Jenny?'

'Of course. And is it OK if I use the computer afterwards? I've got a ton of stuff to sort out if I'm going to apply for college. Plus emails...'

'You can use my computer in my office if you like, Jen. It's much quicker. I'll leave the door open for you.'

'Blimey that's a first, you letting someone into your *den*!' Kath spits out the last word.

I daren't look at her.

'You'll need to switch it on then, won't you, unless you've decided to share your password.'

Tom ignores her remark, picks up his cigarettes and heads for the back door.

– CHAPTER 9 –

Stepping cautiously into Tom's study, I turn round slowly to confirm that I'm alone. I'm not. He is everywhere. I pick up a sweatshirt on the back of his chair and breathe in deeply, then wrap it around my shoulders to enjoy this proximity to him. There's a sudden warmth running through my veins.

His desk is in order. Pens of all colours and sizes stand in the mug I gave him when he went off to university. We'd only been together a few months. I was sixteen and he was eighteen. I pick it up and trace my finger around the rim. It's cracked in a few places and I can see that it has been carefully glued back together where the handle must have broken off. It's got his name on it, which I had custom-made in his favourite colour and typeface. The pantone number of the deep-blue colour eludes me now, but the font, I remember, is Franklin Gothic, a bold, sans-serif no-nonsense font – so typically Tom.

He has already switched on his computer for me. I move the mouse around and it comes to life. The screensaver – a shot of a tiny Rosa running towards the camera in a Mickey Mouse T-shirt – disappears, to be replaced by an image of the desert. Nothing but sand and a blue sky. I wonder if it's somewhere in the Middle East where Tom used to work.

I submit my Masters application and start going through my emails when my phone pings. It's a text from him, containing a link.

'Remember Jeanne? You can find her <u>here</u>.'

Jeanne! Of course he wouldn't have forgotten. Is this the subject of the novel he's writing?

I search for the file entitled The White Cave. Within minutes I am transported to another time and another place where Jeanne, a young medieval shepherdess and daughter of the gentle yet mysterious Baragor, finds a cave while looking for a missing lamb. In it she discovers a scroll and a key, which send her off on a journey to unlock the mystery of the White Cave. I quickly absorb the sixty or so pages Tom has sent me and am left craving more. It's a brilliant tale of mystery and witchcraft. His writing is so much better than I remember.

My legs feel stiff, so I stretch them out, then spin round in the chair to look at the books on Tom's shelves. Dictionaries, novels in French and English, many of which I remember from his teenage bedroom. He was always trying to encourage me to read more, but time was always an issue for me. I know he'd be impressed to learn that I have spent the last eight years reading his top fifty novels, which he wrote down for me once. Waiting in airports, in changing rooms, even lying on a bed as my physio has been working on me, I have been absorbed in the stories of Dickens, Austen and Dostoyevsky.

The tale of Jane Eyre and Mr Rochester is my favourite. I reach out to touch the book's dog-eared spine. It brings back glimpses of Tom and I lying on the grass by the river reading it out loud to one another, willing Jane and Edward to finally admit to their hearts' true desires.

I ease the book carefully off the shelf and open the faded blue hardback cover. A handwritten message inside reveals that Tom was twelve years old when he received this copy from his beloved grandmother, the woman who inspired him to keep reading. I flick through the musty pages to look for the passage at the end when Jane returns to Thornfield.

'Jenny, I'm back!' Kath shouts up the stairs.

Dammit. I haven't even checked all my emails yet. I close the book and put it on the desk. I'll borrow it to read. Tom won't mind. 'Hi Kath. Just finishing off.'

Quickly, I reopen my email account and scroll through my unread messages. There are loads from Scott, all with the same message: to please contact him so we can discuss my future. Am I returning to Australia? I send a reply to the latest one, saying I'll be in touch soon but not to worry. All's well. Then I move all of his mails to the trash basket.

My father has also sent an email. It's one sentence long: 'When are you coming home?'

'Yes, Dad, I'm fine, thanks. All is good here. Thanks for asking.' But that isn't what I type. I simply tell him that I'll be in touch next week once I've got a firmer idea of my plans. I close down the computer and leave the office just as I found it, then put the copy of *Jane Eyre* on my bedside table.

Downstairs, Kath is unpacking some shopping. She turns and smiles. 'Hey, how are Pop and Scott?'

'Fine. Just asking when I'm going to compete again. Can't take no for an answer.' I open the fridge door and reach for the cranberry juice, then hold the carton out to Kath.

She nods her assent. 'Yeah, well, can't say I blame them for asking. When you're that successful...' Her voice tails off. She stands looking out of the window dreamily as though she's watching something a long way away that's slowly moving out of sight.

I pour the deep-red juice into two glasses and hand one to her. Our fingers touch lightly. Now she's scrutinising me, the way she did sometimes when we slept over at each other's houses. I'd wake up in the morning to be greeted by two chocolate-button eyes, wide-awake and staring. She always said that she was penetrating my soul and sharing my dreams. I loved the idea of that. As we got dressed we'd speculate about inventing a telepathic drug, so that we could share each other's thoughts permanently.

'It's so good to have you back, you know. I don't think you realise how hard that was for me to see you go. It wasn't supposed to be like that.'

I seize the opportunity. 'What do you mean, "it wasn't supposed to be like that"?'

The colour drains out of her face, like she knows she's said too much.

I move closer. 'My father told me that you said something to him that influenced his decision to move to Australia. What did he mean? What was it, Kath?'

'That's bollocks!' She picks up her juice, drinks it in one and clatters the glass back on the worktop. 'Your father knew you didn't want to go, so he said he'd find a way for me to come too. Said he'd try to help get me into college there, but he bottled out at the last minute. I was desperate to get away from home and he used me!'

I stand alone in my bubble, my brain ticking rapidly, trying to flick through the images of Kath standing on

84

the pavement, waving and crying as we drove away to Heathrow airport. Would my father really have made those promises to her?

The bubble bursts.

'So, hold on, what you're saying is, you knew he was thinking seriously about this before he told me.'

She shakes her head, bends down to put some cereal boxes in the cupboard. 'Of course not. He only told me the day before he told you. Asked me not to say anything as he wanted to speak to you himself.'

'But why didn't you say anything afterwards?'

'I told you that I was hoping to come too. But you weren't interested. You were too upset about Tom finishing with you. Remember?' She holds out her arms. 'Anyway, it's all in the past. You're back with me now, my dearest darling friend.' She pulls me close and hugs me tight, but I'm still holding my glass of juice and it slops over the floor, forming a blood-red puddle on the tiles.

'Shit!' She rushes to the sink to grab a cloth.

I'm rooted to the spot, still trying to decipher what she's just said, but nothing seems clear. There has to be more to this, I'm sure. I can't believe that my father only told her the day before he told me. She was always round at my house waiting for me to return home from a gala or training. What did she talk to my father about then? She said it was to get away from her mum, so she could do her homework in peace, but now I'm not so sure, especially as she went to Tom's too. I look down at the hand that's taking far too long to wipe away the juice from the same tile – over and over. I'm going to get to the bottom of this, even if it means prising the words from my father's reluctant lips.

'There.' She stands back to admire the clean floor. 'How do you fancy coming to *La Miellerie* this afternoon? I have to pack some orders. I'll introduce you to Sylvie and Bernard.'

I need answers to my questions. That's what I told myself on the train, wasn't it? And I'm going to get them, however evasive she may be. Whatever it takes.

***

We approach *La Miellerie* on the same road that I arrived on two weeks ago. I can see that the vines have grown a little taller in just a short time. Kath toots her horn at a small narrow tractor chugging away in one of the fields. A hand appears out of the open-topped roof and waves.

'Tom always works the vines, if given a choice,' nods Kath. 'He enjoys the solitude. Says the monotony helps him to come up with ideas for that epic novel of his. You know, the one he's writing but won't show anyone.' She grasps the steering wheel in both hands. 'Perhaps it doesn't exist.'

I look straight ahead. By only allowing me to read some of his novel, Tom has put me in a difficult position with Kath. If she asks me whether or not I've seen it, I'm going to have to lie.

We pull up in front of the farm. I fumble for the car door handle and jump out to open the tall iron gates. They groan as I prise them apart and wave Kath through. Flakes of sharp paint from the metalwork dig into my hands. I brush them away on the back of my shorts and close the gates.

Pilot appears out of nowhere. He bounds with loud

yelps to greet us, his dangling tongue a permanent fixture. His coat glistens. I wonder if he's been running through the sprinklers that are watering the field of strawberries next to us. Without any warning, he shakes his coat energetically, spraying me all over with water drops. Roused by my laughter, a woman with short grey hair and a slight stoop comes out of the back door to the house carrying a metal bowl. The glare of the sun forces her to blink. Her grey apron is dappled in purple stains and she wears long black gloves, which extend past her elbows. Her brow is shining and she struggles to wipe it with the top of her arm. I don't envy her working indoors in this gruelling heat.

'*Bonjour les filles*,' she shouts to us and waves.

I wonder if this is Sylvie, the owner. For some reason I was expecting someone more refined, a lady of the manor in twinset and pearls, perhaps. Kath confirms this by taking me over to her and introducing us. I tower over this petite woman with her deeply lined face. She smiles up at me to reveal a gold tooth on each side of her mouth, before kissing me three times. She says something in a regional gravelly French, which I can't grasp, but it's clearly about me. Kath's reply is both abrupt and mumbled. I feel an urge to intervene.

'*Votre maison est très beau.*' I gesture round at the lovely house.

'*Belle*,' corrects Kath. '*Votre maison est très belle. Maison* is feminine.'

Sylvie responds warmly, squeezes my shoulder and motions with her hand to offer me a cold drink. She reminds me of a female pirate – someone who's lived life to the full and has survived to tell the tale. Kath declines and tugs me away so we can get to work.

We walk through one of the stuffy outbuildings. The stench of manure is overwhelming and my head feels dizzy. Thankfully the room we are now entering is air-conditioned. It's filled with bottles and containers of all sizes. These are the beauty products that have just arrived from the factory. Kath and I are to pack them into boxes so they can be sent to various retailers. I unscrew the lid from some body lotion and sniff. It's been delicately scented with honey and makes me think of breakfasts at home with my mother. I loved to watch her dipping her teaspoon into the jar and twisting it swiftly round and round before letting the syrup spiral slowly onto her buttered toast.

Our first job is to line the boxes with bubble-wrap and corrugated card to ensure that they can withstand the bumpiest of journeys. I wonder which far-flung places they will be sent to and imagine Aunt Muriel browsing the local chemist's in Perth, only to come across one of the very bottles I have packed. I must write to her. She has been so kind to me over the years – a gentle voice of reason when my father has tried to coerce me into another race, another medal, another training schedule.

After an hour or so, Kath leaves me to fetch Rosa from school. She's dropped into one of her silent moods. I asked what Sylvie said to her, but she dismissed it as nothing. After years of experience, I know it's not worth pressing her. She'll tell me when she's ready. Or maybe she'll tell Tom. That's what partners are for, isn't it?

Now it's my turn to feel glum. Thinking of the two of them together. In bed together. *No.* I refuse to succumb to melancholy and shrug it off firmly. I knew the risks in coming out here, didn't I? The problem is I've achieved nothing so far, except to let myself fall for Tom again. Did I kid myself into thinking that I'd be able to control my feelings, that it was Kath and only Kath I'd come to see? Did I really expect to come away from this unscathed and heart intact?

I carry on working and force myself to think of a happy face. Rosa's Cheshire Cat grin appears in my mind and lifts my spirits. My legs are stiff from standing up for so long, so I bend down to try and touch my toes with my elbows. My back and shoulders feel like twisted branches creaking in the wind. I must go for a swim soon. My muscles are crying out for some exercise.

Two large trainers appear in the doorway.

'I didn't hear the door open. What is it with you always creeping up on me?'

Tom shrugs. 'You're at your most beautiful when you don't know you're being observed, Jen. Totally unself-conscious.'

He enters the room, body shining with perspiration. His sun-streaked hair is combed back off his face, making his nose and cheekbones seem more angular than usual. Those beautiful eyes are clear and focused on me and only me. I inhale his presence with a deep longing for another time and place, somewhere faraway from here, where we could be ourselves and not have to play this game. *If only it was just a game.* He turns to shut the door quietly behind him. My heart starts to throw itself against my ribcage.

'I love your novel, Tom. Can I read the next instalment? I want to know what's going to happen to Jeanne.'

'Of course, but you have to pay me first,' he says surprisingly, and then he lifts me up and places my flip-flopped feet on top of his own, transporting me back in time. This is a game we often used to play. I'd wrap my arms round his waist, raise my head with my eyes closed and wait for him to kiss me, sometimes a few seconds, never more than a minute. Today, nothing. Unnerved I blink my eyes open to see Tom gazing down into them.

'What is it?'

'I should never have let you go, Jen.' His voice is a whisper, like a gentle breeze that passes through your room on a balmy night.

'So, why did you?' I pull away from him. 'You know you broke my heart.'

'I don't think I realised the enormity of it then,' he says. 'At the time it felt like the right decision. Yet I still can't believe that I let Kath influence me like that.'

I drop my arms despairingly and think back to what Kath said earlier, that my father deceived her by promising that she could come to Australia too. I step away from Tom and walk around to the other side of the bench, tapping my fingers lightly on the grained wood, its rough texture reminding me of my school desk, where I once etched our initials with a compass.

'Actually, Tom–'

The door scrapes open with a jolt. It's Edouard, the barbecue carrier with his wide grin. 'Ahh, *salut les gars*! I thought it was you, Jenny.'

He doesn't appear to pick up on any atmosphere in the room, just comes over to embrace me. He's a head shorter than Tom but the veins in his arms stand out like power cables. This is obviously a man who trains with weights.

'So, you have come to help today? *Très bien*. Come – I have something to show you.'

He winks at Tom and escorts me out of the room into the stifling heat. We head for a dark corner of the shed and I strain to adjust my eyes. Out of the darkness come several tiny mews. A large cat is sprawled out on some tarpaulin, surrounded by tiny kittens kneading away at her tummy, fighting to find a free place to feed.

I crouch down low but keep my distance. 'Oh they are gorgeous, Edouard. When were they born?'

'Only last night. And please, my name is Eddie.'

'Jenny!'

It's Rosa. I beckon her over and put my finger to my lips so she knows to approach quietly. Kath and Tom also join us.

'Oh, Daddy, please can we have one?'

'No, Rosa, Pilot wouldn't like it,' snaps Kath. Her mood doesn't appear to have lifted.

'You know Pilot adores cats. Look at him here. I'm sure it wouldn't be a problem,' mutters Tom quietly to Kath, out of Rosa's earshot.

'Tom, our family is big enough,' says Kath in a loud voice. 'We don't need another bloody pet!'

She turns on her heels and marches back into the cold room where we've been working. We stand and watch her go. Rosa bows her head.

Tom swings her onto his shoulders. 'Come on, missy. Let's go and see Sylvie. I'm sure she'll have baked something sticky and sweet for you!'

I follow them outside into the bright sunshine. Armelle's husband Luc and some of the other men are standing around in front of the house chatting, many of them smoking. It must be the end of their working day. An older man steps forward out of the pack. This must be Bernard, Sylvie's husband. Like his wife, he has a well-weathered face. These are clearly people who spend most of their time outdoors. Grinning from ear to ear, he shakes my hand and goes on to make freestyle swimming actions and gurgling sounds, no doubt to impersonate me. Another comedian. I chuckle along. How do they ever get any work done?

Within minutes, Bernard has organised some champagne and beer so that we can all toast my successes and good health. Tom bends down to whisper that Bernard always likes an excuse for a drink at the end of the day. Kath joins us and looks more relaxed. She flirts mischievously with Eddie, standing close to him, a hand stroking his arm as she chats.

I take a seat next to Sylvie at a small round table where she's shelling peas into her bowl. She's tied a red scarf around her head, knotted at the top. She joins in every now and again with the men's banter. Her voice is strong and authoritative. I can see that the men respect her. I can't understand what they're discussing, although it has something to do with their underwear. A few waistbands are pulled down. Eddie confirms his role as ultimate clown of the pack by dropping his oil-stained shorts to reveal a pair of very skimpy Y-fronts. With his shorts bagged below his knees he enjoys twirling around for all to view. I catch the word *petit* shouted out jovially by Sylvie. Grinning, Eddie dances over to our table, adds some pea shells down the front of his pants and twerks. Tom looks over to me and shrugs happily. He's at home here with his family of friends.

Refusing to allow Eddie to be the only clown at the party, now Bernard attempts to pull down Luc's shorts.

Luc shouts '*Non!*' and holds on desperately to his waistband, trying to slap Bernard's hand away.

Sylvie leans towards me. 'No underwears,' she says, pointing at Luc with her vegetable knife.

Rosa squeals with delight at the play-fighting and runs over to sit on my lap. I put my arms around her tiny waist and jig her up and down. I lean forward to absorb the coolness of her silky hair. It smells of pears.

'*Allez!*' Sylvie shakes her head at me conspiratorially, letting out a heavy sigh. She takes herself back into the kitchen, a slight limp slowing her down.

'So, Jenny,' Eddie sits down next to me, reaching out to tickle Rosa under the arms. She laughs and makes to run away, but looks round disappointedly when she realises that Eddie isn't up for chasing her. Clearly he has another fish to fry, and something tells me that I am that fish.

I look around for help, but Tom is talking to Bernard.

'You and me go dancing tomorrow?' Eddie leans into my face space.

'Did I hear someone mention dancing?' Kath comes over and squats at our feet.

'*Oui,*' confirms Eddie. '*Jenny et moi demain soir.* Tomorrow evening.'

'I'm not sure, Eddie. There's a lot of work to do at the house. And I'm a terrible dancer.' I'm desperately making eyes at Kath, pleading with her to help me out.

'You should go, Jenny. It'll be fun. Eddie goes every week to the local *Ceroc* dance in the village. Tom and I used to do it. It's like rock 'n' roll. Go on, give it a go!'

Thanks Kath. My fate is sealed.

Eddie jumps up and takes my hands, shaking them

around. 'Yes, you come. Don't worry – no hanky-panky. I know you have boyfriend.'

I laugh at his choice of words.

Tom wanders over to join us and Kath tells him about Eddie's plan.

'Good for you, Jen.' His voice gives nothing away. 'OK, let's go!'

Before I have the chance to make my excuses in front of Tom, he has turned on his heels and started walking towards his truck. Rosa skips after him, along with Pilot. I turn back to Eddie who is waiting for an answer.

'OK, Eddie. That would be nice. But I really am a terrible dancer. You will be embarrassed, that I can promise you.'

He whoops and picks me up, whirling me around. When he finally releases me, I step back giddily and see Tom leaning against the truck watching us. What I would give to turn back the clock and put my arms around his neck instead. But then I remember what happened the last time I did just that. The day he broke my heart eight years ago.

– CHAPTER 10 –

I'd just finished my A-levels and had returned from a fantastic holiday in Turkey with a group of friends, including Tom and Kath. I was brimming with happiness, confident with my future plans of university, swimming and living close to Tom. Nothing could dent the elation I was feeling. How wrong could I be?

As soon as I entered the house and saw the unlikely combination of my father, Bob my coach and Tom sitting at the kitchen table, I knew something was wrong. Tom stood up and started to pace up and down the room. There was a heap of papers on the table. No one was speaking.

'What's up?' was my immediate question, but no one answered.

I threw my bag to the floor and went over to the fridge to pour myself some apple juice. My father stood up next, disturbing the papers and sending them flapping all over the floor. Tom bent down to gather them up – a good excuse to avoid my gaze.

'Jenny! Come and sit down. We need to have a chat,' said my father. Perspiration glistened on his forehead.

He proceeded to tell me, with Bob interjecting, of their plans for me to start training in Australia the following month along with some of the younger members of the

British squad. I could stay for a year (perhaps two) during which I could also start my psychology degree. It would be a great opportunity to spend time with Aunt Muriel in Perth and, as a qualified electrician, my father was confident he could get a work visa.

'I know we've already discussed this, Jenny, but please hear me out. The facilities over there are out of this world and the coaches are world-class – one in particular, Scott Morrison,' said Bob keenly. 'The climate will suit you too and I'm sure we'll be able to knock a few seconds off your best.'

I sat down, my gaze on Tom. Finally he raised his head, his eyes holding mine momentarily before he looked away to shuffle the papers around once more.

'And what do you think of this plan, Tom?' I asked him.

He stood up and pushed the hair out of his eyes. The Adam's apple in his neck looked more prominent than usual. 'I think it's a fantastic opportunity, Jen. It'll be the making of you.'

I stared at him in amazement. 'It sounds like you know all about it already.'

Silence. Tom seemed to be waiting for me to take the lead.

'So will you come too, take a year out and join me?'

'I can't do that. I've got my studies to finish. This is something you have to do by yourself. I'll only be a distraction.' This time he held my gaze and it unnerved me. 'Jenny, you've got your career ahead of you. You're on the brink of making it. Don't let me stop that from happening.'

I spun round sharply and walked towards the window. Raindrops were dribbling down the panes. 'I'm not going.

I'm happy where I am here. Home is where the heart is. That's what you always used to say, Dad. Isn't that right?' I turned back to confront all three of them.

'Jenny, you really need to consider your future. I'm convinced this is the only way to secure yourself a place in the British squad,' said Bob. 'Everyone else wants to do this and we've got the funding for it.'

'Well, you'll have to find someone else to fill my place.'

I'd heard enough and ran out of the house into the driving rain. I ran and ran, finally finding myself at our rock. I picked up a handful of stones and threw them one by one into the river. Tom arrived moments afterwards and placed a raincoat around my shoulders.

'I thought swimming was your sport, not running,' he joked.

I didn't respond.

'Listen Jen—'

'That was clever of them, wasn't it? Let's rope Tom in and get him to persuade Jenny. She's sure to listen to him.' My voice was waspishly unfamiliar, even to my ears.

Tom sat next to me on the rock. Rain was rolling down his nose and dripping off his chin. I wondered if it ever rained in Perth.

'Jen, you have to admit this is a fantastic opportunity for you. Come on, I know deep down you want this too. You keep saying that your mum would be so proud if you ever won gold. Well, now's your chance. It'll only be for a year, if that.'

'Or two, they said.' A lifetime.

'It'll fly by and I can come out to see you, can't I?' He turned me round to face him, rubbed his finger over my chin.

'Sorry, but I'm not doing this without you, Tom.'

He shook his head and stood up. I waited.

'To be honest, Jen, this is probably a good time for you and me to have a break from one another.' He kicked a stone into the water. 'We're both young. You're only eighteen.'

'Nineteen in a couple of months.'

'We have years ahead of us and I don't want to settle down yet. I need to get out into the big wide world and experience it for myself. And so do you.'

I stood up and wrapped my arms around his neck. 'I think you're just saying this, Tom, to–'

He pulled away and took my hands in his. 'Jen, stop! I mean every word.' He paused for breath. 'There's something else I need to tell you.' He combed his hair back with his fingers, a familiar gesture that usually indicated a sense of awkwardness. A bombshell was coming. 'My English tutor has arranged a work-placement posting for me in Jordan.' He flashed me a quick look. 'I've decided to accept it.'

'As in the Middle East?'

He nodded slowly.

'What kind of posting? What about us? What about the flat we were going to rent?'

'You're not listening to me, Jen. I'm going to the Middle East and you're going to Australia. Different continents. I could never forgive myself if you stayed here and gave up this amazing opportunity on my account. That would be mad.'

He dropped my hands, turned away and started walking.

'Tom, please. Don't go. I need you!' I was rooted to the spot, stunned by his words. They sounded so final.

But he didn't look back.

I refused to take his calls after that. Things happened so quickly. After I'd finished sulking, I popped round to his house a few days later and his mum told me he'd already gone to the Middle East. She gave me his contact details, but I threw them away and stubbornly refused to contact him. I decided that I'd go to Australia and wait for him to come to his senses and fly out to rescue me – my white knight in shining armour. He never did.

- CHAPTER 11 -

My newly cut hair is beginning to bother me. It won't lie flat like it used to. I made the mistake of towel-drying and now it stands up like a dandelion clock, so I grab the serum Marie the hairdresser gave me and rub a few drops through the ends. It'll have to do. There's a heap of clothes on my bed and nothing feels right. Everything's too long, too short, too low, too skimpy, too everything. Not only will I have to walk into a room full of strangers tonight, whose language I can't speak properly, but I'll have to dance in front of them too. *Ceroc*, whatever that is. I breathe in deeply.

There's a sharp rap at the door. Kath enters without waiting for a reply.

'Hi Jenny. You ready?'

I spin round slowly for her, resigned to wearing an old sundress. On the plus side, it's quite 1950s in style, so hopefully will be fitting for French rock 'n' roll.

'You look lovely, Jenny, and I like your hair all flouncy like that. What about footwear? Just wear something comfortable but keep your toes covered in case someone steps on them.'

Kath's words are the tonic I need to help calm my nerves. I lean in to kiss her on the cheek and she draws me in for a warmer embrace. Her hair smells the same as Rosa's.

'I'm sorry about yesterday, Jenny.'

'Yesterday? What do you mean?'

'Oh you know. Being in a grump at the farm. It's Sylvie. She can wind me up sometimes. You probably didn't understand her, but she said how beautiful you were and how difficult it must be to have such a successful friend, blah, blah. My bloody mother all over again!'

She waves her arms about, clearly agitated by Sylvie's comments, which have struck a nerve. I only heard Kath's mum, Julie, utter similar words once, but Kath said she was relentless with her unkindness.

I reach out to pat her hair. 'Rubbish! It's only because of the Olympics. You were the one who had all the boys knocking on your door, remember?'

'That's because you were out of bounds, *remember*?'

'Well that's all in the past now, isn't it? And it's only right that I've still got it – seeing as I've got a date tonight. Yee-haw!'

I slap my thigh, before sitting down to finish applying my make-up.

She leans in conspiratorially. 'Just be warned, Jenny. Eddie's a real flirt, but he's all hot air. Make sure you don't fall for his charms.'

'OK.' With a mascara wand in my hand I risk clogging my lashes if I so much as blink, which takes all my focus.

She continues to watch my reflection for a moment, then withdraws. She's still behind me, scratching her arm, perhaps forgetting that I can see her in the mirror. Something's on her mind. The weight of it fills the whole room. I sweep powder over my face. Our eyes meet again in the glass for a long moment.

'Seriously though, Jenny. Are you OK about Tom and me? I wasn't sure if you would still have feelings for–'

'Of course, it's fine, Kath. That was such a long time ago.' The chair rocks on its legs as I stand. 'But I still don't understand how you can say that you only knew about my father's plans to emigrate the day before he told me.'

My hand grips the back of the chair to prop up my courage as a door downstairs slams shut.

'Jen, Eddie's here!' Tom shouts up from below.

Kath waits for me to continue, but I wave her away. This needs more time, more thought. She looks relieved as she leaves the room to go downstairs and greet Eddie. I wonder how uncomfortable she really feels about me delving into the past to question her like this. Has she picked up on the doubt in my face? I've tried so hard to mask my emotions. The trouble is, when you know someone so well – have grown up together – you develop a strong understanding of each other's body language. Even now, after all these years, I can sense when she's looking for a sign of my intent. Does she ever wonder if I came here to see Tom?

I squeeze my hot feet into a pair of white plimsolls. No doubt they will be grey by the end of the night. The untamed hair will have to do and is sure to be in far worse a state after I've been spun round the room by Eddie countless times. I feel like a teenager on her first date all over again. Ironically, when I was a teenager my first ever date was with Tom – who has barely uttered a word since we parted at the farm yesterday afternoon. How I wish I could replay my teenage years all over again. Make different choices, keep a watchful eye over Kath, over my father and, most of all, say 'no' in the strongest possible terms when he told me we were emigrating.

***

The community hall is pulsating with music when we pull into the car park. A group of teenagers are huddled together on a cluster of car bonnets, smoking and laughing. A bottle of vodka is passed around merrily to lift spirits and loosen any inhibitions. That was a lifestyle I never really knew at that age. When we moved to Australia, I wasn't allowed a social life. And I guess I didn't want one either. I poured all of my emotions and anger into being the fastest I could be. Of course, with Tom and Kath I'd had a few wild nights. We'd concoct a story to tell my father, which usually involved Kath's mum, bless her, having to pretend that I was staying over. It feels so long ago.

Eddie slams the car door shut and stoops to light a cigarette. He cups the flame between his hands. The amber light flickers to reveal scratches and scars. Most of the workers wear gloves for their work on the vines, but not Eddie. Some people have this incredible ability to withstand pain and I wonder if it's because they don't feel it as much or whether there's something within their psyche that enjoys testing their own mettle, perhaps. He stands up straight, puts the cigarette packet in his back pocket and takes my arm.

'*Allez hop*, let's go.'

I pull my wrap around my shoulders, suddenly feeling shy in my simple attire.

We enter the lobby. Moths flutter around the bright strobe lights to create eerie shadows. The walls are covered with posters and small ads, suggesting an active community. There's a photo of Bernard and Sylvie with a group, holding up a trophy. Eddie explains that they used to be part of the Languedoc *Ceroc* dancing team and have won many awards.

'But Sylvie has problems with her legs now. So they don't dance anymore.'

Eddie pulls me towards the music and we step into a candle-lit hall. People of all ages sit at tables pushed together to accommodate groups of families and friends who have come out for a *soirée* of dance and chatter. Café-style doors are folded back to entice the little breeze there is into the humid room. Several couples are already moving on the waxed dance-floor, swinging their hips seductively, their feet sliding gracefully back and forth as though they're skating on ice. Women are manoeuvred away and reeled back to their partners. Many wear high heels and trot on the balls of their feet like young deer. Small girls dance together, wearing pretty floral dresses and ribbons in their hair. They twist round and round until finally they let go and lurch about, enjoying the dizziness.

The music changes to an acoustic mix of Spanish guitars, which is greeted by loud cheers. Many of the older couples make their way enthusiastically onto the dance-floor. Their steps seem more traditional, almost like ballroom dancing, I think.

Eddie hands me a cool cup of sangria. Ice cubes bob among a sea of fruit. I pick out an orange segment and suck on it. Eddie puts his arm lightly round my waist and leans over to shout in my ear. We are cheek to cheek.

If only Tom was here. He spent all of yesterday evening locked away in his study. I could hear him tapping away at his computer as classical music played gently in the background. I hoped he'd come out so that I could tell him that I didn't want to go dancing with Eddie anymore, but I didn't see him again until Eddie came to the house this evening. Even then, he barely glanced at me when I came downstairs. He told Eddie to drive carefully and not to drink too much. Eddie said that Tom sounded like my father, which, of course, struck a nerve with Tom and he retreated back upstairs to close his study door on us both.

'Come and meet my friends.' Eddie pulls me over to the largest and loudest group of people in the hall. Raised eyebrows and curious smiles are turned towards me. I take in a blur of faces and clasp the edge of the chaotic table for reassurance. Half-filled bottles of wine and beer vie for space, among ashtrays already half-full of discarded cigarette ends, some of which are still alight. The incessant smoke begins to create an ethereal fog around us as I am delivered to each and every one of Eddie's friends for an introduction. I don't stand a chance of remembering all their names. Even though I didn't ask him to be discreet, Eddie introduces me as a friend of Tom and Kath's who's visiting from '*l'Australie*'. Nothing more.

'Come Jenny, let's dance.' He brims with eagerness. Sadly, I feel the complete opposite.

'Oh Eddie, one more drink, please!'

He reaches for the jug he has set down on the table and refills my cup. I knock it back, put down the cup and hold out my hands to him. *Like a lamb to the slaughter.* My shoulders feel stiff, my body awkward. I'm instructed to relax and simply follow Eddie's movements. He's a very good dancer. The mesmeric way he moves his hips so gracefully is a sight to behold. They move up and down, from side to side in a slow and tantalising manner. I, on the other hand, have need of a lifetime of learning. My flipper feet, while graceful and expert in the water, have no idea how to turn and step lightly. Instead they trip over his and show no rhythm whatsoever. Eddie is patient. He coaxes me into a number of complicated twists and turns, helps me to relax and muster something resembling a dance move.

After two bouts, I'm keen to leave the dance-floor, but Eddie is persistent and stubbornly refuses, insisting that we keep going until I have found the 'special feeling', as he calls it. I never do find out what that special feeling is. My feet seem to have a mind of their own and one of them trips over Eddie's leg, twisting my ankle badly as I land in a heap on the floor. A lightning sharp pain shoots up my foot and I know my dancing is over for this evening. A guilty-looking Eddie leads me gently to the table. His friend Laurent jumps up to give me his chair and hurries to the bar. He returns with a tea-towel wrapped around some ice and passes it to Eddie who has removed my now grubby plimsoll. He presses the cold compress gently against my ankle. Feathered lashes graze his cheeks as he concentrates on the task at hand. I'm tempted to ruffle his hair to reassure him that it's not his fault but I don't want to risk being misunderstood.

'You are a charming man, Eddie! Why don't you have a girlfriend? Ouch, that hurts.'

'Sorry, Jenny.' He presses more gently. 'In answer to your question, I am waiting for you to come to your senses and forget about that man you have in Australia.'

I smile back and watch him at work, hoping that the ice will magically mend my painful ankle.

He looks up, pauses, and continues to interrogate me. 'You know, Jenny, I wonder if you have a man. You say you have one, but I don't think you do. It's just an excuse, isn't it, so you can come here and steal Tom from Kath?'

Now I stare at him with total bewilderment. Who told him about Tom and me or is he just guessing? Was it Armelle? Does everyone know? Is it so obvious? He continues to look at me, eyes unblinking. Waiting for a response. The tension starts to rise. What should I say?

'Ha, I am only joking, Jenny!' He breaks into laughter and tickles my knee.

'Eddie, that was so mean! I thought you and I were going to be friends, but I'm not so sure now!'

I slap his shoulder and he pretend-winces playfully and winks.

Warm relief rushes through my veins and I reach for my cup and another mouthful of sangria. 'But seriously, Eddie. When did you last have someone to love?'

'*Bof*, I like to have lots of girlfriends. Every season, lots of beautiful foreign girls come here for the *vendange* and I enjoy many of these exotic beauties. I take maybe two or three at a time, plucking them like cherries from a tree. Then I spit them out at the end of the season.'

His laughter rings out, but it isn't true. I can see a glimmer of something dark hidden within him. I wonder what his story is. Everybody has one, don't they? He probably uses his humour to hide behind the real person. Kath said Eddie was all hot air. I'm certain she's wrong about that. There's definitely more to him than meets the eye.

The evening moves on swiftly, despite my inability to dance. Eddie is besieged by female partners and enjoys throwing a multitude of girls and women from one arm to the other for the duration. His friends are good company and naturally think I'm Eddie's girlfriend, but I'm quick to quash that rumour.

Despite having drunk over the limit, Eddie insists he's going to drive us home. I hobble to the car, leaning on his arm. As we race through dark lanes, he sings loudly and tries to teach me 'La Vie en Rose' by one of his favourite '*chanteuses*', Edith Piaf.

Suddenly a rabbit shoots across the road, its brown bobtail disappearing out of the bright headlights into the hedgerows. Eddie brakes hard and fast, successfully managing to bring the car to a sudden, juddering halt. The wheels squeal on the road, a piercing scream in the thick cloak of night. The seatbelt digs into my chest. I pull at it to loosen the pressure and uncurl my other hand, which is tensely wrapped around the door handle. We sit absorbed in the silence. Stunned. It was so fast, so sudden. However, we are both unhurt. The car is fine too. As I turn to look at Eddie, I can see he's in shock. I reach out.

'*Ça va* Eddie? Are you OK?'

I switch on the overhead light to find that his face has paled. He stares ahead wide-eyed, still gripping the steering wheel. I reach for the near-empty packet of cigarettes in front of the gearstick, hand one to him and bend down to retrieve the lighter, which has fallen onto the floor. Eddie leans over to light the end. Noisily he inhales the smoke, taking it far back into his lungs, his chest rising. He unwinds the window and lets it out slowly, abandoning the phantom-like swirls to the night air.

'I'm sorry. I was driving too fast.'

'Listen, Eddie, it's not a problem. We've both drunk too much tonight.'

'It is a problem. I have a problem. I am a problem.'

He bangs his steering wheel and gets out of the car to inspect the tyres. I do the same. The smell of rubber irritates my nostrils. Now I see how lucky we are. We almost ended up in a ditch which runs narrowly along each side of the lane – a ditch that Eddie should surely have been aware of.

From that moment on, we drive at a more sedate pace. So sedate, in fact, we would probably be overtaken by a rambler. Eddie is quiet, mulling over something and chewing on the inside of his lip. I attempt a few mundane comments about the stars and the winding roads, but my words fall on deaf ears.

I tell him to drop me outside the gate. It's past midnight and I don't want to disturb the others. Eddie stops the car and turns off the engine. He sits quietly, staring straight out into the darkness, still lost in his thoughts.

'Goodnight then, Eddie, and thank you for a lovely evening.'

With nothing more to say, I grasp the door handle. He touches my arm. I hesitate.

'Be careful, Jenny, yes?'

'I'm always careful, Eddie.'

'No, I mean be careful of people. I think you are a nice lady. But, perhaps too... you trust.'

'OK, Eddie,' I say, flattered by his concern for me, a lone woman tourist. 'Thanks for the warning. I hope you are feeling better now.'

His eyes go to another place and his tongue darts across his mouth as I open the door.

'I did love someone once, Jenny. She was very special to me.' He pauses to lick his lips. 'She died in a car crash. Alone. It wasn't her fault. The other driver was drunk. That is why I am angry with myself tonight. I was stupid.'

'Oh, Eddie, I'm so sorry.' My arm coils around his shoulders and he leans into me.

'It was more than two years ago, but tonight I thought about Ute – she was from Sweden. She was very gentle like you.' He lifts his head and teardrops linger on his lashes. Our closeness unsettles me, but I don't want to pull away too quickly. His need for comfort is evident.

We're disturbed by the sound of crunching gravel. My door is wrenched open. Brown legs. Muscular calves. Tom.

'OK, you two, less of that.' The tone is sardonic. Tom bends down and reaches across me to shake Eddie's hand. A few words in French, which I don't follow. Goodnights all round and I get out and accompany Tom through the gate. I turn back to wave at Eddie.

'That was looking a bit steamy in there. Have a good night, did you?'

'Actually I've hurt my bloody ankle, so you'll need to give me a hand going up the stairs. And yes it was a good night, thank you. I like Eddie.'

'He likes you. I can see that!'

'Jealous?'

He turns to me abruptly and the pain shoots through my ankle, but I say nothing. Then he pulls me into the porch where we can't be seen by anyone and pushes me against the wall. His mouth clamps down hard on mine. I caress his head and draw it closer to me without thinking. *You are mine.* Spasms of desire shoot through me like shocks of electricity. My breath quickens and I raise a leg to wrap it round him. He pulls away and looks down at me, a glint in his eyes.

'Yes I am. You should know better than to play with me, Jennifer Parker.' He caresses my chin with his thumb, draws a line across my mouth. I want to bite it, but he's too quick.

'Come on, let me help you up to bed, before this gets out of hand.'

'I wish.' My whispered response vaporises into the night air, unheard.

– CHAPTER 12 –

By the time I return from my swim at the lake the following morning, Tom has already gone to work at *La Miellerie*, taking the truck and Pilot with him. Perhaps he wanted to avoid seeing me, regretting the previous evening. My lips and chin still tingle from where the bristle on his jaw grazed them, just before we kissed. I tremble at the memory. At least I know that he still feels something for me, even if it's only physical desire. I may have had too much to drink, but I'm certain that he was sober.

Kath is in the kitchen munching on an apple when I come downstairs after my shower. For a moment I wonder if she can read my thoughts.

'Hey, how was your evening? I thought we could go to the beach today, just you and me. Rosa's off school from next week, so we should make the most of it.'

'Great. What about breakfast? Do you want anything first? I need a coffee.' I reach for the coffee pot.

'Yes, take your time. I've made a picnic already, so just bring your swimmers.'

With a coffee in one hand and a piece of toasted baguette in the other, I go back upstairs to get my beach gear. Although my ankle is still swollen, I can walk on it normally. *Jane Eyre* is still sitting on my bedside table, waiting for me to pick her up and start reading. She'll be waiting some time. I don't want to risk getting Tom's precious book full of sand, so I grab a couple of French magazines from the pile in the corner instead.

Kath drives us to La Tamarissière, a small beach village close to Cap d'Agde. Situated by the river Hérault and surrounded by pine forests, it's a beautiful crescent-shaped sandy beach, smudged with rock pools and relatively quiet for the end of June. Kath tells me that she and Tom joined the farmworkers here last New Year for the annual skinny dip in the sea.

'It was bloody freezing and I'm terrified of the water, as you well know, so I just dipped my toes in, then ran back to get dressed. Never again.' She shakes her head. 'Luc and Eddie had a competition to see who could stay in the sea the longest. They were in there for nearly an hour. Bernard had to threaten to fire them just to get them out. They looked like a pair of shivering bluebottles when they finally came out. Bloody nutters!'

We lay our towels high up in the dunes to try and get some shelter from the lively sea breeze. Kath takes off her clothes and stands stark naked digging around in her bag for her bikini.

'Careful Kath or a dog's going to come along and take a bite out of one of your juicy buttocks!'

'Ha ha. Bloody better not or I'll set Pilot onto it.' She gets changed, throws out her towel and plonks herself down onto her stomach. 'And when your highness has finished fannying around folding her clothes nicely, perhaps she'd be so kind as to put some cream on me.'

I squirt suntan lotion on her back and legs, sending her into fits of ticklish giggles. It's funny how I can carry on like this with Kath as if there was no tension between us – as if the last eight years never happened...

We lie there, enjoying the summer heat, flicking through our magazines and chatting about nothing in particular. I'd almost forgotten how it feels to be absorbed in a vacuum of inactivity. After a couple of hours, I'm lying peacefully on my stomach, my eyes half-closed, listening to the sea suck in and out of the rocks, seduced by the heat working into the knots of my back and shoulders. I become aware that Kath has sat up and has started to cream her front.

'Jenny?'

'Mmmm?'

'Do you remember when we used to go to the river and play those make-believe games, pretend we were orphans or princesses in disguise? I loved those times.'

'Mmm.'

'Sometimes we'd sit on that rock for hours, throwing stones into the water, just you and me. I hoped that time would stand still and we'd never have to move from that moment. It felt so perfect.'   ●

'You're right, Kath, they were happy times.' A picture of our two pairs of feet dipping in and out of the gently flowing water forms in my mind. We used to pretend that if we kept them still for too long the fish would come along and nibble our toes away.

Kath lies on her back close to me, an arm flung loosely over her eyes. Her breast seeps out of the side of her bikini top. Its white, rounded fullness reminds me of a poached egg.

'I guess I hoped when I married Tom that I'd find those moments again – that a piece of you would be buried within him, you know?'

That snaps me out of my doze. I sit up fast and look down at her. 'Kath, how could you possibly think that by marrying Tom you'd find that connection with me? Don't you realise that you nearly broke my heart when I got your letter? Just going off with him like that, when he'd meant everything to me.'

Kath shakes her head over and over, her hair flapping about her face as though my words have put her in a trance.

'I was going to come back to the UK, try and get back with him. I sent you an email, remember? And you never responded to it.'

Now she looks dumbstruck. 'What email? When? I didn't get it.'

Now it's my turn. 'You can't be serious? The one I sent you just before the 2007 World Championships in March.'

'No, I didn't get it, I don't know what you're talking about. It must have got lost. I changed my email address a few times back then, remember?'

It's true that Kath was always moving around. She sent me countless emails, telling me she'd changed her address. I was never certain that I had the correct one. I never understood why she couldn't just set up a hotmail address like everyone else.

'But I emailed all your email addresses, just to be sure. I can't believe you didn't get it.'

Kath stares at the twinkling water.

'So you really didn't know that I was planning to come back to the UK to try and make it work with Tom?'

'I'm sorry, Jenny. I didn't get your email. Truly.'

She falls silent.

I don't know what more there is to say on the subject, brush off her hand, and run into the sea. I plunge under the gentle rippling waves and swim as far as I can until my breath can hold out no more. Reaching the surface, my lungs gasp for air. For a while, I lie on my back, gazing up at the cloudless sky, trying to empty my head of any negative thoughts, trying to work out my next move.

When I get back to our towels, Kath hands me a cup of coffee from the flask she has brought. I take it and enjoy the sensation of the hot liquid racing down my throat, then sit back down and look out at the empty ocean, willing the feeling of calm to stay with me a while longer.

'You didn't tell Tom, then,' says Kath. 'You didn't email him about your plan to come home all those years ago.'

I look down at my toes. 'We weren't in touch. I blotted him out of my mind. It was the only way.'

'Right.'

A question bubbles to the surface, however, and I can't keep it down.

'So, how are things with you and Tom? From where I'm sitting, you two seem a little distant from one another.'

Kath dips a finger into her coffee and sucks on it before answering. 'We were happy at first, we really were. But, lately it's got hard. All we seem to do is argue about money, Rosa, the business. To be honest, Jenny, if you were to tell me that you were going back to Australia, I might come with you for a bit. What do you think? Or we could go on a road trip in Europe. Rosa can stay with Tom.'

I stare at her, bewildered by her eagerness to discard everything she holds dear (or should hold dear). She's like a small puppy that's discovered a favourite old slipper to chew on.

'Kath, I really don't think you've thought this through properly. You have the most amazing family and life here. Isn't that enough for you? And how could you up and leave, just like that?'

She blows into her cup. 'Maybe you're right. But promise me you'll think about it. We could just go away for a month or two. Just like we planned to do one day. Our "big world discovery", as we used to call it.'

I look at her doubtfully. 'Wouldn't Rosa mind?'

She shrugs. 'Rosa loves her dad. She'd be fine for a bit.'

'OK, I'll think about it, ' I say, and she smiles.

Hopefully, Kath will have forgotten about this by the time she's immersed herself back into her busy home life. I can sense that her mind has wandered already and she's thinking about something else. She never was able to concentrate on one subject for too long.

'Do you remember that time when we made a raft and decided we were going to sail across the Atlantic?'

'Oh crikey, yes,' I say, relieved that Kath is already moving on. 'How could I forget? It's a good thing it broke up into pieces as soon as we threw it in the water. We wouldn't have lasted more than five minutes on it.'

I move into the shade to get some respite from the heat. Kath doesn't seem to worry about sunburn.

'Then there was the time we said we'd withstand an earthquake and be the sole survivors on the planet.'

'Hey, we were such dreamers.'

'Sad thing is, I really believed that those dreams would happen. But, they didn't. In the end, it all went wrong.' Now Kath looks as though she's going to cry. Her hands look tense as she rakes them raggedly through the sand. Something tells me that she's thinking about Tom.

'Kath, what did you talk about to my father at my swimming galas and when I wasn't around? It's a long time ago, I know.'

She glances at me. 'Oh this and that. Nothing really. We both wanted you to become the best you could.'

'Even if it meant encouraging Tom to finish with me.'

Her head jerks up. For a moment she says nothing. Then: 'Maybe. Listen, Jenny, you were so smitten and it was affecting your ability to see the future we'd mapped out for you.'

'We?'

'Your dad, I mean. He shared his dreams with me, that's all. And I listened to him. I felt sorry for him. He missed your mum and he said he hoped that you might become an Olympic champion one day, in her memory.'

'He never put it like that to me.'

'Well, that's what he told me. I don't think he wanted to pressurise you too much. Hey, look at that little girl, she screeches just like Rosa. Drives me potty sometimes that noise she makes.'

We watch a young girl bouncing up and down in the water, trying to find the courage to go deeper.

'You know that Rosa picks up on your disagreements. Even I can see it. She looks so bewildered at times when you argue. I know it's not my place to say this, but it would be better if you didn't argue in front of her. Try and be nice to Tom. I know it's hard sometimes when you're in a relationship.'

Kath sighs heavily and scratches her arm up and down while she appears to consider what I've said.

'You're right, Jenny. I will. I promise. But only if you invite me back to Australia with you.' She jumps up, unclips my bikini top before I can stop her and runs to the edge of the water laughing, daring me to chase after her.

'Right,' I call, reaching round to clip it back up, 'you've asked for it now.' I run after her, whip away her bikini top and run back to our towels, waving it as though it's a flag of victory. 'That'll teach you.'

***

After our picnic lunch, we spend the next few hours walking to the lighthouse and along the riverbank. On the opposite side is Le Grau d'Agde, a little fishing port lined with shops and restaurants. Large fishing trawlers are taxiing along its sides. Kath explains that there's a small fishing and canning industry still in operation here, although many vessels take tourists out on fishing trips two or three times a day.

'That's something you could do with Eddie, if you wanted to see him again. He's always going fishing. Loves staring moodily out to sea, as he puts it.' She laughs.

I almost say something about Eddie's near-accident last night, but stop myself. Perhaps Eddie was right when he said I was too trusting of people. Perhaps I need to pay more attention to what's going on around me, and tread more carefully around Kath, in case she misconstrues my words to serve her own ends.

And an hour or so later, she does just that.

Day is slipping into night when we get back to the house. The sky is streaked in blood-orange ribbons and looks as though it's on fire. Tom is sitting out the front, a beer in his hand. Pilot runs up to the car and barks keenly at us.

Kath bends down to stroke him, then walks over to Tom. She ruffles his hair.

'Darling, we've had the most amazing day. Guess what? Jenny and I are going on a road trip.'

'Kath! What are you saying? I said I'll think about it.' Stunned, I drop my bag at my feet and fold my arms.

'I know, Jenny, but Tom won't mind. And, as you say, we're just thinking about it.'

Tom is still wearing sunglasses, so I can't see what he's thinking. His silence, however, says it all. He knocks back his beer in one and stands up. 'Glad you two have had a good time. Shall I make some dinner?'

'Good idea. I just need to go and get Rosa from Béatrice's.'

Kath puts her arms around Tom's neck and reaches up to kiss him full on the mouth. He pulls back after a few seconds, unwraps her arms and takes a step backwards. She doesn't seem to mind.

'OK, you go and do that and I'll light the barbecue,' says Tom. 'Oh, by the way, your boyfriend phoned, Jen. Nothing urgent, he said. Suggests you Skype him before 8 p.m. our time. After that he was heading off to the pool.'

His words are measured, no sentiment attached. He turns and heads into the kitchen, leaving me to stand and contemplate what he's just said. While Kath gets back into the car, I go through the house into the back garden where Tom is lighting the barbecue. He stands tall and still, watches the flames build into a dancing kaleidoscope of colours. I know he can sense my presence behind him.

I wait. Finally, he turns, removes his sunglasses and looks at me questioningly.

'What's this about a road trip?'

'I only said "maybe" to Kath to stop her from going on about it. She's not thinking this through properly. There's Rosa, the business, you too, of course.'

He goes into the kitchen and returns with two beers, hands me one. 'And where did that "darling" come from? It's been years since she used that term of endearment on me.'

'Actually it was my idea. I told her that Rosa could probably pick up on your disharmony and she should make more of an effort to be nice to you.'

'Yes, well your timing couldn't be any worse.' He throws back his beer, slams the bottle back down on the table and moves closer to me, his mouth twisted into a grim line. 'I told you that we needed to talk because, before your arrival here, I'd been planning to tell Kath that I wanted a separation. I thought you should know. Your timing wasn't ideal.'

It feels as if a thousand splinters of ice have just shattered all around me.

'Of course, that was before you arrived. I've decided to put off telling her until you leave. But there's no way I want to start getting cosy with her again. That stage of our life is over as far as I'm concerned.' He turns away to inspect the barbecue. I follow him.

'Shit, Tom. I'm sorry. I just–'

He raises a spatula at me to stop. 'Jen, you have no idea how hard it's been and I don't have time to enlighten you now. She'll be back soon. To be honest, I'm not even sure you'd believe me. Kath's doing a very good job of being her old self. I just hope that it's long lasting. Did she tell you that she was taking antidepressants?'

'No.' I shake my head, recalling the empty packet on the worktop when I'd just arrived.

'She's been on them for six months or more. Anyway, they seem to be working and hopefully there won't be any further spells of her dark moods. God they were awful. There were some days when she refused to speak to Rosa and me. I sometimes wonder if she actually cares for Rosa. I've never seen much love pass between them in the way you usually see with a mother and a child.'

'I suppose she's not as tactile as you. Rosa has a strong bond with you, Tom. I can see that.'

'I love her to bits. Hence why I've been trying to hold this family unit together. For Rosa's sake more than anything else. But now it feels as though I'm trying to cling onto something that would be better off if I let go.'

He stalks back into the house and returns with the meat and another beer, his face expressionless. I wonder if he's set on getting drunk tonight.

A car engine alerts us to Kath and Rosa's return. He takes some sausages and chicken wings out of the packet, lays them out onto a platter, before drizzling them in a dark marinade. 'Jen, don't say anything to Kath, will you.'

'Of course I won't.'

Tom waves at Rosa as she steps out of the car.

'Dinner will be half an hour or so. Why don't you go and call that boyfriend of yours? I've left the study open. I'm sure he'll be waiting.'

***

'Hello stranger.' The long drawn-out vowels confirm that I'm speaking to Scott. There's something wrong with his camera, so we can't see each other.

'Hello Scott! How are things down under?'

'Yeah, all good, all good. Listen, you've been gone nearly a month now and I've heard practically nothing from you. Just a couple of brief emails and your phone's always off when I've tried you. What's going on, Jenny?'

'I'm sorry, Scott. It's been hectic here. They've got guests arriving next week and I've been roped in to help. Where's Dad? I'm hoping he might be around so he can join in with our chat. There's something I want to ask him.' I lean forward in my seat, hoping to hear the familiar West Country accent of my father's.

'He's out working all hours, assisting the coaches, showing interest in the new Brit, Amanda Berryman. Wants to know when you're coming back. I do too.'

'Not yet. I've agreed to help my friends out until mid-September. I told you that.'

'Yeah I know. And what about your swimming? What's your decision on that?'

'I'm retiring, Scott. Just like I said. This is the end of the road for me.'

There's a long tense pause. 'Are you completely sure, Jenny? Why? You're so young still.'

'Not young enough. Listen, I've applied to do a Masters so I can get into sports management.'

'What, out here you mean?'

'Possibly England. I'm not sure.'

There's a long silence followed by a clicking sound at the other end. I know he's pulling his finger joints as he takes in and absorbs my words, an old habit from when I trained with him.

'Listen, Jenny. You're an Olympic athlete. Why would you want to return to college? We need to talk about things. Face to face I mean, before we even think about sketching out the news for the press. It's a huge decision you're making. How about I come out and see you in France for a couple of weeks?'

'Absolutely not. There's no room – I'm here on a working holiday. You promised me breathing space, remember?'

Now there's another long silence.

'OK, Jenny,' he says. 'Have it your way, then.'

Finally, after some general chat, I end the call. Scott has persuaded me to wait to announce my retirement at the end of the summer, so that first I can speak to my father. Right now, I have other issues on my mind.

Back downstairs, I help Kath make a salad. Rosa is dancing around Tom at the barbecue. I notice that he's switched to drinking water. We sit outside, Kath's and my face tinged pink and glowing from our day at the beach. She and Rosa are both in high spirits and compete for my attention. I just sit back and listen, gazing up at the stars and wondering if my father sees the same ones when he goes on his night-time walks along the beach. Suddenly, he seems so far away – he's even in another hemisphere. I realise I don't miss him and I'm convinced I was right to leave, even though my future still looks uncertain. The thought makes me feel sad.

Tom says very little, avoids looking at me and as soon as he's finished eating, stands up to go and read Rosa a story and put her to bed.

Kath and I clear away the dishes and play a few rounds of *boules* before we finally succumb to tiredness. Tom doesn't come back downstairs. I hear the music seeping out from underneath his study door when I climb the stairs to bed. 'Swan Lake' by Tchaikovsky: one of the pieces of music we used to listen to when we were in a mellow mood, lying on top of his bed, chatting about our future – our far-fetched, unrealistic, never-to-be-realised future. I stand outside the door and put my palm on the cool wood, imagining that he might be on the other side doing the same thing.

'Goodnight Tom,' I whisper, before walking on to my room. Closing the door, I lean against it. The energy fizzes out of me and I drop to the floor, crying silently into my hands until I finally manage to crawl between the sheets.

– CHAPTER 13 –

The arrival of our first guests coincides with the hottest day of the year so far. We spend the morning rushing around to make last-minute touches to the *gîtes* and the communal area outside. Tasked with the duty of making up all of the beds, my arms laden with a tower of bed linen, I negotiate opening the front door with one elbow to step outside. The brightness of the sun startles me and its intensity almost tempts me back inside. A sheer curtain of dust hangs heavy in the air after Tom's efforts to finish cementing the pathway. There's a stillness, an eeriness all around like that split second before a bomb goes off. I can't really see where I'm going and my feet touch something soft on the path. *A dead body*. I scream with fright and almost drop the linen. Except it isn't a dead body lying out in front of me, it's Pilot. Poor chap. He's sprawled out on a diagonal of shaded concrete, his sleek body heaving up and down in a regular rhythm. He raises his head to greet me, but the effort is too much and it flops back down.

I come across a glum-looking Rosa, sitting motionless on the swing, head bowed to her knees. She kicks at the bark chippings, which Tom has carefully laid out around the entire play area. I heard her arguing with Kath earlier when I was upstairs. I think she wanted to bake a cake to welcome the guests, but Kath objected. The last thing she wanted on a day like today was more heat in the house. Unlike the new *gîtes*, the main house isn't air-conditioned and the nights are starting to make sleep difficult for all of us.

Rosa tilts her head slightly when I invite her to help with the beds. I notice her face is red from where she's been crying. She'll shake herself out of it shortly, I'm sure. Something will catch her attention and she'll quickly forget that she was ever sad. Kath was like that. She'd often hit rock-bottom after an argument at home and come to seek me out and watch me training at the pool. She said it was therapeutic to count each length I completed and, usually by the time I'd finished my training programme, she was back to her normal bouncy self.

I'm right. An hour later, Rosa's the first to jump up when a pair of glinting Audis turn into the gateway. Our guests – two families with young children – have driven all the way from a rainy Germany and are delighted to see that there isn't a raincloud in sight. So keen are they for their holiday to begin that within minutes they are freshly showered and on their way into the village for a walkabout. As they disappear out of the gate, one of the young girls, a few years older than Rosa, turns and waves. Rosa is delighted by the possibility of new friendships and skips off to make some ice-lollies for their return.

Tom and Kath are sitting at the outside table poring over a sheet of paper. They've come up with a plan to conduct vineyard tours at *La Miellerie* throughout the summer as a way of drumming up local business. I've agreed to distribute some flyers to the tourist office and local businesses when I go to the market next week with Armelle. The new guests expressed an interest when Kath mentioned it on their arrival, so she's going to take them on a guinea-pig trial tour to see how it works out. Now she and Tom formulate a plan. He's sketched a diagram of the process, which she's scrutinising carefully. I look at their heads nearly touching, voices excited, Tom's flop of hair hanging over his eyes. This is the first time I've seen them like this – genuinely close, animated, happy even. Maybe they'll make it work after all, now that Kath's meds are taking effect – and I'm shocked by the despair this thought triggers in me. Given that I encouraged Kath to be nicer to Tom, I should be soothed by their togetherness, but instead a great sorrow seems to be taking root. All I can do is turn away and take myself to the kitchen to help Rosa.

Several moments later I'm cleaning up Rosa's sticky-lolly mess on the worktop, Rosa nowhere to be seen, when I hear the back door swing open, rattle hard and slam shut.

'He's impossible!'

Kath takes a glass from the cupboard and fills it with water. Her face is red and angry. Without so much as a pause for breath, she bangs it down on the worktop. I watch, fascinated by the rivulets of water which trickle onto the floor.

'Who, Tom?'

'Who do you think? Yes, that ex-boyfriend of yours. Remember?'

The tension in the air is tighter than an archer's bow. 'Is that how you see it, how you see Tom, as my ex-boyfriend? So, why–'

'Jenny, OK.'

'Well, don't bring me into your domestics, Kath. It was your choice to... to marry him.'

She turns away and stares out of the window, her hand to her stomach. Tom's truck pulls away, out through the gateway. 'I didn't feel I really had a choice though, Jenny. I was pregnant. I wanted to bring up the baby, give it security, give it love.' A beat. 'Give it a *real* family.' Her voice is choked with upset.

She had a choice whether or not to sleep with him, though. They both did! But now isn't the time to discuss this. Rosa's in the house somewhere. Kath's volatility sets me on edge. Her moods never used to swing quite so sharply. It's a part of her personality that's new to me and I'm not sure how to deal with it. I want the old Kath back – the Kath whom I could say anything to and it wouldn't really matter, the Kath who would sulk for two minutes then sweep away any negative thoughts as though they were a cloud of willow fluff. I keep my head down and continue to wipe the worktop clean, but it doesn't take long for her to worm her way back into my heart. One tiny glance at her shuddering body sparks my conscience. Her hands grasp the edge of the sink. I'm sure she must have been terrified at the thought of having to raise a baby by herself. I'm glad she didn't have to. I just wish she'd been more selective about her choice of sleeping partner. She knew what he meant to me.

Dammit. I feel as though I'm back to square one. I've accomplished nothing on this journey so far and I too feel like a teenage girl – angry with myself, angry with my father, angry with Tom for pushing me away when all he had to do was tell me how he really felt. Who knows? If I'd stayed in the UK, I might still have got a place on the team and won my medals.

Cautiously, I approach Kath, the one friend I could always rely on to help me through a difficult time. Her head rests on my shoulder.

'I know, Kath, I know,' I whisper.

Together we stand and look out beyond the garden wall, losing any sense of time as we watch the sunset streak paint across the darkening blue canvas – each of us wondering, perhaps, what our future holds.

***

Over the next few days, Tom keeps his distance and spends all of his time working at *La Miellerie*. Kath muses to me that perhaps she pushed him too far with her criticism of his plan. She adds smugly that he's handed over the vineyard tours project to her entirely.

'He'd be rubbish anyway. Would probably end up giving away the wine because he's so bloody charitable.' She pauses from drying a plate, and looks at me as if debating the divulging of some new secret. 'I've just found out that he's lent Luc some money for a down payment on a house. Hasn't told me, of course.'

I stop wiping the hob. 'From Armelle?'

'Doesn't matter how I found out, I just did. He'll say it's his money; money he earned before he met me. He'll use some argument to try and shut me down, like he always does, using those big words that he thinks I don't understand.' She sits down opposite me at the kitchen table, chin in hands, brooding. I notice her nails are bitten to the quick.

I always admired the way Tom handled my father so deftly and chose to ignore his rudeness. Of course, my father didn't approve of our relationship, arguing that it got in the way of my potential to be a world-class swimmer, and he made that clear to Tom, often practically shutting the front door in his face when Tom came to call for me, offering up some excuse that I was way too busy with my training schedule. Now, as I gaze at this bold and complex woman in front of me, I wonder how Tom plans to talk to her about the separation he says he wants. I'm glad he's decided to wait until after I've left at the end of the summer. It's difficult to know how she will react, but I don't think it'll be easy. He's right, Kath has changed. I don't know what's brought it on but I've noticed how she often looks deep in thought, as though she's plotting something.

Often, after my morning swim at the lake, I return home and see her through the window sitting alone at the kitchen table, staring into space, her hands wrapped round a cup of tea. Yet as soon as I open the door and drop the breakfast pastries on the table, she shrugs off her shroud of mystery and jumps up to prepare a pot of coffee. Perhaps I should try and take her away for a few days so that we can talk properly; somewhere with no distractions and we can relax fully. But I'm no longer certain she would open up to me. From the little she's said, Kath has obviously had a serious falling out with her mum. She used to relish discussing in great detail the arguments she had at home. And, even though I've prompted her a few times, she refuses to be drawn into explaining exactly what happened this time, except to say that she can never forgive her mum.

I'm not even sure I want to spend time alone with Kath – not anymore. Of course, we have a strong bond, almost like a blood tie, which is rooted in our childhood friendship, a bond that runs so deep on so many levels. But sensing the dark cloud of gloominess that seems to now be part of her, I'm starting to realise that we are poles apart in most respects and that it's only our shared history that holds us together. And I don't think that's enough.

***

A day or two later, Kath takes Rosa to a friend's for the day and says she'll be out all morning to run some errands. After doing the chores, I head to Tom's study. I asked him at breakfast if he would leave the door open for me, so I could check my emails on his computer. On his way out, he handed me the key, eyes burning into my soul, his finger gently stroking my palm – or maybe I just imagined that's what happened.

I'm excited to see that he has sent me several updates to his novel. Ignoring the rest of my inbox, I settle down to read his words and am immediately transported back to Tom's fantastical world of thirteenth-century southern France. This girl, Jeanne, feels so much a part of me as she must be a part of Tom. His prose is beautiful, almost poetic. It conjures up the mysticism surrounding this epoch in rural France so brilliantly. How witchcraft, religion and faiths of all sorts played such a major part in shaping France's future. At the same time, he makes small but utterly convincing observations about the human mind, the power of fate and destiny. I feel as though I'm reading a subliminal message about my own life and the fact that I have to take control of it and make my own decisions now. His words empower me.

Reluctantly I check my other emails and am relieved to read that Scott has told the swim team that I won't be returning until after the British summer. If I'm planning on retiring, he confirms that I'm going to have to break the news to my father myself. I can't say I blame him for not wanting to take on that task. It won't be easy. He's also going to try to get some time off, so he can come out here to see me and meet my friends. I need to let him know if that's OK with me. Of course it isn't. I've already told him that. The last thing I want is someone around me from that other life who's going to jostle me back into my reality.

I'm also pleased to see that I've been offered a place at a London university to do a Masters. It'll mean sorting out my finances to check I can afford it, but I'm glad I've got another option for the future.

I go back to re-read one of the chapters in Tom's novel. Although I don't hear the door open, the creaking threshold rouses me.

'What's that you're working on, Jenny?'

I peer up, still lost in the world of Jeanne, to find Kath standing there with a questioning look on her face. Before I can formulate an easy lie, she's edging forward to see the screen. The document title at the top will give it away instantly.

I have to make a decision. Fast.

'Oh shit, you've caught me out Kath. I've found an excerpt from Tom's novel and was having a quick nose. But, please don't tell him or he won't let me use the computer again. I was going to draft a press release about my retirement and came across it by chance.'

My words are garbled and I can feel that my face is burning. I can see that she is curious – desperate even – to read Tom's work, as he's made it out of bounds to her. The look on her face unsettles me. But she's not angry with me. No. She can barely control her excitement.

'Let me see, Jenny. What's it all about then? Hold on a mo'.'

Kath rushes into her bedroom to get a chair and it's in those precious few seconds that I grab the only chance I've got to delete Tom's email trail. However, I leave the text document open. This chapter is about five pages long. Hopefully enough to keep her satisfied.

She returns and sits alongside me, grinning with excitement.

'It's just a few pages of his novel. Hard to tell what it's about exactly. A shepherdess who loses some of her flock,' I say with feigned nonchalance.

'What? Is that it? I thought it was going to be much more mysterious than that. All that secrecy to keep it away from me.' She peers closely at the screen to scan through the document, as if she's looking for some incriminating evidence to use against Tom.

I stretch and yawn. 'I wouldn't bother if I were you, Kath, it's only one chapter. Shall we go and make some Pimm's to have with lunch? I got a bottle yesterday in the British section of the supermarket.' I hang around the study door, willing her to leave the room. I doubt that she has the patience to sit and read Tom's work. I've never known her to finish a novel in her entire life – this unspicy tale about a medieval shepherdess is not going to change that.

I'm right. Soon, I hear her footsteps on the stairs as she comes down to join me.

A few hours later, we've shared a jug of Pimm's and lemonade, and are playing *boules* in the back garden. I launch my coloured ball at the jack and knock Kath's ball out of the way. 'Gotcha!'

The rumbling sound of Tom's truck can be heard around the front of the house. 'Remember, Kath. Don't say anything about his work!' I say, squeezing her arm.

'Sshhh,' she laughs complicitly, putting her finger to her mouth. She bends down to retrieve her balls and almost topples over.

'Hey, girls, any of that for me?' Tom and Pilot bound out of the kitchen in unison. Dog and his master, both full of vitality.

'Sure, I'll get you a glass.' I hurry to the kitchen, not daring to leave Kath alone with Tom for too long. Not in the mood she's in.

Too late. Before I even shut the cupboard door, I hear raised voices. Kath's laughter rings out loudly and untrue. She's taunting him.

'Who the hell gave you the right to go looking for my work?'

Sensing my presence, Tom swings round to confront me. His face carries a look of thunder.

'Sorry Tom, it was my fault. I just came across it when I was emailing.' My expression pleads with him to believe my obvious lie.

Kath steps closer to him. 'I can't believe you've written such a nonsense story. Jenny said it was, didn't you, Jenny? Little Po Beep who lost her sheep. Well that's really going to be a bestseller, isn't it?' The words spray out of her mouth like acid rain.

Tom stands tall, unflinching.

'I don't know how you can call yourself a writer,' she jibes with her forked tongue. 'It must take great self-belief to think what you've written is worth reading. Is that why you wouldn't share it with me?'

He says nothing in return, just looks out beyond Kath's bobbing head to a place in the distance, somewhere she has no hope of reaching, as if he's one of those Benedictine monks who flog themselves with horsehair whips. Why doesn't he just walk away? He reminds me of a Samurai warrior, silently psyching himself up to deliver the fatal blow. But that doesn't happen. After a moment, when she starts ripping the characters apart, he inclines his head towards me. *Let her think she's in control*, he seems to tell me silently.

Unable to watch any more, I go indoors. This is too much. When Tom has invested so much time and effort into writing something so deeply personal to him, how dare she be so spiteful and take such pleasure in humiliating him? And it's now that I finally wonder if this is what she has done all of her life. To think that I used to be complicit in some of her endeavours. When she wasn't in control of a situation – that time with our PE teacher or when she played pranks on her brothers – she'd do her utmost to ridicule them in some way or destroy something they treasured. I remember when she put salt in her brother's orange squash simply because he wouldn't run an errand for her. At the time, her actions seemed like a bit of fun, but now I can see how small things like that can build up to far more significant events.

I enter the sanctuary of my room, to my shells, mementos from a summer holiday eight years ago. I pick one up and hold it closely to my ear. The sea at Kalkan in southern Turkey pulls me towards it. I let it draw me further and further away from shore until I am lying on top of it like flotsam, enjoying the foamy, undulating waves, moving closer to the horizon.

***

'Careful, Jen, you're getting too close to the rocks.'

I lifted my head out of the water and spat out the snorkel. Tom was treading water next to me, mask stretched over his forehead, his eyes showing gentle concern. I wriggled close to wrap my arms and legs around him.

'Hey, hold on a moment or I'm going to drown.' He started to sink and splutter beneath my grasp.

'That's fine, so long as we go down together. I couldn't bear life without you.'

I let go, laughing, and he swam away from me towards an anchored raft bouncing in the turquoise water. Hauling himself up, he turned to pull me up alongside him. Together we collapsed on the warm wood, flat on our stomachs, head to head, not touching. I opened my eyes to see him looking at me intently.

'What?'

He didn't respond.

'You know, I'm so happy here, Tom. I don't want this holiday to end.'

'So let's float away on this raft, shall we? Cut the rope and off we go.'

'Seriously, Tom, have you had any more thoughts about us living together in October?'

I was planning to study psychology at Bath, which

had excellent sports facilities, meaning I could train at the same time. It was close to Bristol where Tom had secured a work placement on the local newspaper as part of his undergraduate course, and he and I had discussed the feasibility of us sharing a flat somewhere between our respective cities.

He'd been enthusiastic when we'd discussed it several weeks ago, even though it would involve some commuting on both our parts, not to mention having a car. But I could see now that something had changed his mind. He didn't answer straightaway, just continued to look at me, unblinking.

'Tom, did you hear what I said?'

He cupped his head in his hand, stroked my prickling arm gently up and down. 'Of course I heard you. You know, Jen, there's nothing I want more than to be close to you.'

'Let's do it then. Deal?'

I sensed that he was hesitant to agree. His thoughts were lost somewhere. I didn't want him to spoil our last days on holiday, so tickled him under the arm, forcing him to jump up quickly. He patted me on the backside and stood at the edge of the raft.

'Last one back to shore's a sucker.' He dived into the clear water and free-styled away, back to where Kath had made a base for our group on the beach. As if he really thought he could beat me.

***

I dive into the sea, but don't hit water. Instead I am flying high above the wind-sweeping clouds like a kite, twisting and twirling. I hear the laughter of small children beneath me. They pull my string and the momentum forces me higher. The heat of the sun intensifies as I draw closer to it. This is the warmth of happiness, of freedom. I look down and see two people below me. They're fighting. I can't make out their faces but I know who it is. Unexpectedly, my ribbons start to flap and I am losing height, jerked into a nosedive towards the ground, faster and faster, out of control. Then, bang.

My afternoon sleep is broken by the sound of cupboards being opened and closed downstairs. A feeling of sorrow casts a black cloud over me. I don't want to wake up. My eyelashes are glued together and there is drool on my pillow.

It can't just have been the shells that triggered the dream about that holiday in Turkey. What was it? Perhaps it was the image of Kath taunting Tom earlier. On that holiday, I remember, he'd been reluctant to commit to our future. I recall him and Kath having a heavy discussion on the raft one day. Tom had said it was 'nothing' when I pressed him about it later. But, now I'm sure that she was nagging at him to 'release' me. I wonder if they'd both been aware of my father's plans to take my career to the next level at that stage. We'd even joked about getting married, although it wasn't a joke to me. Tom had already said that if I managed to win at least one gold medal at the next Olympics, he was going to whisk me away and put a ring on my finger. I was only eighteen, but it still made complete sense to me.

'I'll hold you to that promise,' I laughed back as I came out of the shower, wrapping a towel round myself.

He didn't reply. He just winked at me in the mirror as

he slowly shaved away his beard of shaving foam.

'Seriously though, Tom, for me there's no point getting married unless it's for the right reasons. I mean it's all about being with your true love – your soul mate – isn't it? And I couldn't contemplate loving anyone more than I love you.'

I wrapped my arms around him and stroked his chest. Now I wonder if he knew then that our future was swinging in the balance. Perhaps that's why he silenced me with a long foam-faced kiss.

***

My eyes blink open to confront the reality of today. The light streams through my window, telling me I haven't slept for long. I need to stick my spinning head under a cold tap. Drinking alcohol in the afternoon was not a good idea. And look at the consequences: another battle between Tom and Kath. These outbursts are becoming more frequent, or maybe they're just more prepared to have them in front of me.

Kath is singing an old nursery rhyme as I descend the stairs. 'Little Bo Peep'. She carries on droning in a flat monotone, stirring a pan of bubbling pasta with a wooden spoon. Something tells me she's hasn't stopped drinking since I left her. The only person she hasn't openly humiliated yet is me. Although, perhaps she has. Perhaps, I'm her ultimate victim and I've been blind to it all my life. From the moment Tom knocked on my door with that message in a bottle in his hand, she might have been hatching a plan to take him from me. Perhaps she did get that email I sent her and sought out Tom before

I returned home, so she could take him for herself. Or, perhaps I'm running away with my thoughts. I shake my head. I need to stay rational.

Kath continues to stir her spoon round and round. A witch crafting a spell, I can't help thinking, then admonish myself. Even so, I move towards her quietly, tempted to give her a fright, until a noisy Rosa rushes through the door, her cheeks tinged red, full of merriment. Just behind her comes Tom, smiling. I'm impressed by his ability to cast aside those deeply personal remarks of Kath's. But he's right to put aside his feelings for the sake of their daughter. Kath's words count for nothing. I go to pick up Rosa and spin her round and round. Tom laughs and raises Kath's glass to his mouth.

'On the subject of sheep, since it seems to be the theme of the day, who fancies a lamb steak for dinner?' he says, looking round for takers.

Rosa jumps up and down with her hand held high. I raise my hand as well. Tom nods at us both. Kath has turned her back on him and continues to stir the pot.

'Rosa and I will see to it, then. Let's go outside and get the barbecue going, shall we?' He picks up the plastic bag he had dropped on the table and takes Rosa's hand. *Touché.*

Kath throws herself down on a chair after they've gone outside, deflated. I can hardly bear to look at her.

'Come on, Kath, what's up? You're lucky he forgave you so easily for some of the things you said earlier. That was unnecessary. It's hard for a writer to share their work, and to get shot down like that, well...'

She shrugs. 'I didn't want him to forgive me. That's the point. I want him to suffer in the same way he's made me

141

suffer by not showing me that stupid book of his before now.' She swings a crossed leg up and down on top of the other.

I survey her with my arms crossed. 'That's ridiculous and really childish, Kath. You're making me feel uncomfortable about being here, you know. If you carry on like this, I'm not sure I want to stay here much longer.'

'Jenny!'

I twist away from her outstretched hand and go outside to join Tom and Rosa, happily playing *boules* while the meat starts to sizzle on the grill. Tom hands me a couple of balls and we are soon locked in a competitive game. A few minutes later, I turn towards the door and see Kath coming outside. She walks over to Tom first, reaches up to peck him on the cheek, then does the same to me.

'Sorry about that, guys. I think I drank too much. Will you both forgive my immaturity?' she says, almost sweetly.

Tom nods and moves to attend to the barbecue. I pat Kath on the arm and turn to help Rosa gather up the balls.

– CHAPTER 14 –

Finally my body clock has accepted its new routine and allows me to wake up later than the dawn chorus. It feels as if the shackles have been released and the next chapter of my life can begin at last. My bed makes a comforting creak as I stretch my feet and toes and enjoy this joyful moment. How I loved those times when I was young, listening to my mother making breakfast downstairs, my father filling the basin with water for his daily shaving ritual, the gentle hum of the milk van turning into my road, followed by the clink of bottles as the milkman set them down on our front doorstep. Here, the sounds are completely different, yet equally reassuring: the chatter of birds in the pine tree outside my window, a door banging, feet on gravel, Pilot barking.

A car engine starts up. It's probably the German families going out. They spend most days at the beach, returning early evening to sit outside supping on local wines and laughing late into the night. Tom often spends time with them, enjoying a nightcap and more intelligent chat than I can offer him. He's always had an inquisitive mind, keen to absorb information, ask questions and offer opinions about anything from pop music to world economics. Often, I curl up in bed, listening to his deep voice in the garden, its tone pitching higher the more animated the discussion becomes. He plays the part of a holiday host well: the guests enjoy his easy-going manner, but at the same time he carries a certain authority, which commands respect. It hasn't missed my attention that women find him attractive too. Yesterday, when I leant out of my bedroom window to push open the shutters, he wheeled his barrow past the two German women who were outside having coffee. They watched him keenly until he turned the corner, and then one of them said something and the other laughed.

My hand reaches for my watch sitting on top of Tom's *Jane Eyre*. It's 8.45 a.m. Perhaps I'll read for a while, before I start on the laundry. It won't take long to dry a line full of washing in this heat. The book is cool to the touch. I hold it to my nose and breathe in its history, the pages now yellowing with age and travel.

There's a knock. Expecting Kath to come bustling in, I don't respond, but just put the book back on the side and climb slowly out of bed. I expect she's wondering what's happened to me. Normally I've been swimming at the lake and returned with fresh croissants before breakfast. The knock repeats, more pressing, so I walk over to open the door. Tom stands there, running his hand through his hair. He pushes past me and comes in, closing the door softly behind him.

'Jen, can you take Rosa out for a bit. She's got her holiday club at lunchtime, but I need to speak to Kath – alone. She's just popped out to the *boulangerie*.'

'Of course, I'll grab a towel and have a quick shower.' I hesitate as I move towards him. Straightaway, I'm drawn to his warmth and solidity, and have a strong urge to pull him towards me, feel his arms around my back, rest my head on his torso while he kneads the base of my spine, just like he used to. I don't, of course.

'Is everything all right?'

He shakes his head, looking beyond me through the window. 'No, I think she must have stopped taking her medication. I could tell yesterday when she was goading me about my novel. The hard stare of her eyes. I've got to talk to her. She's probably decided that with you here, she doesn't need to take it anymore. You're the only drug she needs.' He attempts a laugh, but it sounds more like a snort.

'What if she refuses?'

'God knows. I'll have to threaten to call the doctor, I guess.' He shakes his head and turns back to look at me. 'Thanks, Jen. If you could be quick. I need to have this conversation before any of the guests return. I'm not sure how she's going to take it.' He shrugs his shoulders and leaves me to get ready.

ж ж ж

Rosa and I drive into Béziers, where I treat her to a strawberry ice-cream. We stroll to the Fonserannes Lock and watch the canal boats queuing up to make their way through the nine gates. It's an amazing spectacle. Rosa is happy just sitting on the wall, legs swinging, licking her way round her cone.

'Jenny, do you think Daddy's going to leave us?' She throws me a darting look as if she is trying to appear nonchalant, and bites into her crispy cone.

I put my arm round her and draw her close to me, quickly recomposing my expression. They don't miss a thing, children.

'Of course not, Rosa. Your daddy loves you very much. Why do you think that?'

She jumps off the wall, almost dropping her ice-cream, and looks down, kicking the gravel with her blue plimsolls.

'Mummy said this morning that if I don't behave, she'll send Daddy and Pilot away, and I'll never see them again.'

'Oh, Rosa, she doesn't mean it. It's just... well, sometimes parents say things they don't mean when they want their children to behave well. Mummy and Daddy would never leave you.'

'Good, because I was going to ask if I could come and visit you in Australia, if Daddy leaves.'

'Well, that's a nice thought, Rosa. Maybe one day.'

She smiles and attempts to get back on the wall with one hand. I can see that she doesn't want me to take her ice-cream in case I decide to eat it for myself. However, the task is too great and she is forced to hand it to me. I test her reaction by pretending to take a lick.

'Hey!' She laughs and snatches it back from me.

'Ah, I thought you'd given it to me, Rosa. Just joking.' I cuddle her once again.

Poor little girl. The things people say to their children to get them to do what they want. Kath used to tell me that her mum often threatened to send her to a children's home if she didn't behave and here she is now doing exactly the same thing to her own daughter. I'm sure it isn't easy raising a child, but Rosa isn't exactly difficult.

Strong-willed – yes, proud – yes, and definitely stubborn, but never unbearable.

***

At midday, I drop Rosa at the holiday club. There are lots of children there already when we arrive, some running around playing tag, others climbing on the different apparatus set up outside. Rosa kisses me and disappears as soon as she spots her special friend Béatrice. I sit in the car for a few moments and wonder if it's a good time to return.

How long will Tom need to have this difficult conversation with Kath? And what if it escalates into something unmanageable? If Kath has a mental health problem, and from what Tom has told me, it sounds as though she does, we both need to be on hand to support her through this. I think Tom should continue acting as though everything is normal, until she's back on track. The last thing Kath needs is to feel unsettled. Those comments she made at the beach about our friendship makes me realise how she must have felt threatened by my relationship with Tom back then – as though she couldn't see a future for herself outside the comforting walls of our childhood sanctuary.

It isn't a good time. As soon as I drive through the gateway, I sense that they haven't finished. Tom's truck is parked in front of the house, with both windows half down. Pilot is on the front seat and barks at me to let him out. He jumps free as soon as I open his door, so I take him by the collar and walk him over to the garage where his food is stored. It's gloomy. The bulb needs replacing, but I manage to find a spare dish and fill it with water from the outside tap. I sprinkle a few treats on the ground next to it. He snacks away with greedy enthusiasm.

Suddenly, there's a loud smash and raised voices. I rush across the yard and through the open front door, afraid of what I might find. Kath is standing at the worktop, a shard of glass in her hand, watching Tom crouched on the floor picking up pieces of broken glass. She looks over at me, her eyes dark and angry, almost snarling. Startled, I stand still, hesitant, scared that she might thrust the glass into Tom's neck on an impulse.

'Kath!' I come to my senses and move towards her. 'You've cut your hand. Let me take a look.'

I take the glass from her and walk around Tom who's managed to pick up the larger pieces of glass and is carrying them outside in a dustpan. Blobs of blood drip onto the tiles as I walk Kath to the sink and thrust her hand under cold running water. Thankfully, I can see that the cut is small. She must have just nicked it when the glass shattered.

'Ouch, Jenny.' She tries to pull her hand away from the tap, but I grip her tightly and hold it under.

'What happened? Did you break a glass?'

'Two actually.' Tom walks back in with the emptied dustpan and puts it back into the tall cupboard by the front door. His face is flushed – with worry or anger, I can't tell.

'Tom's told me that I have to start taking my pills again – my happy pills.' She pouts as she speaks, mocking his suggestion.

'I don't think it's wise to stop taking them without getting professional advice first,' he says.

I grab a paper towel and dry Kath's hand while Tom bends down to get the first-aid kit out of the cupboard.

'Jenny, what do you think? Do I seem normal to you?' She thrusts her face into my line of sight. There's something unnerving about her behaviour. I'm glad Rosa isn't here.

'To be honest, Kath, you have seemed a little on edge, particularly during these past couple of days.'

Kath shakes her head, unhappy that I've apparently sided with Tom.

'Which is normal, Kath. You must be exhausted. All the work you've been doing on the house and garden.' I hold her hand carefully between the pieces of paper towel. She pulls it away.

'It is bloody hard work. But I don't need those pills to get through it. They make me dizzy and thirsty. I hate them.'

As tempted as I am to tell Kath to stop acting like a baby, I bite my bottom lip. Tom reaches for Kath's hand, and after a moment she acquiesces. She visibly relaxes as he wraps the plaster around her cut finger, then smoothes it down gently for her.

'Listen, Kath, why don't you try them again and at the end of each day, we can have a chat about how you're feeling? If you're not happy after a week, then I can come with you to the doctor's. Or Jen can if you prefer.' He continues to hold her in his grip and bends down to force her to look at him.

'OK, OK, I'm not a baby.' She turns away to look out of the window, pulls her hand away and folds her arms in front of her.

Tom and I make rapid eye contact, a silent pact to look out for her and, most of all, to ensure that Rosa is kept safe.

– CHAPTER 15 –

14th July, Bastille Day

We've been invited to Bernard and Sylvie's for the celebrations that evening. Rosa's full of beans and excitement. I offer to help her get ready for her sleepover party and into the red, white and blue dress, which Kath has run up on the sewing machine. Rosa explains that she's supposed to be Marianne, the goddess of liberty, the symbol of the French Republic. She had someone more current in mind, like Katy Perry, but Kath has insisted that she play along with the theme of the day. I've made her a crown of sorts out of aluminium foil to put on her freshly washed, silky hair, which I need to plait and pin up for her. I greet her at the shower door with a towel at the ready. With her hair scraped back from her face, she is the spitting image of Tom. Those large hazel eyes set slightly wide apart dominate her pretty face, which is open, yet playful. She moves her head about a lot, in the same way as Tom – curious minds always on the lookout for something to discover or explore.

The bathroom is steamy from the shower. Rosa hops up and down gleefully as I pat her dry. The skin on her back is sunkissed and unblemished. She swivels round to face me, pecks my nose with a rosebud kiss.

'Rosa, sweetheart, you've still got dirt on your arms. Let me rub it off.' I reach for the flannel.

Rosa studies the top of her arms warily. 'It isn't dirt,' she says.

'Let me see.'

Reluctantly, she puts out an arm for me. Her mouth is downturned. She almost looks ashamed. They're bruises. Fresh.

I look into her eyes, but she's avoiding mine. 'Did someone do this to you, Rosa?'

'No. I fell over.' Her reluctance to open up sends out warning signs to me. I draw her towards me and hug her tight, yet she hangs limply in my embrace, no tears.

'Listen, Rosa, if anyone is hurting you, you must say something. This is wrong. A child shouldn't be bruised by anyone, big or small.'

I hesitate and hold her at arm's length. Her eyes jump up to look at me. In them I see fear.

'Come on, sweetie, let's put this lovely dress on you and we won't discuss it again tonight, but I think I'm going to have to tell Mummy and Daddy, OK?'

That rabbit-in-headlights look once again. This time a small, barely audible whisper. 'Please, Jenny, don't tell. It was an accident. I was rude to Mummy and she pulled me.' She hurries to put her dress on and cover herself. Fortunately the capped sleeves cover the dark bruises.

'What, Mummy did this?'

Her arms are so small. I could easily encircle each one with my finger and thumb.

'She said sorry, honestly Jenny, and she promised me a kitten if I didn't tell people. You know, one of Sylvie and Bernard's.'

That little face is so excited at the thought of a new pet, I daren't spoil it for her.

'OK. But Rosa, promise me if it happens again, you'll tell me, whatever?'

Our eyes meet and a tacit agreement is made.

I'm sure Tom would have noticed if this had happened before. Perhaps Rosa's simply a child who bruises easily. It was the look in her eyes, however, which tells me that something's not right. Should I mention it to Kath or to Tom? It's so difficult to know the right thing to do, especially since Rosa has asked me not to say anything.

***

There is a lot of noise and laughter coming from the back terrace when we arrive at *La Miellerie*. Armelle rushes to greet me and walks me around to meet the residents of this small community, including the mayor, a barrel of a man with cheeks so ruddy, their colour matches the glass of rosé he is holding. He growls at me amicably, but I've absolutely no idea what he's saying.

Eddie, whom I haven't seen since our evening of *Ceroc*, steps out of nowhere holding a chicken leg, and guides me by the elbow to the barbecue, where we help ourselves to glasses of wine. We nudge past Tom who's engaged in conversation with a group of farmworkers. His eyes follow us as he talks to his friends. I wish I could go up to him right now and plant a kiss on his lips. That would shock him. Such a clandestine thought fills me with sparkle. Eddie reacts by drawing me in close to him and I pull back fast, accidentally trampling on his foot with the pointed heel of my sandal. He yelps with pain, holding onto his foot. I can see that I've also hurt his feelings.

'Sorry, Eddie, you surprised me.'

He puts his foot down slowly and pulls a wry smile. 'Jenny, we are friends, yes?' His arm finds its way back around my waist.

'Yes, Eddie. You are a good person and I want us to be friends. Just friends, OK?'

'Of course, Jenny.' He withdraws his hand and takes a slurp of wine. The skin on his neck is pale and smooth. Dark hairs peep out of the top of his T-shirt. 'So, how are you getting on with Tom and Kath?' He puts down his glass. 'An interesting couple, I think. Both filled with melancholy before you arrived and now both full of hope.' He bites into the chicken drumstick, smacks his lips and gives me that ironic smile again.

'Eddie, what are you trying to say?'

'As I said before, Jenny, be careful. Look around you at all times. Often there is someone watching.'

Someone puts a song on and Eddie puts his food down and takes my arm. He doesn't learn. Once again, I am coaxed onto the terrace. In my high heels, I feel like a stork on stilts. But the alcohol has relaxed me and I throw myself into the dancing.

'I hope your ankle is better,' he shouts into my ear.

I twist even more frenetically. The terrace quickly fills with partygoers and I beckon at Tom to join in, but he shakes his head, unsmiling, now talking to the mayor.

The music changes to a chart track I know. Eddie signals to me to come and have another drink with him, but I prefer to carry on dancing, losing myself in the moment. Word seems to get round that I'm new in town and soon I become a source of interest. Drinks appear in my hand and a string of men – young and old – offer to partner with me on the dance-floor. The calloused hands of men who have worked the land all their lives compete with the smooth, clammy hands of the younger generation – a generation that has embraced office work or has seen the financial benefits of selling unprofitable farmland to property developers.

The song ends abruptly and I thank the man I'm dancing with. Time alone at last. The alcohol has taken root now and I feel relaxed and confident. I take off my sandals and giddily walk through the kitchen garden into a large paddock filled with machinery and what look like metal barrels of varying sizes. The air is heavy with farmyard smells, yet quiet, apart from the wind in the trees and the thumping backdrop of music coming from the farmhouse. I often crave these moments of stillness where I can imagine that I'm the only person on this planet. Just me and the stars above my head. That's what I love about swimming: when you reach what I call the zone, and all that matters is the amplified sound of your breath in the water.

A small crack breaks the silence and tells me I'm not alone. Tom stands a short distance away. His silhouette is edged in the twinkling light of the farmhouse. He moves towards me.

'What are you doing here, Jen? Are you lost?'

'No, I just had a strong urge to be alone. Probably because I've drunk too much.'

'Here, let me help you.'

He comes closer and reaches for my shoes, his chin grazing my arm. I touch his full mouth with my finger, stare up at his long straight nose, those volcanic eyes. I can feel my own simmering with lust.

In the concealing darkness he groans and nuzzles his nose deep into my neck. I press myself against his hardness. His breath shortens as he caresses me, kneading my thighs with those strong hands. When he lightly strokes me through my pants, my knees weaken and I start to fall towards the ground, pulling him down with me.

Just as I'm about to gasp in ecstasy, he stands up abruptly and grabs my wrists. 'No, Jen, this isn't a good idea. Not now.'

'So when is? I need you.'

'Jen, I'm sorry, but you've had too much to drink. I don't want to take advantage of you. You'll regret this tomorrow.'

I stand up again and brush down my clothes. Feeling a huge sense of frustration, I have this desire to lash out at him all of a sudden.

'So why did you call me "Mouse" when I first arrived here? Was it some sort of test, to find out if I was still in love with you? You know what that used to mean for us, so why say it?'

He looks down at me and rubs my shoulder, coaxing me to look at him, but I refuse. 'You're right, Jen, it was stupid. Stupid and selfish. Seeing you again sent a rush of crazy – and erotic – thoughts through my head. I was drunk on lust. I'm sorry.'

'Tom, I'm not with Scott anymore, just so you know. We finished a while ago. I told Kath we were still a couple to reassure her. I didn't want her to think that I'd come here to steal you away.'

'But, I–'

'Scott and I, we're just friends. Good friends, actually, but that's all it is now.'

He looks down, and it's hard to read him in the darkness. 'Thanks for enlightening me.'

A small sound – a snapping twig perhaps – comes from behind Tom. He drops his arm and steps away from me, but nobody's there.

'I'll wander down this path a bit longer while you go back to the party. It's probably not a good idea to raise any suspicion. This is a small community and people like to gossip.'

I nod, put my sandals back on and walk back towards the house, feeling emancipated by my confession. It's liberated me, given me a courage that I'd forgotten I had. As I step back along the unfinished path, I'm careful not to trip up on the gulleys between the slabs. The forlorn hoot of an owl invades the night. Hidden up high, it waits patiently for its prey to make an appearance. The combined scent of rosemary and lavender is intoxicating. I stop, stand still and inhale deeply. A feeling of calmness touches me, like a blanket of frail poppies falling from the sky.

The party is in full swing when I return. As I get closer to the open doors of the house, I realise that the Spanish guitar music I can hear is live. A couple of men, farmworkers I recognise, are playing in the cavernous living room. A brunette struts around them. Her dress sparkles as she twists and turns, claps, stamps her feet with laughter, as if to say, 'Don't take me too seriously'. She has drawn a crowd of people who clap and yelp around her. I slip into the house through the kitchen door, hoping that I haven't been missed. After using the bathroom, I find some bottled water in the fridge. The cool liquid trickles down my throat and swishes around my empty stomach. I must remember to eat something.

It's difficult to pick people out in the flickering candlelight of the living room. I can just make out Kath in the corner in deep conversation with Luc. She spots me, says something to him, then walks over. She looks very drunk, her mouth more lopsided than usual, her eyes darker. The large tumbler of sangria in her hand swishes about, threatening to spill.

'Where've you been? I was looking for you,' she slurs in an accusatory tone.

'I was gazing at the beautiful starry night,' I reply. 'Remember? Your mum loved that Van Gogh painting, didn't she?'

'How could I forget?' Kath's tone is sharp-edged, even malevolent. 'You were such a goody-two-shoes, always playing up to my mum for favours.'

Before I say something I'm going to regret, I turn and head back to the kitchen.

'Hey, Jenny, I'm sorry. I didn't mean anything. It's just you were always such a hard act to keep up with.' She links her arm in mine and leads us out of the kitchen door.

'Kath, we weren't in competition! You were my best friend. We looked out for each other.'

She plonks down on the low wall outside and pats the space next to her, but I'm not in the mood for reconciliation yet.

'Those were the good old days,' she laughs. You, me, Tom, your neighbour Mrs Holt and her cats. Hey, whatever happened to Mrs Holt? Oh yes, that's right, she died, poor old dear.'

Kath takes a mouthful of sangria too fast, and starts to choke on it. My hand enjoys giving her a good smack on her back. Hopefully that'll sober her up. The red liquid splutters everywhere.

'Oops, pardon me.' She burps and leans against me. 'You know, Jenny,' she breaks off, 'I'm so glad you're here. Eight years is a long time.'

'It is.'

Eddie appears in the doorway and raises an empty glass. I shake my head and he disappears. Kath continues.

'At first, I was worried that you might breeze in and try to take Tom back. But I think seeing you again has made him realise that what he's got here is pretty damn good. A beautiful daughter, good lifestyle and the potential for a successful business. Don't get me wrong, but realistically what can you offer him?'

Her words have the desired effect. My shoulders sag. 'Nothing, I guess.'

'Oh, he's still got feelings for you, I'm not stupid. But he knows that he'll never get to see Rosa again if he leaves me.'

The triumphant note in her voice makes me sit up. 'She's not a possession you can fight over, Kath. This is your daughter you're talking about. Your own blood. She loves her dad.'

Kath waves her glass around as she speaks. 'I know that, but like I say, he doesn't stand a chance of seeing her grow up if he leaves me. *I* get to say when we're finished.'

I wonder if this is a veiled threat to me as well. I stand up and her hand, which has been resting on my leg, falls off me.

'Are you taking your medication, Kath? You know you really shouldn't be mixing alcohol with prescription drugs. Not to this degree, surely. And I don't feel comfortable when you're like this.'

'Yes, I am taking the *bloody* medication, don't you worry. I've got Mr Spymaster watching my every move.' She also stands and starts swaying to Serge Gainsbourg, whose gravelly voice plays out over the warm night air. 'Come here, let's not fight, please.'

Kath gestures for me to come and dance with her and I allow myself to be led onto the small patio. Together we move back and forth, just as we used to in my bedroom when we were thirteen or fourteen, excited at the possibility that someone might ask us to dance for real one day. She rests her head heavily on my shoulders, then, perhaps sensing my ill ease, looks up at me.

'Actually, Jenny, talking about Mrs Holt, just now.'

I nod. 'Such a lovely woman. I miss her.'

'I know she meant a lot to you. That's why I never said anything. You see, I was with her when she died.' Kath's voice trembles.

I stop dancing and focus on Kath. 'What do you mean? We found her at the bottom of the stairs – together. I was on a swimming camp for the weekend when she died.'

She staggers over to the wall for another slurp of sangria, pretending to pick bugs out of it, so she won't have to look at me. I follow her, trying to put the pieces together.

'You and I went round to see her as soon as I got back from the camp. Although I remember you didn't like visiting Mrs Holt as a rule. So what do you mean, you were there when she died?'

'Actually I went round to her house to see if she was doing OK and wasn't missing you.'

'Go on.'

'I'd had a shitty day at school. Mr Ferris wouldn't stop picking on me – just because I hadn't done my homework.'

'And?' There seems to be a whole ants' nest in that glass of hers.

'Well, Mrs Holt opened the door and looked really disappointed to see it was me,' says Kath. 'She thought you were back, you see. But it was me instead.'

I shake my head. Mrs Holt would never have been so obvious about showing her feelings.

'Mrs H invited me in and I offered to give the cats some fresh water. God, that sink was disgusting – filled with tealeaves and brown stains. I retched when I saw it. Had to hold my breath to stop myself from puking.' Kath takes another slurp of sangria and offers her tumbler to me.

I shake my head. 'Keep going, I want to know where you're heading with this.'

'Oh Jenny, I knew you'd be mad at me, which is why I kept quiet all this time. You were so besotted with her and those mangy cats.'

'I cared about her, yes Kath. She was good to me.'

Kath pats her hair, a familiar gesture I remember, perhaps forgetting that her teenage curls no longer exist. 'I told Mrs Holt off for not taking more care of herself. I guess I might have been a bit hard on the old dear.'

I put my hand to my mouth. Kath sees my reaction and grabs my arm tightly. Too tightly. I shake her off and she stumbles.

'Oh Jen, I didn't mean to be horrible to her, but she set

off upstairs. I asked her where she was going and she told me to leave. I'd never seen her look so determined – she moved quicker than she'd ever done before. So I'm sure those bunions didn't play her up as much as she'd have us believe. Anyway, I followed her up the stairs. She said she wanted to lie down. I was a bit concerned. I thought she might do something silly, so I told her to come down again and we'd forget about it. But she pushed me away, like she was mad, or something.'

Kath stops again, pulls herself up tall. Her face is stripped of guilt. It scares me.

'While she was pushing me she lost her footing and started falling. I tried to grab hold of her but couldn't get to her in time. She was like a rag doll, bouncing down the stairs.' Kath's voice slows to a paced monotone. 'One by one.'

'But why didn't you run and tell someone? Why didn't you call an ambulance?'

'I was scared. I thought I'd be blamed for pushing her.'

'She could have still been alive.' I shake Kath's arm.

'She wasn't alive. She was just lying on the carpet at the bottom of the stairs. I checked her neck for a pulse, like they do on TV. There wasn't one. So I decided to leave her there.' Her eyes evade mine and return to her drink.

'What, for someone else to deal with? Someone like me? So that's why you suggested we knock on her door and see how she was after I came back from camp. So I could deal with her death.'

I'm starting to feel sick, really sick, and push past Kath to get to the bathroom. There are Rosa's bruises to consider too. I really should have told Tom about them so that he can ensure it doesn't happen again. I rush to the toilet, my chest heaving. How could I have not seen the clues? How did she manage to hide her real feelings from me all this time? I splash my face and drink cold water from the tap until I start to feel more sober.

When I come back downstairs, my world feels completely changed. The music has moved on to more contemporary rock and pop. Tom is in the middle of the dance-floor, swaying around in mock fandango style, his arm wrapped protectively around Sylvie's waist. He waves me over to join in. I force a smile and shake my head, stumble to the table laden with food and cut myself a slice of *Gruyère*, placing it on a thick piece of French bread. I try to blink away the tears welling up in my eyes. When I think how close Kath and I were, how we told each other everything. At least, that's what I thought.

Angry voices rise up in a crescendo against the music, then ebb away intermittently. At first I think it's part of the song, but a movement in the corner of the room catches my eye. Armelle and Luc are arguing. Their body language tells me that she is on the attack. He is imploring with her, but her arms are folded against her body. She refuses to look at him. I glance round and realise that a few others have noticed too. I instinctively start to walk over towards them, but an arm reaches out to pull me back. 'Leave them, Jenny. It is not your business,' says Eddie.

'What are you, Eddie, some sort of village oracle? Always there, all knowing.'

His responding chuckle lies deep in his throat. 'Maybe, Jenny. Maybe.'

A sharp sound like a belly-flop on water forces us to

turn. The story of Luc and Armelle has played out. She is striding away, fists clenched at her sides. He is holding his cheek. She joins a group of girlfriends on the dance-floor, raises her arms above her head and moves sensuously from side to side, swishing her curtain of hair about like a horse's tail sweeping flies off its back. Luc has moved to the edge of the dance-floor and glances over at her from time to time, beer bottle in hand, cigarette hanging out of his mouth as if he hasn't a care in the world. Still, the wound lies in his eyes and he can't shake that away easily. Hopefully it was just a lovers' tiff as, from what she's told me, Armelle is deeply in love with her husband.

The combination of what I've heard and seen tonight leads me from one drink to another. Finally my thoughts stop on my own frivolous behaviour with Tom, a lustful fantasy that re-energises me. After several tracks, I look round for Armelle and Luc, but they must have left. The party is still lively even though numbers have dwindled. It must be late, but I don't feel tired. I start to enjoy the attention I'm getting from some of the men at the party and throw myself into my dancing. I don't think I've ever been in this situation before – the only woman among men on the dance-floor – and for the first time in my life I am relishing it. Of course, there are disadvantages and I see them at polar opposites of the room, watching me silently. Tom, his mouth set to a grim line, Kath watching him watching me and getting drunker in the process. Finally, she trips over and is helped to a chair by a couple of bystanders. I wonder if we'll all be regretting this party tomorrow morning.

– CHAPTER 16 –

The taxi lurches along the dark road, headlights on full, negotiating the abrupt turns and potholes, throwing us around in the back. Prayer beads rattle from the rear-view mirror. Something about them reminds me of sardine bones, the ones you crunch when you eat them mashed up on toast. That was a favourite snack when I'd just completed a morning's training. Tom's mum made it for me sometimes when I dropped by on my way home. Often, she was hungover after a night out with the latest boyfriend. Tom didn't approve, of course, but, despite her poor choice in men, he and his mum were very close.

A snore breaks my chain of thought. It comes from Kath who has drifted off on Tom's shoulder. Her eye-liner has smudged and her mouth is open. Not a pretty sight, but then neither is watching her get more and more inebriated during the evening, making threats. It was a good thing she collapsed when she did. Tom is sitting stiffly behind the driver, looking out of the window. He's barely moved his head since we got in the taxi. I'm not sure who he's annoyed with. Perhaps I did go over the top with my flirtatious behaviour on the dance-floor, but it was a bit of fun and nice to get some attention. He should experience what it's like to be shackled up in bed by 10 p.m. nearly every night for eight years.

***

I'm not sure how long I've been asleep, but a noise wakes me. A door closing. Laughter (Kath), a groan (Tom?), then nothing. I relax back on my pillow and try to rekindle my dream. I was walking along a beach with my mother. We were bent over, studying a strange blue object, our bare feet sinking into the squelchy sand, unsure whether it was a shell or just a piece of plastic. She looked at me and laughed, the crinkles round her eyes reminding me of the branches of an olive tree. Her laughter continued and carried on relentlessly. I couldn't understand why it wouldn't stop. Then I woke. The laughter was real – *is* real. It's Kath. At first, I try to ignore it and cover my head with a pillow. But it gets louder and more out of control. It sounds like a hungry seal, gulping and barking. Perhaps I should get up and check everything's OK. It's a good thing Rosa isn't here. I just hope the holiday guests haven't been roused awake.

Perhaps they're having sex. The noise stops abruptly. Silence. A door opens. Someone going to the bathroom. Her footsteps are heavier, quicker than Tom's. The toilet flushes. The tap is turned on and off. A door opens once more and the same footsteps shuffle down the hallway, but the wrong way. They stop and hesitate outside my door. Or perhaps it's Rosa's door. I'm not sure. Next thing I hear another groan and faster footsteps, this time back to the bathroom. Retching. Water tap on again. Kath being sick, I'm certain of it.

***

The morning can't arrive quickly enough. I keep staring at the shutters, willing them to reveal flecks of glittery light. Wild thoughts spin out of control. What does Tom want from me exactly? He's keeping me at arm's length, yet the way he caressed me last night felt so real, as though I meant something to him still. I desperately want to believe that there might be a future for us again, once he's sorted things out with Kath, but I think I'm fooling myself. He won't leave Rosa if Kath wins custody. And she'll do everything in her power to ensure he doesn't have any rights. There is her depression and Rosa's bruises, however, to take into account, but something tells me she'll find a way to misconstrue the evidence. Perhaps they won't separate after all. Perhaps they've rekindled their passion for each other.

An internal door opens and shuts and I creep out of my bedroom into the bathroom, still half asleep with a thumping head. Fortunately, the medicine cabinet offers up some painkillers. As soon as I exit the bathroom, Tom's study door swings open. I hesitate. Our eyes meet and he looks as tired as I feel. I go downstairs and his footsteps follow mine to the kitchen. I hold back my questions until he closes the door behind us.

Pilot makes a friendly yelp and jumps out of his basket. I bend down and smother my face into his silky neck and he tries to lick me. Tom stands quietly behind us. Doubt is setting in once more and I wonder what the hell I'm doing here. I need to get out to think things through.

'I'm going out for a swim. In fact I'll get Rosa if you like and take her with me.' I rise and turn away from Tom to get a couple of towels from the dresser.

'God you teased the hell out of me last night, Jen. You need to be careful you know or those single men might start to think that you're interested.'

His voice is gentle, yet I detect an undercurrent of controlled anger.

'Perhaps I am, Tom. I am a free agent, remember?'

His face darkens.

'And I don't need any advice from you, especially after the whole neighbourhood was probably woken up by you two in the middle of the night.' There's no juice in the fridge, so I fill a bottle with cold water.

'Shit.' He groans and runs a hand through his hair. 'Kath tried to have sex with me, but I said no way. For some reason she wouldn't stop laughing at me and then she was sick. What a night.'

'Tom, I really don't need the details. You are a married couple, I know that.'

He tries to pull me round to look at him. 'We haven't been intimate for a while – since you arrived, in fact.'

I want to believe him, but my head is still fuzzy with exhaustion. Anyway, it's not my business. I no longer have any claim over Tom, do I?

I march through the wall of solid comfort he's offering me and straight out of the front door.

***

Rosa seems thrilled to see me when I arrive at her friend Madeleine's house. She folds herself up in my lap before we drive to the lake. It's very quiet here today. I suppose most people will be recovering in bed from their 14th July parties. Rosa's swimming technique has improved enormously and she confidently laps the shallow end of the lake several times without her armbands.

As I sit watching her, my mind drifts back to the events of last night. I wonder what's going on between Armelle and Luc for her to be so upset. Perhaps she'll confide in me when I see her at our regular market slot on Thursday. As for Kath, now I'm not sure whether she was telling the truth about Mrs Holt or whether it was just the alcohol talking. She always liked to spice up a story to make it sound more interesting than it actually was. She'll probably tell me she made the whole thing up when I see her later. Oh Kath, what a complex person you are.

The warmth of the midsummer air wraps around me like a cashmere blanket. I lie back on my towel and finally begin to relax, concentrating on my breathing. Something rouses me from a daydream. A splash. Something's wrong.

Rosa.

Where is she?

'Rosa!' I run to the edge of the lake and scan the water for any sign of movement. 'Rosa!'

Rings of water pulsate on the other side of the lake. I can just make her out below the surface. Quickly, I dive in and throttle through the water, dive under and grab hold of Rosa's arm. It's lifeless. *What have you done?* It takes all of my strength to tug at her and throw her tiny form out of the lake. I pull myself out and drag her up the bank. Chest compressions, breathe into her mouth – *Come on, focus!* There is a fog in my brain, which is trying to throw me off kilter, but I shake it off. Her delicate limbs lie inert in the still heat. How could this have happened?

'Come on, Rosa, come on,' I whisper.

Finally a cough, a splutter and a puddle of lake water oozes out of her mouth. She cries out, her eyelashes fluttering as she tries to work out what has just happened. I carry her to my towel where I wrap her up and rock her gently. My tears of relief stain her face as she weeps gently into the cloth.

'I'm sorry, Jenny. I thought I could get to the other side without you seeing me. I wanted to wave to you, show you that I could do it. But a weed touched my leg and I got scared. I swallowed lots of water. Loads. It was disgusting.'

'Oh my poor baby. It's not your fault. I should have been watching you.'

'Everything went dizzy.'

'Hush, sweetie, don't say any more, just relax. In a minute, I'll call Daddy, OK?'

Rosa flicks me an anxious glance. 'Just Daddy. I don't want Mummy to come. She'll be angry with me.'

'Rosa, I'm sure she won't be angry with you, but yes I'll phone Daddy.'

Fortunately, Tom picks up straightaway when I ring his mobile. I tell him to come quickly and bring some sugary tea and plain biscuits.

Minutes later he turns up on his bike, throws it to the ground, takes Rosa from my arms and holds her close, talking to her softly as though she's a newborn baby. I reach into the bag he dropped and take out the flask filled with tea. He takes the cup from me, refusing to look into my eyes. Hugging my knees close to my chest, I'm filled with guilty wretchedness at the thought of what could have happened. What was I thinking, drifting off like that?

After a while, like a foal she stretches and breaks out of her father's arms to stand. At first, she's a little wobbly on her feet. She lets the towel drop to the ground and smiles. Relief runs through me. I don't think I could have lived with myself had she drowned.

Rosa begs Tom to take her back into the water, so she won't be scared. He looks at me for advice. Gratefully, I nod my agreement. There's no sign of her having been traumatised by the event and no vomiting or chest pains, which are the main symptoms to look out for. However, I'd still be more comfortable if Tom got someone to examine her.

Tom lies on his back and encourages Rosa to dive underneath him. We both watch her attentively for any outward signs, but she seems all right. Her eyes have lost that scary bewildered look, which they had when she came round.

'We'll just tell Kath that Rosa swallowed a little too much water,' Tom says out of Rosa's earshot when they're getting dressed. He still hasn't looked at me directly, so I guess he's angry. I know what he's thinking. I've been negligent.

'Are you sure, Tom? I—'

'It's fine. She'll be so hungover that she probably won't notice a thing.'

'OK. I'll take Rosa back to the house right away then.'

He nods his assent, and Rosa and I drive back, leaving Tom to make his own way.

He's right about Kath. She's just got out of bed and stumbles into the kitchen, bleary-eyed. She can't seem to remember too much about last night, thankfully, so I leave her lying in the shade, fanning herself, while I take over and serve us all a late lunch – a Ploughman's of sorts with bread, cheese and a salad fresh from the kitchen garden.

'You seemed to be enjoying yourself last night, Jenny.' Kath trowels butter onto her piece of bread and pops it into her mouth.

'It was fun. Everyone was so welcoming despite my terrible French.'

We sit in silence listening to Kath chomping on her greedy mouthful. Tom keeps glancing down at Rosa, checking on her, no doubt. She's polished off her plate of food in no time, which is a positive sign that she's recovered from that awful experience.

'You know, Jen, don't feel you're tied to us here. If you want to get away for a few days, feel free.' Tom puts down his fork and sits back, arm casually thrown over the back of Rosa's chair. His eyes hold mine. I know him so well. The calm before the storm.

'What are you talking about, Tom? We need Jenny right here.' Kath leans forward and puts a possessive hand on top of mine.

I don't know how to respond. Does Tom really want me to leave?

He ignores Kath and addresses me again. 'All I'm saying, Jen, is take a break. Don't feel obligated to us. You've worked relentlessly for God knows how many years. We can manage this place.'

'Thanks. I'll give it some thought.'

Before anything more can be said on the subject and thrown by Tom's words, I rise to clear the table. He follows suit. Kath wilts back onto her lounger.

'Jen.' Tom almost crashes the plates into the sink.

'Listen, Tom, I'm so sorry about today. I was tired. It

was stupid of me to let Rosa swim by herself. I should have been watching her like a hawk.' I daren't tell him that I dozed off. A wisp of hair falls over my eyes.

Tom reaches out and strokes it behind my ears. 'I wasn't angry with you. I was angry with myself for letting you take Rosa to the lake. We're all tired after last night. Plus there's the heat, the work, the atmosphere. It's starting to drive me nuts, being here.'

He takes the coffee pot from the shelf, untwists the top and fills the base with water. His fingers are etched with scratches from the vines. He puts several teaspoons of ground coffee in the filter and screws on the lid, his tongue licking his lower lip – a sign that he's deep in thought. Metal clatters on metal and the hob flame sparks into life. It fans out around the pot which emits a gentle hiss.

'Tom, I think you're right about me going away. I'm getting too involved in your lives here and it's starting to feel awkward. I thought that I could come and see you all and leave unscathed. But it isn't that easy.' My voice wobbles with emotion. I'm not sure he understands what I'm trying to say – that I've fallen in love with him all over again.

He studies the coffee pot with great intensity. Then, finally: 'It's your decision, Jen. I just wanted to give you an opening to leave, if that's what you want.' His eyes bore into mine. His smooth knuckles grasp the worktop. 'Please believe me when I say that you've made an enormous difference coming back into our lives again – not just mine and Kath's, but Rosa's too. She adores you. Having you here has forced me to think long and hard about Rosa's happiness, Kath and me, the business. I'm going to be making some tough decisions over the next few weeks.'

He squeezes my hand and I bow my head to look down at our fingers entwined. Two vines twisted around each other, strong and unyielding. That's what we are. The coffee pot steams and whistles loudly, a hint that we've had long enough alone.

– CHAPTER 17 –

Picking up on Tom's suggestion, I decide to go away for several days to see the famous fields of lavender in Provence that Florence told me about. It'll give Tom and Kath some space to try and work out their future. Perhaps I'm the catalyst who has shaken things up a bit – set the wheels of change in motion. However, whatever that change is, that's for them to decide and better they do it when I'm not around.

Kath's eyes narrow with suspicion when I tell her. 'You're not going to see that woman are you?'

'What woman?'

'The one you met on the train – the lawyer.'

'Florence? Of course I'm not.'

'So who are you going with – Armelle?'

'No.'

'Someone you met at the party the other night, then?'

'No, Kath. I'm going alone. Is that such a surprise?'

***

Two days before I leave, I accompany Armelle to the market. She makes a good attempt at trying to appear her usual animated self as we chink along with our jars in the back, but there are telltale signs of anxiety in her mannerisms.

The morning is very busy. It's now the height of the tourist season and even with triple the quantities of honey and other products from *La Miellerie*, we sell out before midday. Armelle's brother isn't at the café today, so I have her all to myself. I know this isn't going to be an easy conversation but I want to reach out and offer her some support, even if she rejects it. We sit in the shade at the last available table. Two waiters jostle among the hot, weary customers, taking orders and delivering trays laden with cold refreshments. I pick up the dog-eared menu to fan my face. Slugs of hair stick to my neck and I run my fingers through it.

'So, are you going to tell me what happened at the party or do I have to tease it out of you, Armelle?'

'Oh Jenny, it was terrible. The worst night.'

She reaches into her bag, takes out a water spritzer and passes it to me. I spray the fine mist all over my face and neck.

'Luc told me that he's been having *une liaison*, an affair, with someone.'

'What? Are you serious? But he adores you.' I place the spray on the table between us, not totally believing what she's said. Still, I remember Luc's eyes, how wounded he looked, perhaps at the thought of losing Armelle.

'He wouldn't tell me who it was, but he said he was going to finish it. I keep looking at all of the people around us and can't believe it might be someone I know. Actually, he claimed I didn't know her, but I'm not sure if he just said that to calm me down as I'd have probably slapped her too!'

She heaves a huge sigh, which seems to ripple through

her from top to toe. Her little pink toenails remind me of matches in a box, waiting to be plucked out and lit.

'I haven't stopped crying. I am angry, I am sad. But Luc has been trying very hard and in a way I'm glad that I know now what the problem was between us.'

I'm amazed by her mature approach. 'So, do you think you are going to be able to work it out together, put it behind you?'

Sniffles break out of Armelle's nose. I pass her the napkin underneath my glass and wait for her to finish blowing.

'I love him so much, Jenny, and he promises me that he was just stressed by having to try for a baby and worrying about not having enough money. I suppose I want so badly to believe him.'

'OK.' For a moment I wonder if he's told Armelle about his loan from Tom and if I should tell her. But that might impact on me.

I pat her arm. 'I'm sure you'll get through this, Armelle. I think it's good that he was honest with you. It shows how much you mean to him and how he's scared of losing you. I could see that on his face when he was watching you dance with so much energy and fury.'

Reaching over to hug me, she clings tightly for a second or two. For a moment I want to tell her how I really feel about Tom. But that would be foolish. I've got to work things out for myself.

***

That evening, I send Scott a quick email. I suppose I've been avoiding a direct phone call with my father – I don't want to get grilled about my future career plans – so I'm hoping that Scott might be able to catch him at the right moment when his guard is down. I want to know exactly what promises my father made to Kath – if he made any at all. So far, I've only heard her side of the story, and doubt is now gnawing away at me, compounded by recent events, including Rosa's bruises.

Tom pulls into the lane as I'm coming back from my morning swim, my head filled with so many anxieties that I almost crash my bike into the side of his truck.

'When are you off to Provence?' He leans out of his window, his hair still damp from the shower.

'Tomorrow morning. Listen, Tom, I need to tell you something important. I think I should have told you before, but I promised Rosa I wouldn't unless it happened again. I don't know if you know about the marks on Rosa's arms. You might have seen them the other day at the lake.'

He stares at me. 'What marks?'

'Bruises. She said that Kath pulled her. I think Rosa was rude or something. But—'

'She what?' He stops the engine, his face reddening. He makes a movement to get out of the truck, but I hold his hand to stop him.

'Tom, don't bring it up with Kath now. Rosa asked me not to say anything as Kath's promised her a kitten.'

'How can I not say anything?' He shakes his head with repressed anger. 'Kath's been overseeing Rosa's baths recently, so how would I know about these marks?'

'I know, I know. OK, can I suggest that you take it up with her once I've gone? I'm sure the bruises will still be there if you look closely.'

'Of course. Let me handle it.'

He starts up the engine and pulls away without another glance at me. I just hope he's calmer when he speaks to Kath. Pouring anger onto her will just fan the flames. Calm reasoning has always worked better with her, but I'm sure Tom knows that already.

***

The following day, I leave the stillness of a sleeping household to walk to the bus stop. Although I'm sad to be leaving the house and garden, it'll be good to spend time by myself and make some firm decisions about my future.

The road is quiet except for the rustle of long dry grass, which reaches out to stroke my legs. I sit on the weathered bench by the bus stop and wait. Several minutes later the bus arrives, the driver welcomes me aboard and we cut through the solitary landscape, stopping along the main road to pick up early-morning workers.

At the station, there seems to be a delay – a signalling problem is what I think is announced over the loud speaker. I order a *petit café* and sit in the waiting room, next to the window so I can observe what's going on. There's a smudge of red on one of the panes of glass – lipstick, perhaps. It makes me think of the heart I drew on the misted-up train window seven weeks ago. *Seven weeks*. How unsure of myself I was then. It feels as though I've lived through a lifetime of emotions here already. Is it possible to change so much in such a short time? I wish I could gaze into a crystal ball and see the future. Will Kath be willing to let Tom move on? Or will she fight tooth and nail to maintain control over both him and Rosa – as she has tried to control me and influence my father? Or will

Tom decide to work things out with Kath? He must have loved her once.

A bespectacled man with white hair enters the waiting room, a pile of paperwork in one hand and a drink in the other. He clears his throat for a '*Bonjour*', smiling warmly at me, before sitting down at the next table. I return his greeting, the door blows open and his papers flap about like a cage of white doves newly released into the air. I rush to help him, just as my phone rings.

'Hello, Kath?'

'Jenny! Are you on the train already?' She sounds upset.

'No, there's a delay. All OK?' I try to sound calm.

The old man takes the papers from me and lets them fan out messily over the table. '*Merci, merci chère Mademoiselle.*' I smile back at him.

'Problem is, Jenny, I've gone and twisted my ankle badly.'

'Oh dear, so...' Kath wants me to return to the house.

'Well, we've got new guests coming tomorrow, haven't we?' Her tone is sharp. 'Jenny? Are you still there?'

The old man sips his coffee. I envy him his solitude. 'Yes, I'm here.'

'Oh. So, yes, can you come back? You can always go to Provence next week, can't you?'

I remain silent. I wanted to spend time by myself, away from her.

'Listen, Jenny, there's something *really* important I need to discuss with you,' she whispers down the line.

And, of course, she's succeeded in rousing my curiosity so I tell her that I'll be on the next bus back. But this time I'll be on my guard. I wonder if there's another secret she's been withholding. Or has she decided to confess everything to me? Perhaps she's worked out how I feel about Tom. My stomach starts to turn over and over, until I have to rush outside to take in some fresh air.

During the bus journey I mull over Kath's threats at the party – at what she would do if Tom tried to leave her. It's hard to see how it can happen without Rosa being used as a pawn, but people make all sorts of threats when they're in pain. Maybe Kath will come round and it will all be fine. They may even become friends. And where does that leave me? Even if they do separate well, Tom will stay in the Languedoc to be near his daughter. Should I tell him how deep my feelings are? He might just laugh in my face.

Maybe I should just leave on the next train and never come back.

***

I spot Tom's truck parked in the lane as soon as I alight from the bus. I'd managed to convince myself that I should just tell him how I feel and see how he reacts. But, seeing him like this, looking agitated, pacing up and down, I know that now is not the best time. I walk towards him slowly, reluctant to hear bad news.

'We need to talk,' he says as soon as I reach him.

We jump into the truck and he drives us back onto the main road towards the beach.

'Sorry she had to break up your trip. If it's any consolation, I think the twisted ankle is for real, although whether she did it deliberately, I don't know. Maybe I'm just too cynical.' He pulls over into a lay-by and turns the engine off. 'I've just told her I want a separation.'

'Jesus. How did she react?'

'She didn't take it too badly. I thought she'd explode, but actually she was very calm. Asked me if it was because of you.'

My heart skips a beat. I open the window. 'What did you say?'

'No, of course. It's not because of you. It's because of her and me. And that's what I stressed. I've told her that after the *vendange*, the grape harvest, I'm going to move out – temporarily, of course – I didn't push it that far – so that we can both have a break. In the meantime, I want to go and see her GP with her to ensure that she's stable.'

'Good idea. And when did she twist her ankle?'

'Straight afterwards. She said she stumbled on the path.'

Very convenient, I think, but I don't say it.

Tom turns the truck around and drops me back in the lane. Rosa is already at *La Miellerie* helping Sylvie to make fig jam. Wearily, I enter the gateway. The dread starts to creep up inside me and my feet feel heavy as they step up to the front door. I drop my bag onto the floor and walk through to the back door, which is open.

Kath's sitting outside, one foot propped on a chair, a pen and jotter in front of her on the table. She's staring into her lap. I stand in the doorway, just looking at her bent head, its auburn colour flecked with gold from the sunlight piercing the surrounding trees. For a moment I'm transported back to that first week of our childhood friendship. Kath had invited me round to her house for tea and we'd agreed to meet at the playground benches after school. As soon as the bell rang, I rushed out of my English lesson, down the six flights of stairs, giddy with the excitement of having a new friend to play with. As I raced down the stairs, I could glimpse Kath through the smudged glass sitting on a bench, head bowed in the same way it is now. She looked up and smiled with relief when I skipped towards her, as though she hadn't expected me to show. As if she's plugged into the same memory, Kath looks up and immediately winces with pain.

'Poor you. How's it feeling?'

She sighs deeply. Changing tack, she dazzles me with her '100 per cent smile' as Tom used to call it. The smile that seduces, coaxes and persuades all in one.

'Sorry about having to get you back like this. It's a bugger, that's what it is.' She attempts to get up.

'No, don't move, Kath. Let me get you something. What would you like? Coffee? Tea?'

'I'm fine. Sit down here beside me.' She pats the empty chair. (The confession chair or the seat of torture?) 'Have you seen Tom?'

I try to look confused. 'No, why?'

'He said he's leaving me,' she says, with a blank expression. 'Going to move into town, so he remains close to Rosa. Over my dead body.' She tries to push herself up in her seat.

'Oh, gosh.' I pretend to absorb the information. 'I'm sorry. How do you feel about that? I mean, do you still love him, Kath?'

Kath appraises me. 'Oh, come on, Jenny. Who knows what love really is? Thought I did at the beginning but he's never been interested in me really. Only has sex when I want it. Never told me he loves me. Not with meaning anyway.' Her eyes flick back and forth as though she's speed reading words on a screen.

'But do *you* love him, Kath?' I want her to answer that question, but she squirms in her chair and I know she won't answer me.

'He can go where the hell he likes but he's not getting his hands on Rosa. I'll always win – whatever it takes.' She pauses, then pulls me towards her. 'Have you two been going at it behind my back? Is that what this is about?'

Our eyes meet. Hers are strangely empty. I pull away from her. 'Of course not. I'm with Scott, remember?'

'Oh yes, Scott.' A small smile appears on her lips.

'Why do you say that?'

'Oh, I don't know.' Her attention is taken away momentarily by a small gecko that's moving up the wall. She turns back to me. 'I'm just wondering whether your relationship with Scott is for real, that's all.'

'I don't know why you'd think that.'

A sigh. 'Maybe, it wasn't such a good idea, you coming here, after all. The past being raked over again.'

'If that's how you feel, Kath, I'll pack my things and go now.' I start to turn away from her but she reaches out for my arm again. I shake it away from her.

'No, sorry, Jenny. Don't go. It's just that...' Her voice tails off. 'If you must know, before you arrived here, I was definitely planning on visiting you in Australia at Christmas. You know, to see if there was a chance we might emigrate, so we could be closer to you. Rosa and me, I mean.' Her words tumble out like a set of dominos falling on top of each other, one after the other.

'You know, it's not that easy to move to Australia. And what about your business here? What about Tom? Rosa's his daughter.'

'I'd give them both up in a heartbeat if you want me.

Tom and the business.' She starts to scratch her arm.

'You can't do that to Tom, Kath. You can't take Rosa away from him. She needs her father too.'

'Oh blow that!' She kicks out at the table leg with her good foot. 'I'll get some legal advice. He's not getting his dirty mitts on Rosa. And that's another thing. He accused me of hurting her, which is absolute bollocks.'

I say nothing.

'Probably saying that to threaten me over custody.' The fine down above her lip glistens. 'He's got some front, telling me he's leaving me.'

'Why? Because you wanted to do it first?' She doesn't answer. 'I can't believe how childish you're being, Kath. And there *really* is a child to consider in all of this. You have to put Rosa first.' I get up too fast and my chair crashes to the ground.

'Careful! Hey, where are you going? I need you to help me get up. Jenny!'

'I'll be back in a sec. I just need to unpack, remember?'

I head upstairs with my bag. She can sit there and rot for all I care. I'm sure I'm right about why she's so upset with Tom – she's treated him with utter disdain since I arrived. As usual she wants to be the one in control.

– CHAPTER 18 –

Kath's swollen ankle couldn't have come at a better time, as it means she has to stay put and rest during the days that follow. I relish keeping busy, cleaning the *gîtes* for the new arrivals, taking Pilot and Rosa for walks around the many villages surrounding the house and staying away from Kath as much as I can, so I don't have to listen to her pouring her frustrations out on me. Tom works late at the farm, probably for the same reasons. It does mean, however, that I don't have a chance to speak with him properly. I start to doubt myself and lose the courage I'll need to deliver the words that I'd rehearsed on the bus. What was I thinking? *How ridiculous, Jenny. Why would he be interested in you? He dumped you, remember? He never tried once to see you.* The words go round and round in my head, until I convince myself that I dreamt the whole thing up, that there is no future for Tom and me, it was a stupid idea and as soon as the summer is over, I'm moving on and away from here. Away from them both.

Then something happens which puts us all on edge. Several days after my cancelled trip, I come downstairs before breakfast to find Tom in the kitchen crouched over Pilot's basket. He looks up as I enter, his eyes filled with sorrow.

'Tom! What is it?' I drop my swimming bag and walk over to him.

Pilot is curled up in his basket as though he's asleep, yet he isn't moving. I peep over Tom's shoulder and spot white foam on his coal-black nose. Tom strokes his silken paw gently.

'He's dead, Jen. Poor little mite. Not sure what did it, but at least it was peaceful.'

'Where's Kath and Rosa?'

'Still in bed. I'm going to take him to the vets, to see if they know what killed him. Just for peace of mind.'

He stands up and wraps his long arms around me for comfort. I respond instinctively. He is still a huge part of me, whatever I try to tell myself, and at this moment, seeing him like this, filled with grief, I know that I cannot give him up so easily. I may have tried to kid myself otherwise, but he is the main reason why I came here.

I help him carry Pilot to the truck. He's quite a weight. His paws hang out stiffly and it's a struggle to wrestle him into the back. Tom covers him with a blanket and drives away, his face still knotted with upset. He was so attached to that dog. I turn back towards the house and see Kath looking down at me from their bedroom. She waves as she pushes back the shutters. I go inside to break the news to her. She'll need to console Rosa who will be devastated.

We bury Pilot in the garden, close to the cherry tree. Dark patches of sweat have chequered across Tom's chest while he has worked tirelessly to dig a hole in the dry, unforgiving earth. He carefully lowers Pilot, still wrapped in his blanket, into the womb-like cavern, and we all take turns to sprinkle the dusty soil onto the dog's body. Rosa is beside herself with grief. She runs upstairs at one point,

I think because she can take the pain no longer, but she quickly returns with her favourite doll, Alice, and throws her into the hole, so that Pilot has 'a friend to talk to when he's lonely at night.' Kath stands solemnly with her arm draped across her daughter's shoulders. She reaches out for my hand with the other and squeezes it tightly. I turn to see tears rolling down her face. Tom mutters a small prayer for Rosa's sake, asking God to take care of the best-loved pet in the world. He returned from the vet's with no real resolution as to how Pilot died. The vet thought that, given the foam in Pilot's mouth and nose, he probably ate some rat poison, which is a common product used on farms around here, especially where there's livestock.

'It's just unusual for Pilot to have gone anywhere near that stuff as it's everywhere, here and at *La Miellerie*, and he was always so careful to steer clear of it.'

'Perhaps someone left some tasty food out laced with the stuff and he couldn't resist it. You know how he was always disappearing into other people's gardens on his walkabouts. He wasn't exactly a house dog, was he?' says Kath.

She's right. Pilot did wander off by himself at times, although not very far from the house from what I've observed.

***

August arrives and brings with it a few nighttime showers. The damp smell of soil and roots fills my nose when I step outside into the eerie early-morning quiet. My bike squeaks and rattles down the lane, moving closer towards the sunrise, which is the colour of pale-pink rose petals. I have to concentrate to avoid the potholes filled with rainwater. At the lake, the morning birdsong is at its liveliest. I picture hundreds of birds above me, chattering over their early-worm breakfast. The water sleeps on in the shade. I dip my toe in. Gentle pea-green ripples move towards its centre.

I dive into the cool, inscrutable depths and begin my routine. As my arms move over my head and dip in and out, all I hear is the sound of the water lapping with each stroke. This feeling of tranquillity is like no other and I am totally absorbed in my quiet meditation. After a frantic weekend of changeovers, new arrivals to settle in, I need this.

A car engine purrs somewhere not far away, but I blot it out and continue with my lengths. Shortly afterwards, a streak of red breaks my concentration and I see birds flying away from their treetop resting place. I stop and lift my head to see what has disturbed the stillness in the air. It's Kath. She's by the water, shaking out a towel. She doesn't usually come to the lake. I sense a confrontation and continue to plough the water with my arms. I need to get my thoughts together.

I dive down deep, breaking through the luminescent green seal of weeds which covers the water in places, and holds the lake's secrets beneath it. My legs kick up and down and I flap my hands gently at my sides to move between the reeds, slowly like a fish. I can't see the bottom, it's so deep. Shadows jump out of nowhere, air bubbles fizz around me. It's like looking through a fogged-up lens. But, at least I'm safe to think down here. No prying eyes to unnerve me.

Finally I'm ready. I surface and there is Kath sitting

on the bank, waiting. Her anxiety is obvious. She pulls on blades of coarse grass and throws them into the water.

'Morning, Kath. What are you doing here so early? Is your ankle better?'

'Yes, much,' she says in a monotone. 'Thought I'd come and find you for a chat.'

'What about? Can't it wait until breakfast?' I swim towards the lake's edge and tread water, looking up at her.

'Jenny, please can you get out? All I can see is your head bobbing up and down in that vile green liquid. I don't know how you could swim in that when you can't even see how deep it is. There could be a monster living in there for all you know.'

'Having a summer's break from Loch Ness you mean?' I laugh as I pull myself out.

Kath grabs my towel and throws it over my shoulders. She stands there watching me as I dry myself. Anyone could see that she's twitchy, the toes in her sandals moving up and down. She sits down and starts pulling on the grass again.

'Shit.' The blade of grass is sharper than it looks – a red dot of blood appears on her finger. She sucks at it. 'Bloody hell.'

'So, what's up?' I ask, taking a seat next to her.

'It's Tom. Something isn't right with him and I want to know if you have any idea what it might be.'

'I don't know what you mean.'

'It's just that... oh, piss off!' She hits out at some tiny flies buzzing around us.

I reach for my clothes so that I can start to get dressed. The beauty of my surroundings has been tainted by this unwelcome visitor.

'Jenny, someone might see you.' She grabs her towel and uses it to shield me from the empty car park. 'Every time I look up, he's studying me. I don't like the way he looks. It scares me.'

I sit down on my towel to put on my plimsolls. 'What sort of look?'

'Like he wants to kill me. It's pure hatred, that's what it is.'

'Kath, of course he doesn't hate you. Why don't you just ask him what's up?' I lie back, gaze up at the whitening sky, wishing she'd go away and leave me in peace. Kath lies down next to me but jerks back up again almost immediately.

'Jenny, you've got to help me. Are you listening to anything I've said?' She is scratching her arm again. The sound is like sandpaper rubbing a chair leg. 'I think he wants to hurt me.'

I sit up on my elbows and take a calming breath before responding. 'Kath, just relax. I think you're tired. No one wants to hurt you. Tom isn't that sort of person. You know that.'

'Perhaps he knows.' She throws me an anxious look, then hides her face in her hands.

'Knows what?' She gets up and paces up and down, scratching that arm again.

'Knows what, Kath?'

Now I start getting my things together, my eyes fixed on her.

'Oh I don't know, Jenny.' She attempts a smile. 'You're right, I'm just tired.'

'Is there something you want to share with me, perhaps?' My voice is gentle, yet persuasive. 'I mean everyone has a little secret, don't they? Something they don't want their partner to know?'

She throws her arms wide and continues with the pacing. 'I don't have any secrets. I'm an open book. You know me.'

'Do I?' I stop and stare deep into her eyes.

Time stands still as we hold each other's gaze. Finally, she looks away.

'Of course you do, Jenny. You know me better than anyone. Best friends, remember?'

'In that case, Kath, you've got nothing to worry about, have you?' I hand her my dripping things and jump onto my bike. 'Can you take these for me please? I'll get breakfast. See you in a few minutes.'

Back at the house, nothing more is said on the matter and Kath seems to want to forget that we'd even spoken when I ask her if she's feeling OK.

'Of course, Jenny, why wouldn't I be? I think I just needed to see you. I had this weird dream about Pilot.' She looks at me as though she wants me to say something about that.

'What sort of dream? That he was still alive, you mean?'

Kath opens her mouth to speak, but stops when Tom and Rosa come outside to join us. I'm thankful for her silence. Rosa especially has been subdued this past week.

'Oh, it was nothing. I just wanted to make sure that you were safe at the lake. I was worried that something had happened to you, that's all.' Her eyes seem to sparkle with the reassurance that all is well.

Tom stirs a teaspoon of sugar into his coffee, looking at Kath questioningly. 'All OK?' he says.

'Fine,' she says tersely, taking a bite out of her

croissant. Her eyelashes fan up and down, like a cow's chewing on cud.

***

The following morning I return from my swim and visit to the *boulangerie* to witness an unlikely truce. Kath and Tom are eating breakfast outside, chuckling, laughter in their eyes. There's no sign of Rosa, so I assume she's playing in her bedroom with her doll's house.

'Jenny, come and have some coffee, won't you? Tom and I have been talking. We're going to stay together and try to work things out. Then we'll see how we feel at the end of the summer. Yummy, those croissants look good.'

She puts her cereal aside, rips open the bag I've placed on the table and takes a bite out of one of the warm buttery croissants. This distraction gives me the opportunity to raise an eyebrow at Tom while she is eating. He doesn't respond.

'That's good news. So what brought this decision on?' I look from one face to the other.

'I realised I was being too rash.' Tom leans over and takes a croissant, dips it into his *café au lait*. 'I think Kath and I should wait until the end of the summer, once the season is over. Then we can see if we can settle the differences between us. For Rosa's sake – and ours, of course.' He puts the pastry into his mouth.

'Good for you.' I mimic his actions to try and appear relaxed. This is a confusing state of affairs.

Kath is watching me closely. 'Perhaps you should do the same with Scott, Jenny. Try a bit harder to make things work between the two of you.'

I glance at Tom and will him not to say anything. I'm not ready to tell Kath the truth yet about Scott.

'I'm not sure what you mean by that. Scott and I are fine, although our work's always been more important to us. In fact, we spoke to each other the other day and he's coming to meet me in September when I leave here. That's if you still want me to stay on until then?'

'Of course we do. Couldn't survive without you now.' She clears her throat, looks down to brush the crumbs off her lap. 'And that's great news, Jenny – about Scott, I mean. I didn't realise he'd already made a plan to come out here.'

'Why would you? We've only just arranged it.'

'Good, we'll finally get to meet him. Right, I'm going to take a shower, get Rosa dressed, then I've got to sort out Saturday's bookings.' She gets up slowly and hobbles away into the house.

I look down at my plate.

'Listen, Jen.' Tom's voice is a whisper. 'I was premature in asking her for a separation. I hoped that she might be OK about it. I was wrong.'

'I don't understand. She seems fine to me.' I pour more coffee into my cup and watch the bubbles popping on the surface.

'*She* might seem fine, but Pilot isn't, is he? That was her way of getting at me. A message.'

I stare at him while his words sink in. 'Are you saying that you think she killed Pilot? Oh come on, Tom, she loved that dog.'

'Jen, when the hell are you going to see things for how they are?' He gets up too quickly and a plate crashes to the floor. We both wince at the sound. 'You've been here, what, two months now and you still think her behaviour's normal, don't you?'

I crouch down to pick up the broken fragments of crockery, shocked by the strength of Tom's anger. 'Of course not.' I stack the pieces carefully. 'But I struggle to believe that she's unhinged. The timing could just be a coincidence. We can't automatically think Pilot's death is Kath's doing, surely?'

'Can't we? Don't be so sure.' He passes me a serviette. 'I should have waited to talk to her at the end of the summer, after you'd gone. I don't trust her anymore. I think she's capable of anything to get what she wants and you need to be far away from here on the day I tell her what I really think of her, that I don't want a break, I want out. Rosa needs to be away too, but I haven't worked that bit out yet.'

'Well, I'm here for as long as you need me, as far as Rosa's concerned. I'm more than happy to take her off for a few days while you two work things out. If that's what you need.'

'Thanks, Jen. I'll give it some thought.'

He goes off to repair one of the air-conditioning units and finally change the light-bulb in the garage, which Kath reminded him about at breakfast, leaving me to clean up the mess and ponder over what he's just said. There is the issue of Mrs Holt's death that has been hanging over me ever since the party. In this mood, Tom is certain to believe that she pushed Mrs Holt down the stairs. I decide not to fan the flames by mentioning it to him for now.

– CHAPTER 19 –

A few days later I'm cleaning the communal terrace, where we've set up some outdoor barbecues. The guests we've had so far have been a melting pot of nationalities: Swedes, Dutch, Germans and the odd British family. For the most part, they keep to themselves, content to be out sightseeing or at the beach. The weather has been consistently fine so nothing to grumble about, apart from the odd flurry of ants when food or drink hasn't been cleared away.

I received an email yesterday from the London college that's offered me a place on its Masters programme in September. They're pressing me for a decision. I know what all of my options are and still I'm undecided. I wonder if there would be anything for me here – in Montpellier perhaps – and realise what a stupid thought that is right now. I've got to leave at some point and let Tom work this out first. That's when I realise that I've been mopping the same bit of terrace for five minutes.

Tom stroked my shoulder this morning when I was washing up. He was reaching over me to get a glass from the cupboard. My skin still tingles where he touched me. Kath and Rosa were upstairs getting dressed at the time – I could hear them arguing about what Rosa was going to wear today. Before he came into the kitchen, a sensation, like static, travelled through the hairs on my arms, making them stand on end, and I knew he was close by. The touch only lasted a few seconds but it feels as if he's marked me forever. I touch the spot with my finger, losing my thoughts to the usual daydreams about my future. A scraping chair jolts me out of my reverie.

'Kath!' I plonk the mop and bucket on the kitchen floor.

'Just checking my emails. Be down in a sec!'

I move around the kitchen, putting the coffee pot on the hob. Morning coffee at 11 a.m. has become a habit for Kath and I. It's unusual for her to be upstairs on her laptop. She usually sits downstairs with it at this hour. The bottom stairs creak and she enters the room and looks at me for a moment longer than is usual. Her mouth is a straight line. She fidgets awkwardly in the doorway, as if reluctant to enter. I can sense that her arm twitches to be scratched, but she resists. There's something about that pattern of movement that's familiar as she sits and reaches for her cup. Another look at me. No words spoken. As if to say, *I know*.

The day after Tom and I went to the river during that first summer when we met, Kath turned up at my house early to see if I wanted to go into town. We shopped until the heat drove us into a café for a cold drink. Kath had been slightly moody all morning and had given me that same look, I remember now. I asked her then if anything was wrong and she hadn't answered. She took her time sipping on a bottle of lemonade, her lips puckered around a straw, eyes fixed on me. Watching. Thinking. Finally, she bit the bullet and asked me if I was using contraception. Somewhat fazed by her directness, I considered lying, but affirmed that yes I was. It didn't take long to get to the bottom of it. She was upset because I hadn't told her that I was sleeping with Tom. How did she know I was? I asked. Turned out she was upset that I had asked Tom to go with me to the doctor instead of her. But wasn't that the right thing to do? She seemed to accept my reasoning, and then announced that Mark Butler had asked her out, so she was planning to put herself on the pill. She was curious to know what sex was like.

I discouraged her from rushing into things, to wait until she and Mark were comfortable with each other. The way that Tom and I had. She ignored my advice and slept with Mark after a couple of dates. Some weeks later, she finished with him. Said that sex wasn't all that it was cracked up to be and blow jobs made her gag. We'd had a good laugh about that. I was concerned, though. Why had she felt this compelling urge to rush into a sexual experience with someone she didn't really know? Tom thought it was probably because she wanted to share the same experiences as me and not feel left out. He said we should be more concerned about how she found out about us.

'Do you think she saw us at the river?' he asked.

I blushed at the thought of her following us, watching our intimacy through the hanging canopy of the weeping willow. We had chosen the spot carefully, knowing that hardly anyone went to that part of the riverbank.

'Maybe. Or she saw your pills in your bag. You know how you always leave your rucksack gaping open.' He laughed and pulled me towards him for a kiss.

And here we all are a decade later and she's wearing the same expression.

'Are you coming for lunch at Sandrine's today?' I take a sip of coffee and lean back in my chair.

'No, I'm doing a wine tour today, remember?' Kath picks up a leftover croissant, tears it into small pieces and dips it into her coffee. 'So, Jenny. Have you discussed with Scott your plans to settle back in the UK?' I mean will you get married, so he can live there too?'

'He's got to ask me first, hasn't he?' My attempt at humour falls on deaf ears. That look continues to wear me down. I hear myself babbling on. 'Scott's very driven, I'm not sure I can see the two of us living under the same roof in the same country with his work commitments. He loves Australia, I prefer the UK.' I've got to hold my anxiety in check. Why is she nosing around my life in Perth? She hasn't shown much of an interest before and that's how I liked it.

'So why don't you ask him to–'

There's a tap at the kitchen door. It's Miriam, one of the guests. Greeting her like a long-lost friend, I offer her coffee but she declines, explains that there's a problem with ants in the bathroom. Reluctantly, Kath gets up to deal with it. They leave together.

The open door stares back at me. What next?

***

The intensity of the mid-afternoon August sun is strong today. The air is motionless and has a gauzy haze to it. Apart from the growling of a tractor in the distance, there is a siesta-like stillness all around, imposed by the pounding heat, which forces us all to retreat indoors behind closed shutters.

My bike tyres wheeze when I turn into the gateway and seem as keen as me to find some respite. There's an unfamiliar truck in the yard, the windows open. Perhaps Tom's borrowed it from someone.

Lunch at Sandrine's was a merry affair with lots of chatter about one of the girls who helps at the holiday club. Apparently she's pregnant and there was some speculation about the father's identity. I couldn't follow everything that was discussed, but I enjoyed sitting back and listening to the animated voices trilling out over the street as we sat outside on the shaded balcony, sipping rosé. It feels good to be included in this local community and now I admonish myself for rejecting similar invitations in Perth. How foolish I was to cut myself off from people like that. Sandrine tried to ply me with several glasses of wine, but I insisted on only one, knowing I would suffer for it later when I was cooking dinner.

As I walk my bike round to the side of the house, I hear raised voices – shouting – in French. One of them is Kath's, the other male – a familiar voice, but I can't yet place it. I don't know whether I should stay put or continue to the back door, where the voices are coming from. The French is too fast for me to understand, but Kath's voice is unrelenting. I've never heard her tone so hard-edged. She cuts through the man's pleas as though she is ripping off his shirt with a sword. Just as I check the provisions I've bought in my bike panniers, the back door slams and Luc appears red-faced and glowering. Instinctively, I duck out of sight. I don't want him to think I was eavesdropping. Fortunately he chooses to leave by the other side of the house so I remain undetected.

I wait until I hear his truck pull away, then walk

casually to the back door. Kath is standing at the kitchen sink, her back towards me. The door handle heralds my arrival and she twists round to confront me. Her face is flushed, her chin poised for battle.

'Oh, Jenny, sorry, I thought you were an intruder or something.' Her arms drop to her sides and she turns back to busy herself at the sink once more.

'Wasn't that Luc I just saw leaving?'

'Yes, he dropped by to see Tom.'

I take a breath. 'I could hear shouting.'

She turns towards me. I see the hesitation on her face before she smiles to cover it up. 'Actually, he was worried about Armelle. I think he feels under pressure to perform in the baby department, if you know what I mean, so I was trying to offer support. Maybe the shouting you heard was him voicing his frustration. But I think I managed to calm him down. What've you been up to?' She turns to the washing up once more to signal that the conversation about Luc is over. Her ability to turn the tables so seamlessly is impressive.

'I went to Sandrine's for lunch, remember?' I don't give up so easily. 'So don't you think Luc and Armelle are getting along now? Armelle seemed happy when I last saw her.'

'Oh, I'm sure it'll be fine.' She turns to smile at me. 'Hey, I was thinking we should have a cheese and wine party next week. My wine tour group loved tasting all of that plonk earlier, so we could do something more – invite other holidaymakers who are staying in the area, sell a few dozen crates of wine. What do you think?'

'Sounds like a good idea, but–'

'OK, that gives us five days to leaflet the area. I'll send

out an email too.' She wipes her hands on a tea-towel, moves to the table, taps her nails on her pad, and starts to hum.

'Is there something you're keeping from me, Kath? You seem distracted at the moment.'

'Oh, you know me. I always like to have a plan, keep the boredom at bay. I've been thinking about the autumn. Our road trip, remember?'

I stop unloading my shopping. 'God, I thought that was on the back burner. Anyway, that's going to have to be put on hold if I go to London.'

'Are you sure that's what you really want, Jenny? I mean, come on, you're an Olympic gold medallist! Surely you don't want to do more studying. And England, when you can have Australia. Those big open roads, sunshine, the outdoors.'

'It's a long way from here, though. I'd like to be closer to my roots.'

Her mobile phone rings. She takes it off the counter and looks to see who it is. Her face reddens slightly. Her smile is secretive. She glances up at me. 'Sorry, Jenny, I've got to take this call. Let's talk about it later.' She rushes out of the back door, leaving a breeze in her wake, and all I hear are the words: 'Hello, yes, thanks so much for calling back. I'm so excited!'

***

The following morning at the lake, I reach for the two large stones by the bank, which I always use to haul myself out of the water, only to find a strong hand in their place. I am pulled out into the air and crushed against Tom's chest. He wraps my towel around me. There's something ritualistic about this moment. Those times we spent at the river and he'd be waiting for me on the bank after my swim, a book in one hand, my towel in the other, ready to wrap me in my 'cloak', as he used to call it. This moment is so intoxicating, so comforting, that I raise my eyes up to his in hope. Nothing. It seems he has only come to deliver an errand from Kath.

'Can you go to the pharmacy and pick up this prescription please? I've got a lot on at the farm. Thanks.' He hands me the piece of paper and turns on his heels to go.

'Tom!'

He hesitates and turns round to face me.

'Is that it? Is that all you've come for?'

I wait and feel the silence wrap itself about us. He doesn't respond and I turn my back on him and gaze out over the lake. A grey dog is sniffing around in the long grass on the opposite side, its ears pricked up.

I sense Tom moving back towards me. He places his hands gently on my shoulders and turns me around slowly. There is a small light in his eyes. It's as though he has pulled back the curtains to allow me to take a peep into his soul, but only a peep.

'For the moment, Jen, yes, that's all. I'm sorry.' He bends down to place his brow on mine, his hands still resting on my shoulders. I absorb his thoughts, his strength, his smell. We waver in the still air like two blades of trampled grass reaching out to the breeze. 'There's so much I want to say, Jen. But, can we leave it for now?'

A whistle rouses us both. The dog's owner approaches his sniffing pet, a lead in his hand. He waves at us both and shouts a '*Bonjour*!' across the lake.

We both return the wave but before I can reply to Tom, he is already on his way back to his truck. His empty truck. And then it hits me and I start to shiver.

The whole household still feels a huge sense of loss for Pilot, but especially Tom who is without his daily companion. I wonder if he'll ever discover the truth or whether, like so many secrets in this world, the cause of Pilot's death will be lost to the earth and buried like the bones of his beloved pet.

– CHAPTER 20 –

'Jenny, you're still asleep!' Rosa jumps onto me, still dressed in her pyjamas, and wriggles into the free space next to me. She strokes back my hair and kisses me all over my face. 'Come on, lazybones, wake up!'

'Mmm, that's nice. What time is it? Have I overslept?' My eyes struggle to open, still enjoying the warmth and comfort of slumber.

'It's eight o'clock. Daddy's going to work and Mummy's in the shower.'

'Oh, dear, I was supposed to be up earlier than this. Are you going out somewhere?'

'No, silly, I'm not dressed, am I?' She giggles and pretend-slaps my arm. 'I want to read a story with you. I've brought *Cendrillon*. Here, look!' She thrusts a small book into my face, just managing to avoid poking me in the eye with it.

'Careful, Rosa.'

'Sorry.'

'Cinderella. Great. Girl gets boy but has to pretend she's a princess first. Just my type of story.'

I shake myself awake and pull myself up so that I can put my arm around Rosa, drawing her in close. I've been doing a routine check on her for bruises, but so far so good. Nothing more. Maybe Kath is learning how to control her emotions.

After ten minutes of Rosa reading to me followed by me repeating back in my terrible French accent, Rosa races off to have breakfast. I lie back listening to the morning activity, enjoying this moment and wishing that my life was as simple as it feels today. I have little planned – housework, laundry, a swim. It's a world away from my old life. By now I'd have swum for two hours, been to the gym, had a power breakfast and would be getting ready for another round of pool training. No wonder I fell out of love with it. How can anyone sustain that sort of strenuous activity for so long?

An engine powering up splutters away my daydream. Doors slam and off go the Swedish guests for the day. They're always up bright and early. They like to have breakfast at the beach, they've told us. Kath says they're naturists and come to this region every year. I can hear her moving about downstairs in the kitchen. I turn over to place Rosa's abandoned book on the bedside table.

Poor *Jane Eyre* still lies untouched under my alarm clock. I pick it up and flick through the first few pages. It's a Penguin Classic, reprinted in 1985, the year Tom was born. There's a sketch of Charlotte Brontë on the cover. I trace her face with my finger, in an attempt to revive the memories of Tom and I reading it together at the river. The book opens at exactly the page I'm looking for, as though it's been expecting me to recount my favourite scene when Jane returns to Thornfield. A piece of pale-blue paper lies folded between the pages. Some old note of Tom's from school, perhaps. I unfold it and find it's an airmail envelope addressed to 'Miss Jennifer Parker' in that familiar spidery handwriting of his. I turn it over. Why didn't Tom post it to me? He always preferred letters to emails. It's still sealed. I start to prise the seal open with my nail, and then I stop. What if it contains something that Tom wouldn't want me to read now? The envelope trembles in my hand. I tear it open carefully, trying to keep the gummed edging intact, but that's impossible given the number of years the envelope has spent forgotten between the yellowing pages of a best-loved novel.

The letter inside has been written on two sheets of airmail paper. I unfold them gently and scan the contents quickly to get a sense of the message and its implications.

'Oh God, please no!'

I slap the paper down on the bed and close my eyes to take in this bombshell, but all I can see are images from the past flickering like a home movie. My chest aches and I realise I feel paralysed with worry. I breathe deeply until a feeling of calm descends over me, then I sit up straight and adjust my pillow behind my back. This time I absorb every word.

20ᵗʰ December 2006
Amman, Jordan

Dear Jen,

I can't shake you out of my thoughts, my daydreams, my nighttime mutterings.

I thought I could let you go, that being hard on you was the kindest thing I could do for you and your future. But I didn't consider the pain I'd have to put myself through in doing so.

I've been to hell and back with the bottle and

pills. Life in Jordan can be very lonely, especially when you spend a large part of it trying to forget. Actually, a lot of it is about trying to remember – to hold onto your beautiful, laughing face, before it dissolves into dust in my mind. I saw you competing on TV the other day. You are doing brilliantly. I hope you're happy, but selfishly on my part I know, I hope that you still think of me. You see, I've decided to take a colossal step into the abyss, to take a fool's chance and come to see you. Jen. My Jen. My little Mouse.

I daren't say that I'm coming to win you back but that's what I'll be hoping. I know I deserve to be kicked away by you, after the way I treated you and, believe me, I have lived to regret that moment ever since. First, I've got to go home as Mum and Paula are moving to Canada in the New Year. I need to help them pack up and clear out my old room, which is filled with so many memories of you.

I have to confess I brought an old T-shirt of yours with me. Every day, I hold it to my nose and breathe you in. The trouble is, it's been so long since you wore it that there's no scent left. That's when I decided. I'm coming to see you, to find out if there's any remaining hope for us.

I'm running late so I'll post this letter when I'm back in Bristol next week. I don't have any contact details for you, but my mum said she heard Kath was working in one of the smart hotels there so I'll pop in and get your address from her.

*'A fervent, a solemn passion is conceived in my
heart; it leans to you, draws you to my centre.'*
Tom

So why didn't he come? I turn the pages round for clues.
Nothing. I don't understand. What stopped him from
coming? Then I spot a yellow post-it note stuck to the
inside of the envelope, obviously written after the letter.
I pull it out.

*'P.S. Kath's told me that you're with someone else
already, but I might take my chances anyway.
Email me and let me know.'*

The grey mist starts to dissolve in front of my eyes and
everything becomes clear.

Tom wrote this letter just over a year after I arrived
in Perth. But he didn't send it, because he didn't have my
new postal address. Kath had it, though. So why didn't I
receive this letter?

I run down the stairs two at a time, the paper rustling
in my hand. Kath is humming to herself, peeling apples at
the sink.

She stops what she's doing and looks up. 'Good
morning sleepy head. I thought you were at the lake.'

'Where's Tom?'

'He's at the farm. Why?' The moist blade of the small
vegetable knife glistens at me like a warning. 'What have
you got there, Jenny?' She nods at the letter as the house
phone begins to ring.

Kath darts around me to go and answer it so I lean
back on the table and wait, trying to breathe slowly.

A minute or so later she comes back into the room.

'Our Swedish guests have been involved in a road accident with a motorcyclist on their way to the beach. No one's hurt but they need an interpreter at the police station.' She tells me all of this as she tears the end off a baguette, pushes it into her mouth and grabs her bag. As she pulls the door open, she turns towards me. 'What was that paper you were holding, Jenny?'

I stuff the letter into my dressing-gown. It presses against me, but the moment for candour is lost. First I want to see Tom, tell him that I understand everything.

'It's nothing, just a page I found. Don't worry, I'll pop it under Tom's study door.'

'Is that all? By the look on your face, I thought it was something more intriguing.' Kath eyes me carefully as if looking for clues. 'Can you take care of Rosa? She's picking cherries by the swing.'

'Sure.'

She waves, gets in the car and drives away. I run my tongue over my lips and watch her disappear in a cloud of dust.

No doubt roused by the departing car, a chirpy Rosa arrives back with her basket full of deep-red cherries. She's just the distraction I need right now. I find a recipe online for a *clafoutis aux cerises*, a cherry flan. Rosa's lips are stained red from where she's been snacking on the cherries, reminding me of when I used to sit on my mother's stool to try out her lipsticks. Her dressing-table had three mirrors and I would adjust the outer two so that I could see three of me at the same time. I'd use her hairbrush for a microphone and pretend we were the Parker Sisters, all wearing the same smudged lipstick.

I wish Mum were here now – she'd tell me what to do.

Kath phones to say she'll be back shortly. The motorcyclist was thrown off his bike, but only has a few bruises. Witnesses said that he was driving dangerously, so the Swedes won't be prosecuted, thankfully. That would have put an end to their holiday.

To take my mind off the letter from Tom, I sit down with Rosa to play cards. I teach her gin rummy and soon she's beating me hands down.

Kath returns home mid-afternoon with the Swedish family who are clearly shaken by events. Olle the husband decides he must return to the beach today, so that he doesn't have any hang-ups about driving in the future. He takes the children with him, including a delighted Rosa. Astrid, his wife, her skin as smooth as a tan leather belt, chooses to remain at the house.

We sit quietly under the cherry tree. The heat is all around us and plays tricks with my eyes. I get up to make us some coffee and serve the *clafoutis*, which looks nowhere near as good as Kath's. Rosa and I got carried away with our card game and left it in the oven too long. Now I try to salvage it by sprinkling icing sugar over the top to mask the blackened blobs of batter.

Astrid has been telling us about how she and Olle met several years ago at a medical clinic in Stockholm. She's a trained psychiatrist and Olle was one of her patients.

'My heart still jumps sometimes when I look at him,' I hear Astrid say while I'm in the kitchen.

Just as mine does every time I see Tom. How I wish I could say that out loud to someone. Instead I have to hold it in – internalise it – and neither can I share the erratic dreams I've been having lately. Sometimes I've woken up after such a vivid one about Tom and Kath, even Pilot, that for a moment or two I am confused about what is real and what isn't.

As I put the cups on the tray, I hear Astrid remark, loud and clear in her clipped accent: 'So you are saying you don't love your husband anymore?'

I step away from the windows in the kitchen. I don't want my presence to affect Kath's ability to reply honestly.

'I'm not sure I can answer that, Astrid.'

'OK, so when were you happiest?'

I hear Kath's chair scrape on the gravel. 'Oh that's easy. The look on his face when I told him I was pregnant.'

'He must have been delighted.' Astrid sounds relieved.

'You could say that. Shocked at first. The delight came later.'

And what about the look on my face when you wrote and told me you were both head over heels in love?

My desire to drop the tray in the middle of the kitchen floor there and then is so great that I have to use all of my willpower to stop myself. Instead I take a long deep breath and walk serenely to the table. Astrid gets up to help me. She looks as if she wished she had never started this conversation.

'But I wouldn't bother asking Jenny about her love life, Astrid. Jenny's very secretive, and I'm not convinced that she is telling us the whole truth about her boyfriend, are you Jenny?'

A teaspoon clatters off my tray, giving me the opportunity to take another slow breath. The yellowing grass is crying out for some rain.

I smile as I bob back up. 'Oh Kath, my love life is just too dull for you, isn't it? You just want to spice it up –

make Scott and me more interesting. But I'm afraid we just aren't.'

I raise my eyebrows at Astrid, who looks grateful for the opportunity to respond with a laugh. I'd love to ask her what she really thinks of Kath, who has little alternative but to join in. I can see from the arm scratching that she has something to say on this topic and won't let it lie until she does. What more can she possibly know or want to know about Scott and me? Tom won't have said anything.

Truly, there isn't a lot to say. In the early days, Scott and I used to have fun together, take drives along the coast, sit on the beach to watch the sunset. Lately we've had little time together, especially since he's coaching more swimmers. Occasionally we'll share a meal and catch up with each other's lives. He's my best buddy, but no longer my lover.

We all head off to our rooms for a siesta. Kath and Astrid are exhausted after their morning at the *gendarmerie*. I lie on the bed, fidgeting, trying to imagine how different things would have been if Tom hadn't gone to find Kath at the hotel. It's impossible to imagine a story that didn't happen, though. There are so many alternative outcomes in life and who knows what fate – or Kath, rather – would have set up for us instead.

I want to re-read the letter, but not here. I need to be alone at the lake. It's the one place that feels like my own space, a place where I feel safe, among the whispering trees and the chattering birds.

A few families are picnicking in the shade when I arrive on my bike. I wheel it over to the far side and prop myself up against a tree trunk. The bark scratches at my back gently as I start to read. I absorb each and every word, over and over until I am certain of the letter's contents. No mistakes. He meant every word. My hands are shaking so hard that I have to cross my arms to hold them still.

> *'A fervent, a solemn passion is conceived in my heart; it leans to you, draws you to my centre.'*

I recognise the quote that closes his letter from *Jane Eyre*. I'm not sure how I feel by the end – there are so many emotions running through me that I'm starting to feel queasy. Except I know there's one thing I have to do and I have to do it now. I tuck the letter carefully away into my backpack, jump onto my bike and pedal hard along the winding back road.

The tractor is there with Tom at the helm, bobbing through the undulating waves of upturned dirt, signalling to me that I've timed this right. My bike struggles to negotiate the potholes in the field. In frustration, I throw it down and start to walk through the vines, waving at Tom, hoping he'll see me and stop. His head turns and I start to run towards him. My arms scratch on the vines each time my hopeless espadrilles catch on the dirt, but I don't care. There is stillness in the air except for the sound of my feet. He has turned the engine off and is getting out of his cabin, pushing his hair back, eyes squinting at me in the sun.

When I finally reach him, I feel awkward. My chest heaves up and down like a steam train. Sweat is running down my back.

'Jen, is everything OK?' He runs his hand through his hair once more.

'Oh God, Tom. No! Nothing is OK. In fact, this is a

horrible dream and I want to break out of it. But promise me you'll come too!'

'What the hell are you talking about, Jen? You're speaking in riddles.'

'I found this in your copy of *Jane Eyre*.'

I wave the envelope at him. He takes it from me and reads the front of it. 'You wrote it to me in 2006. Remember?'

He takes it out and starts scanning the contents, biting his bottom lip.

'She lied, Tom. Kath lied.'

He looks up at me quizzically.

'I wasn't with Scott then. I wasn't with anyone. Just before the World Championships, in February or March 2007 I think it was, I sent her an email to tell her that I was coming back to find you. She said she didn't receive it, but finding this letter convinces me that she did. She never sent your letter to me, so I never knew that you felt that way. So she did everything she could to stop you and me from being together. Kath never forgave me for taking what she believed was hers and she was determined to have you, at whatever cost.' My voice is trembling. I turn away from Tom and wrap my arms around my waist, to steady myself.

'Jen, come here.'

I don't respond. I'm too scared – scared that this won't play out as I'd hoped it might.

'Jen, look at me.'

I turn round and gaze up into his bright eyes. I see my reflection in them. I see hope. He pushes the letter into his back pocket and pulls me towards him, hugging me tightly. I wrap my arms around his neck and kiss the full softness of that mouth, willing him to respond so that I know that this is for real, but he doesn't.

'No, Jen.' He unbuckles my arms.

'Why can't we? Because you're married? Because you don't feel anything for me? Why, Tom?' Part of me wants to punch him in frustration.

He pulls the letter out of his pocket and waves it between us. 'Jen, this changes nothing. As I said before, I need to work things through – for all of our sakes.'

'But why? Just think, if I hadn't found your letter, I might never have fully recognised Kath's duplicity. But now I see her motivations so clearly.'

'I know. So do I.'

We stand a few inches apart. I can feel the heat from his body.

'Why didn't *you* get my address and post the letter?'

'I asked Kath to post it for me, but as you can see, she didn't. I found it on the day we moved in together. By then it was too late.' He grasps hold of the tractor door and kicks one of the wheels in frustration. 'All this for a stupid one-night stand.'

He looks at me with his haunted expression and I know that he is telling the truth.

'But why didn't you just tell me you wrote the letter?'

He just looks away. 'As I said, we were already expecting Rosa. Things had changed.'

'You didn't have to accept it though, Tom. You could have walked away.'

But, of course, even saying that, I know it isn't Tom's way. He would naturally assume responsibility, just as he did after his father left when Tom was a child. He looks at me gently.

'Rosa is my child too. Of course I couldn't do that. We needed to give her a secure start in life. And now we have to keep things as normal as possible, while I plan what to do next.'

I shake my head, furious at myself. 'I should have contacted you instead of telling Kath my plans to come home. What a trusting idiot I've been.'

'That makes two of us,' he says, and I know he's trying to make light of the situation.

'She needs to understand the pain and the hurt she's caused us.' I try to kick out the dry dirt rolling around inside my espadrilles.

'It won't make a difference, I assure you. And we have to consider Rosa. She's the most important person in all of this.'

'Of course. I understand.' But I know I don't, not really. Intellectually I know that children must come first, but in my heart I feel differently. At every turn there is an obstacle in the way.

I walk away through the furrowed soil to my bike, hoping that he might run after me, scoop me up in his arms and declare his love. Wishful thinking. It's as if we're re-enacting the final scene of eight years ago, when he left me sobbing on that rock in the rain.

An hour later, I'm back at *Les Olivades*, playing Kath's unknowing, unsuspecting best friend. No one would guess that underneath the good humour and playful banter, there's a banshee struggling to break out.

And now that I finally understand the extent of Kath's deceit, I wonder if and how Tom's going to tackle her over it. It started with her manipulation of my father, tapping into his anxieties about my career and encouraging him to emigrate. Her plan went awry when my father didn't arrange for her to come and join us in Perth, so she set out to get Tom for herself instead. I almost scuppered her plan when I told her I was coming back to the UK, but she laid a new trap, binding Tom to her, and kept hold of the letter she promised to post to me. In that way, she remained in control of both our destinies and she had the ringside seat. I wonder if there's a final act to come. Something tells there is and I need to find out what it is before it's too late.

– CHAPTER 21 –

Despite Tom's and my best efforts to keep things calm around the house, tensions soon start to build again. Kath talks about our road trip when Tom's not at home, as if she really believes it's going to happen. When he's here, she's eager to discuss the next phase of work on the house, which includes two more *gîtes* and a swimming pool. However, Tom refuses to discuss it.

'Let's wait until the summer is over, then we can sit down and look at where we are financially. There's too much to focus on at the moment.'

He won't be drawn further on the subject and it's clear by the way she bangs the cupboard doors afterwards that Kath resents him shutting her out.

Small things seem to bother her more and more: a misplaced object, Rosa wearing inappropriate attire, even me forgetting something on the shopping list can put her in an unpredictable mood. The atmosphere in the house is so oppressive that I do all I can to keep Rosa away from it by taking her to the beach or on bike rides into the verdant countryside. We often hang out with Sylvie at the farm, helping her to pick fruit in the orchard. Figs and apples are in abundance at this time of year, and I love biting into the velvety softness of the purple-cloaked figs that Sylvie serves with hunks of bread and goats' cheese to the workers. I like Sylvie. She epitomises a true matriarch to me, a strong woman who speaks her mind, yet is sensitive to others' feelings. She works hard to keep the farm running harmoniously. Sometimes I catch her watching me as though she's trying to work me out, but she never says more than: '*Ça va, Jenny? T'es contente ici?*'

She'll squeeze my arm, willing me to let down my guard and talk openly, and I reassure her lightly that of course I'm happy here. Who wouldn't be happy in such a wonderful place where the sun is usually shining and the fields and vines are bursting with ripe harvests?

Since our rendezvous at the vineyard, Tom and I tiptoe around each other like two wary cats. After his refusal to kiss me, and his reminder about Rosa, I'm resigned to assuming that we may never be close again. Whatever the outcome at the end of my stay in three weeks' time, one thing for certain is that I never want to see Kath again. From my point of view, our friendship is over. She played a very clever game to keep Tom and I apart, and I'll never forgive her for it. When I think of the effort I made to include her in anything I did with Tom – even setting her up on double dates with his friends – when she was just manipulating us for her own ends. As Tom said, it's all about control, and it's taken me all this time to realise that he's right. But I have to continue to pretend the opposite – that she and I are close.

'Why don't you take some time off, Kath? I can manage the guests for a few days,' I suggest to her when she shouts at Rosa for spilling her juice one morning, sending her daughter scuttling upstairs in floods of tears.

'Where would I go?' she snaps. 'Better still, who would I go with?'

That cuts me short. She's right. She doesn't have any close friends here.

'She used to,' says Tom, when I ask him about it that evening, after Kath has taken a mobile call outside to discuss a *gîte* booking. 'Armelle, Sylvie, Sandrine. I've lost count of how many. But, didn't you notice, when you were younger, how she couldn't commit to anyone? She wins them over and then drops them. Everyone except you, Jen. I wonder why that is.'

He leans towards me. We're still not touching, but I can feel the warmth radiating out of him.

'Because she wanted to get closer to you, Tom. She wasn't going to drop me until she got you.'

I lay my arm on the kitchen table, hopeful that he might stroke it. Instead he moves towards the door. 'Be careful, Jen. The way she's acting at the moment, she's not going to hold a meltdown in for much longer. Trust me. We need to be prepared.'

He goes upstairs and shuts himself away with the novel he's determined to finish by the end of September.

'That's the deadline I've given myself,' he said cryptically one breakfast time. Kath didn't ask him what he meant by it, so I chose to ignore it too.

As Tom's study door closes, Kath comes back in to the kitchen with a smile on her face.

'Drink?'

I nod.

She goes to the fridge and takes out half a bottle of white wine. She looks like the cat that got the cream. I'm almost scared to ask her why she's looking so pleased with herself.

'Was that a booking?' I take a glass from her and try not to look anxious.

'Yes, a last-minute enquiry. They sound nice. Hopefully, they'll confirm tomorrow. Cheers!'

***

On the morning of the cheese and wine party, Kath announces that she has to run some errands in Montpellier so might be a bit late getting back in time. Armelle has already offered to help, so I assure Kath that we'll be fine.

As we start to prepare the food, the difference in mood in the house is in sharp contrast to the tensions of the past few weeks. Armelle looks relaxed and pretty in a new mint-green sundress she exchanged in the market today for four jars of honey and some nougat. She's wearing silver sandals with a small heel, giving her legs an enviable boost. I am glad to see that Luc is appreciative of his wife's efforts. As he sidles up behind her and pretends to nibble her ear, she rolls her head back, briefly nestling on his shoulder.

I lay out cold meat and cheese onto plates, accessorising them with fresh figs. The *fromagier* at the market has helped me to put together a wonderful selection of regional cheeses, including one that's threatening to ooze all over the board. I transfer it to a plate of its own, stopping to lick the thick gunk from my fingers.

'Hey, that's for the guests!' murmurs a voice in my ear. Tom has arrived with the wine and gets to work uncorking the bottles of red.

I laugh and, for a brief moment, pretend that he's mine. *If only she wasn't here.* Intuition tells him that he's being spied upon and he stops what he's doing to turn his head and hold my gaze. If only I could read what he's thinking. If only he could hear my heartbeat.

The moment is interrupted by the arrival of Rosa who skips across the terrace to join us inside.

'Rosa, there you are. Wow, don't you look beautiful in that dress!'

She twirls round and round for me until she stumbles over with laughter and giddiness. I hug her tight, feeling a wave of strong emotion for this small ball of innocence. I don't want to play any part in breaking this little girl's heart, but I know that it will be impossible to keep it entirely intact, if Tom decides to leave Kath. I shake those troubling thoughts from my head. Tonight I want to let my hair down and be merry. With Kath out of the way for now, I can fully relax without that constant niggling feeling that I am being observed. Hopefully she'll return in the same good mood that she left in and won't sulk in front of the guests.

I wander outside to find Luc preparing the oysters on a trestle table. Armelle is unwrapping some delicious-looking onion tarts she's made. Bread is in ample supply and will help to soak up the alcohol, which I know the holidaymakers will want to enjoy to the full. We decide to serve drinks outside on the terrace. The *mistral*, which was blowing earlier in the day, has died away, leaving behind a few upturned chairs and a pile of leaves, but it takes no time to make it right.

The guests begin to arrive and throw themselves onto the feast laid out before their eyes. Luc has put on some of his Spanish guitar music and soon the atmosphere is buzzing. Tom sets up a game of *boules* for the children.

Rosa joins in and before long she is ordering them all about, laying down the rules to ensure fair play.

'She is so cute, isn't she? Everyone wants one like her.' Armelle laughs.

'And I'm sure you will.'

'Oh yes, I hope so. Now that things with Luc are better.' Armelle sips on her glass of wine and looks over to him. He's chatting to a couple of guests. 'I love him so much, it hurts,' she whispers, her lip trembling slightly.

I put my arm around her shoulder and give her a brief hug. The moment is quickly taken over by the arrival of more guests and there's no let up for the next two hours as we serve wine, nibbles and successfully sell most of our cases.

'Let's hope they don't regret buying all that wine when they're nursing their hangovers tomorrow,' Tom laughs.

By midnight, we've ramped up the music and Luc has everyone dancing. I've danced with most of the male guests, including Eddie who's popped in for a drink. I haven't seen him for a couple of weeks and he explains that he's been to Sweden visiting the family of his late girlfriend.

'I hope it wasn't too painful for you, Eddie.' I hand him a large glass of red wine. He chinks my glass and smiles.

'Actually, no, it was therapeutic to talk about Ute and to share our different memories of her. She was very close to her family.'

Luc comes over to join us and refill his glass. I catch Tom's eye and he pulls me into the dancing circle. As Tom leads me confidently from one move to another, I think we make quite a good couple. I've managed to get the hang of the rhythm and my feet are working properly. Several people stand on the edge of the terrace clapping as our moves get more and more frenetic. He teases me by spinning me round as if I'm a cotton reel and, just at that point when I think we're out of control, he grabs my arm and reins me back in, pulling me against his torso. Twists and turns, back and forth, I am dizzy with laughter as I go round and round. Suddenly Tom stops.

'Surprise!' Kath steps out from somewhere to the left of me. I didn't see her come back.

'How ya doin', Jenny?' says a familiar voice.

I look up into piercing blue eyes.

Kath moves into the middle of the terrace and turns down the music. That sickly smile is plastered all over her face. What I would give to wipe it off at this moment.

'Hi everyone! I'd like to introduce you to Scott.' She pauses momentarily for maximum effect. 'Jenny's husband.'

– CHAPTER 22 –

I sense curiosity from some of the people who know me here. I daren't look at Tom, so instead turn to Kath, who comes over to hug me. That smile doesn't extend to her eyes.

'Scott wanted to surprise you. Isn't that sweet of him? You didn't tell me he was this gorgeous.'

Her laughter is a little too loud.

The next half an hour is a complete blur – people coming, people going, people eating and drinking. The music is put back on for the stragglers to have one final dance. In the meantime, Armelle and Luc embrace me goodnight with big smiles on their faces. Of course, they're bound to think that I'm happy about Kath's surprise, although Armelle must be a little bit confused that I haven't bothered telling her I'm married. Meanwhile, Kath has left to take Rosa to bed. And Tom – *oh lord, what have you done* – has disappeared before I could explain anything.

He won't trust me now if I've lied about Scott. And how did Kath find out about it? I can't believe that Scott told her. He knows my reasons for marrying him had little to do with romantic love. Not on my side, anyway. Hence, when I look at this out-of-place man standing awkwardly on Kath and Tom's terrace, I'm confused as to why he's even here. I told him not to come. Has my father sent him to try and persuade me to compete?

'So, Jenny, do I get a hug?'

It's actually nice to see Scott, to know that he's well. Although now that his messenger has arrived, my father feels more omniscient than ever.

'Why didn't you tell me you were coming, Scott?'

We hug a little stiffly and I pull back at the sound of footsteps approaching.

'Scott just rang the house one day and we thought it would be nice to surprise you. It's so good to meet your husband at last!' Kath has returned, her face flushed and shiny from the heat. She turns towards Scott. 'Jenny has told us absolutely nothing about you, but I'm sure that's because she's been missing you. Haven't you?'

That butter-wouldn't-melt expression. A more innocent person, the Jenny of old, would have mistaken her words as genuine and heartfelt. But this is the new Jenny, the Jenny who can clearly see the cracks, the deception and the lies that her best friend weaved throughout their entire youth and who even now refuses to tell the truth.

'Of course, I've missed you loads, Scott. That voice shouting in my ear every morning to get in the water, to swim faster, harder, further. Who wouldn't have missed that?'

Scott winks back at me. We've always been good at banter.

'I bet you're hungry though, aren't you? All that travelling.'

'No, I'm fine, Jenny, I ate already. Wouldn't mind a beer though.'

We take a seat at a table, the three of us, chatting away about Scott's flight, the weather in Perth. Scott explains that he has to be in London tomorrow for a two-week coaching programme, and he suggests coming back here for a break when he's finished. Tom doesn't reappear. I don't want to risk revealing my feelings to Kath. Completely oblivious to the disquiet of the past few days, Scott asks the question for me.

'So where's that husband of yours, Kath?'

'He said he was going over to Bill's for a few beers — his Kiwi friend,' she says.

I nod vacantly, remembering hearing about the surf instructor who looks after rental properties for absent owners.

'That's what living in a house full of women does to you.' I take Scott's hand to keep up appearances while feigning a yawn. 'It's good to see you. Shall we turn in? I'm pooped.'

***

I lie awake listening out for the sounds of the truck pulling into the driveway, but there is nothing. Nothing except a gentle rumble, like distant thunder. Scott's fast asleep. His bottom lip hangs open and vibrates when he breathes out. We haven't shared a bed in years. He had the good grace to laugh when I told him we had to keep up the pretence for Kath's sake.

'She's such a romantic,' I lied, 'that I didn't want to spoil things for her.'

We talked for hours about what I've been missing in Australia — my father who's still working as an electrician and general handyman at the swimming club, and Amanda Berryman, the latest darling of the swimming team.

'And you thought you were driven. Well, you should see this girl.'

Morning doesn't come quickly enough. As soon as I sense that the sun is rising, I jump out of bed to check outside. There's still no sign of Tom's truck. Perhaps he was too drunk to drive home from Bill's and he got a taxi home.

I find my bag in the kitchen and try his number but it goes straight to voicemail. The kitchen door opens and a sleepy Rosa stands yawning and stretching in her vest and knickers. She has creases in her cheeks where she's been lying on her pillow.

'Morning sweetie, would you like some apple juice?'

Her hair tickles my nose when I reach down to kiss her.

'Where's your husband, Jenny? Mummy says that you're married.'

'That's right, honey, I am. Scott's in bed asleep. He had a long journey to get here.'

'And I wonder what's happened to that husband of mine?'

Kath appears in the doorway, her hair standing on end as though she's spent hours applying gel to it. She shuffles in, wearing Tom's huge espadrilles, which struggle to stay on her tiny feet.

'Must have had a wild night with Bill,' I suggest, turning away to fill up the kettle. 'What do we need to do today, Kath? We don't have any guests arriving this weekend, do we?'

'No, we're fine. Why don't you shoot off somewhere with Scott to catch up. We can get by.'

'But what about Tom? I can't go anywhere until... I mean, do you need me to hang around and help?'

'Tom'll be home soon, don't worry. He's done this before, often when he's struggling with his addictions. Anyway, he's not yours to worry about, remember?'

She crosses her arms and looks me in the eye.

Addictions? I can't believe she used that word. Perhaps she's storing up artillery for when she and Tom might have to fight over Rosa in the divorce courts, and has already started to spread wild lies around the community to anyone who will listen. *How could you have deceived me?* I want to shout at her. But I know it won't do me any good. She'll just deny everything. So instead, we face each other across the silent room, bodies straight and tense, more words unsaid.

A familiar twang breaks the spell.

'G'day everyone. Hey, and who's this? Hello buddy, how ya doing?'

Scott steps into the kitchen, already showered and dressed. He bends down to shake hands with a timid Rosa. She'll soon come round, once he's bounced her round the garden on his shoulders. I remember to breathe and head out of the room to take a shower.

Jets of water pummel away at me as I go over the previous evening in my head. I can't believe that Kath would surprise me with a visit from Scott unless she was feeling threatened in some way. After all, I told him not to come. Has she worked out how I feel about Tom? Is it that obvious? What am I even still doing here? Tom's made it clear he's not a free man. I hear laughter downstairs and wish I could run away from it. I need to find Tom and tell him the whole story, so that he understands that Scott isn't a threat. But I've got no idea where to look without drawing attention to myself. He probably doesn't want to see me anyway. He probably thinks I'm as duplicitous as Kath.

When I get downstairs for breakfast, it seems that Kath has already told Scott about her plan for a road trip around Australia.

'Perhaps Rosa and I could come and stay with you in Perth before we set off.'

'Sure. You're welcome any time. There's plenty of room for all of you.'

They look up when I enter the room.

'Don't get carried away making plans, Kath. I'm not sure what I'm doing at the moment,' I remind her.

She closes her mouth, which was about to say something more on the subject, her smile down-turning into a glum look.

Picking up on the change in mood, Scott jumps back in. 'Jenny, shall we pop out and do a few sights before I have to leave for London?'

'Sure.'

Kath starts to clear the breakfast things. 'I need to go to the farm and sort out a few bits and pieces. Let us know when you're coming back, Scott, and we can talk some more about our "maybe" plans, can't we, Jenny?'

I nod vacantly, now lost in my own thoughts. Why doesn't he send me a message? Something. Anything.

An hour later, Scott and I are on the train to Montpellier. He spends most of the journey asleep, as he tries to catch up on his jetlag. I noticed Rosa observing us both curiously earlier, no doubt wondering how I could have conjured up a husband out of nowhere. When Scott first suggested we marry so I could settle in Australia permanently, I rejected his proposal on the spot, explaining that I was a romantic and could only marry my true love. Scott seemed to take it on as a challenge. But, several months later, when I heard about Kath and Tom, I decided to take him up on his offer. I could see the benefits of remaining in Australia, especially as I no longer had any desire to go anywhere else – least of all back to the UK to be subjected to the picture of love and happiness that, I imagined, was etched on Tom and Kath's faces. So I broke the one promise I made to myself and, the day I married Scott, I cried during the ceremony, fooling my father and Aunt Muriel that they were tears of happiness. Scott and I shared a bed for a couple of years, but there was no real spark between us, so we became more like brother and sister. As well as being my coach, he was my only real friend out there. We laughed, we yelled and we drove each other to distraction with our mutual determination to go for gold, whatever it took.

Now I'm too ashamed to admit that I'd got married for the wrong reasons – and most of all too ashamed to tell Tom.

As the scenery zips by, I make a decision, to accept the place on the Masters programme in London – if it isn't too late. It'll give me something to focus on when I move on with the next phase of my life, whatever that is. I can't imagine life away from here – away from him – and now all I want to do is curl up into a corner and cry my eyes out, just like those times when Scott pushed me too hard in training and made me feel weak and rubbish.

I look down at his head, which is on my shoulder, and pat it gently. We might not be a real couple anymore, but his whistle-stop trip out here confirms that he still cares about my welfare.

I stare out at the rambling countryside, fiddling with my rings, forcing myself to count the lumpy hillocks that rise up from the ground like an infestation of mumps. I want to phone Tom again, to hear his voice, to beg his forgiveness, but something holds me back. Fear? Part of me is scared that he'll treat me with the disdain I deserve.

The gentle rattling of the train is soothing and I drift off into my snow globe of happier memories, shaking each one awake until finally I too fall asleep.

***

We put Scott's bag into left luggage at the station and stroll through the busy streets of Montpellier. Having become accustomed to living in the remote countryside these last few months, I feel completely overwhelmed by the traffic noise and smells of the city. Scott is happy to sit in a café and chat, so we select one with a large covered terrace in a quiet back street, off the main square. Our waiter is a stocky man with grey hair thinning over a pink scalp. As he bends over the table to open our bottle of white wine, I'm reminded of a piece of streaky bacon and nearly giggle inappropriately. Scott looks at me whimsically, reading my mind, then mimes taking a bite out of his head, the waiter none the wiser.

I'd forgotten what a fun person he could be outside of training. Once, we'd taken a holiday to the Great Barrier Reef. We hired a car and drove up the coast to Cape

Tribulation. Scott had me in stitches all the way up there. Now, as I look at him, I realise how much I've missed his banter – the way he would just talk while I sat shivering with a towel wrapped round me, not really listening, just dreaming about the cup of hot chocolate I was going to make as soon as he'd finished.

'So, what's the story with you, Tom and Kath, Jenny? I mean, I know that you and Kath were best friends and Tom was once your boyfriend. But how did it end up like this? And what are you really doing here? You and he looked a bit cosy on the dance-floor when I arrived last night. Maybe other people didn't notice, but I know you.'

I glance at Scott's inquisitive expression. He's been holding this back for a while. I sip my wine, almost stumped for words.

'You remember I told you about the day that someone appeared at my front door with the message in the bottle I'd written? Well, that was Tom. I was only fifteen – nearly sixteen. He'd knocked at Kath's door first as her name and address was also on the message. She wasn't in, so he came to mine and a few months later we started dating. He was from my town but we'd never met. I'm unsure whether Kath's ever forgiven me, Tom or even herself for not being in that day. She probably thought that if she had, the love story would have been about her and Tom, rather than me, you see. Anyway, that's where it all started.'

'But what about now?'

'Now I don't know. It's clear that they aren't happy and perhaps never have been. But who knows where they're heading.'

Scott looks thoughtful. 'I have to say I'm surprised

Kath's even with him, given his past. I'd have thought she'd have steered well clear.'

Now it's my turn to lean forward. 'What do you mean by that?'

Scott refills my glass. I try to hold it steady, but I can sense that he's going to reveal something that I'm not going to like.

'You asked me to talk to your dad about his reasons for moving to Australia. Well, I did. Not easy I can tell you. Like trying to squeeze blood out of a stone.'

'What did he say?'

'He said that Kath had told him that Tom was two-timing you. You know, seeing other girls behind your back.'

I put my glass down and stare at him with my mouth open. 'What? Are you serious?'

'Yeah, he had quite a few on the go, according to Kath. She told your dad not to say anything to you, but thought it might be wise to think of a plan to get you away from Tom. So, when Bob, mentioned the Australian training programme for British swimmers, it didn't take long for him to make a decision.'

'There's no way Tom was seeing anyone else. No way. And I can promise you that if he was, Kath would have been the first person to blab it to me. She told my father not to say anything because it was a blatant lie.' I reach for the wine bottle and pour myself a fresh glass.

Scott whistles in wonder. 'D'ya reckon? Actually, your dad did say that he wasn't convinced. Not after Kath claimed that he'd promised to take her to Australia. He said he hadn't said anything of the sort. He'd said he'd look into it once you were out there, but he never got round to it.'

'So, either she made that up or misconstrued his words. Thanks for doing that for me. I've got my eyes wide open now as far as Kath is concerned.' I take his hand between both of mine. A 'club sandwich' we used to call it. 'So why have you really come to France, Scott?'

'To see my wife, of course. You don't seem to have handed out that piece of information to anyone, do you? I've never seen so many shocked faces in one place.'

'Scott, you know that you twisted my arm into marrying you.'

His face falls, and I regret my words already.

'I guess at the time I hoped that you might grow into loving me. But, it didn't take long to see that was never going to happen.' He picks at the label on the wine bottle. His clean fingernails are a marked contrast to Tom's dirt-filled ones. A part of me wishes that I could have fallen in love with Scott. We were good together in so many ways.

'So, why are you here, really?'

'To check you're OK, first and foremost.' He pauses for breath. 'And to ask you for a divorce.'

− CHAPTER 23 −

I have to admit that when Scott told me that he and Amanda Berryman had fallen in love, there was a pang of jealousy. Just a small one. A purely selfish thought on my part, knowing that I was no longer the focus of his attention. He spoke dreamily of Amanda, outlining how he and she had got close to one another after I left. How it made him realise that the two of us were just biding time.

Now as we stroll back to the station to collect his bag, I sense that we are both completely at ease with each other. If only I'd felt the spark.

'Jenny, you must go and see your dad. He's missing you.'

'I'm not sure I believe that. More like he's missing watching me win.'

'After he talked to me about Kath, he actually shed a tear for you − a small one, OK − but it was definitely a tear.'

'What was that all about? Dad crying? Really?'

I stop in my tracks, spin round to Scott and almost collide with a scooter on the road we're crossing. He quickly pulls me back to the pavement. The rider shakes his head at me grimly and takes off again.

'Jenny!' Scott cautions me. 'Are you all right?'

'Yes, fine. What did my father say?'

'I think he's realised that he's been too hard on you over the years. Dare I say that he actually used the word "regret"?'

'No, really?'

'He said that he hopes you'll find what you're looking for out here.' Scott looks into my eyes. 'Something tells me he's talking about you and Tom. Am I right?'

I can't hold his gaze. 'I don't know, Scott. There's definitely something still there – for me anyway. Let's just says it's complicated.'

Scott laughs. 'OK, I think I know you well enough to know when you don't want to talk anymore. Just be careful, won't you? You mean a lot to me, Jenny.' He pauses. 'As a friend, of course.'

We take a seat on a nearby bench, both of us glowing in the midday heat. This moment feels so special to me. I've missed Scott, more than I thought I had. He's such a gem.

'I will go and see my father, I promise. You will stay in touch with me, won't you, Scott?'

He nods, takes my hand and strokes the palm gently. Tears well in his eyes and he pulls me close.

On the way back to *Les Olivades*, I feel calmer. Scott's words may have shaken me up but at least I can now see the full extent of Kath's treachery, which has had the desired effect and made me feel stronger. I'm still going to leave France, as planned, after the *vendange*. Tom and Kath can separate amicably, if that's possible. Then I will just have to wait.

***

The house feels ominously quiet when I arrive back late afternoon. The bright sky has disappeared and clouds hang heavy like a pile of dirty laundry, scrunched up and ready to be washed away by the impending rain – a sign that autumn is drawing close. I almost expect to see Pilot jumping out of his kitchen basket to greet me, but then I remember.

A forlorn cup has been left on the table outside, a puddle of coffee left in the bottom. I touch the porcelain. It's slightly warm, telling me that its owner is about. A sound of breaking glass comes from somewhere behind me, followed by swearing and a door banging. I sit at the table and wait. Kath appears with the mop and bucket, looking flushed and harassed.

'Ah, there you are. I was wondering when you'd turn up.'

'Did something just break? Are you OK?'

Kath waves away the question. 'It's nothing. So, how were things with Scott? Did you kiss and make up?'

'Yes. Then he flew to London – to be with his new girlfriend.'

There's a crash as the bucket hits the ground.

'What?' She sits down next to me and reaches out, but I refuse to play along. Her hand feels uncomfortable on my knee. 'But I thought... Jenny, what's going on?'

'We fell out of love, that's what.' I move away from her.

She watches me in silence, scratching her arm, brooding. I decide not to say anything about the lies she told my father. There's something in her eyes that warns me off.

'Where's Tom and Rosa?'

238

I swing my head round to listen for a playtime squeal upstairs or in the garden, or the sound of Tom's electric drill. But the afternoon offers up nothing except a brisk wind whistling through the tree behind us, whose branches seem to reach out to grasp any sign of life.

'Tom and Rosa have flown to Bristol. His mum has gone there with her partner Stanley for a conference. Tom only found out she was in the UK this morning, so he quickly packed some things and left with Rosa. They might all come back here afterwards, but I'm not sure. Tom doesn't tell me anything.'

She looks dejected. The web spinning has begun. *No.* I close my eyes and search for Tom's face in my muddled head. His mouth forms first. It turns up gently. I wish he'd left me a message. Anything. Either to hold on and wait for him or to pack my bags and go. Silence is worse.

A gentle pitter-patter of rain starts to fall onto the table, sending us into the house to close some of the shutters. Then Kath remembers the washing still drying outside, so we hurry back to bring it in, flinging pegs to the ground and wrenching armfuls of rain-smudged linen off the line, as the rain gets harder and the rumble of distant thunder threatens. I run away into the house, to the sanctuary of my bedroom, leaving her to bring the basket in.

I cook supper for us that evening, a simple pasta dish served with garlic bread. Even after a few glasses of wine, there's an invisible barrier between us now – and that will never go away. I wonder if Kath can feel it too. It's that moment when you're talking to someone and rather than just putting your mouth into autopilot and letting it run away with itself, now your head is in control and previews your words one by one. The delay is too subtle for most listeners to notice, but Kath and I are so tuned into one another that I almost expect her to reach out with her fist and try to smash the barrier. It doesn't stop us from talking well into the night. Mainly gentle banter and memories of people we went to school with. Kath tells me about the school reunion she went to over a year ago and how dire it was.

'Everybody asked after you, of course, but then they would. You were the only one who went on to do anything interesting.'

I sit back and watch her suck a tube of spaghetti into her mouth.

'Look what you've achieved, Kath. You've moved abroad, speak fluent French, have your own business up and running. This is much more than my short-lived career.'

Her response is a sad smile. 'Not according to my mum. I'm her big embarrassment.'

The silence hangs heavy between us while I think about Kath's family. I imagine her parents live alone now. Her brothers must have settled down with families of their own. A tiny spark leaps out of nowhere in my head and I refill Kath's empty glass. I need her to talk.

'Kath, did something happen between you and your mum when you went back for the school reunion? Did you go and see her?'

For a moment she looks so vulnerable as her eyes move to her shorts and she picks at a bit of thread hanging from the seam.

'Did you go and try to make things right with her, Kath?' I press her. 'What happened?'

I move my head closer, encouraging her to look up at me. Tom said that Kath changed about a year ago and started to suffer with depression.

Finally she speaks. 'Yes, I went to see her. I wanted to give her a photo of Rosa. Show her what she was missing.'

Kath stops to take a breath. Her mouth opens in silent laughter. She stands up and walks towards the window, peers out into the dusk as if looking for someone.

'And do you know what my bitch of a mother did?' She spins round on her heels and marches back to the table. Now there's real anger in her eyes. 'She gave the photo back and told me that she hoped Rosa wasn't like me. She said she had never loved me because I was a mistake. An accident. Had she not had me, she'd never have got married and ended up washing people's hair for a living in a kitchen sink.'

A small patch of red has appeared on her neck as she spits out her words. I sit there staring at her, trying to take this revelation in. So this is why Kath has changed – because of her mum. Poor Kath. And yet, suddenly I'm afraid. What should I do? How should I respond? Kath seems so full of fury. I decide to sit silently and wait.

After a moment or two, she seems to register that it's me she's talking to – she's not back at home, face to face with her mum. Then her legs give way and she drops back onto the chair.

I lean forward. 'I'm so sorry, Kath. Really I am.' My hand finds hers and covers it for a moment, realising how hard that was for her to tell me this. 'You didn't tell Tom?'

Kath shakes her head over and over, then stops. 'So are you going to take him with you when you leave, Jenny?' she says. It's almost a whisper.

I collect up the bowls and move towards the dishwasher. 'Bloody hell, Kath.'

'I was just wondering if you still wanted Tom. That's all.' Her voice is almost plaintive.

And there it is. The opportunity for me to confess that I'm still in love with my ex – her husband. But I can't do it. I can't admit that I'm only this far away from betraying Kath. 'I don't know what you're talking about. I've only just parted ways with Scott. You and Tom need to decide your own future together, and that decision doesn't need to involve me.'

She sits rubbing her finger around the edge of her glass, making it sing. Pondering. She raises her eyes and I see tears. 'I don't want you to go, Jenny. I need you here. There's no way I can face going back to how things were before you came.'

'You looked so happy when you came to pick me up. So settled.'

'You know me. Just putting a brave face on things.'

At that point she breaks down and starts sobbing. I wasn't expecting that. For a moment, we're back on that street corner in the pouring rain on the day we first met, and I start to thaw when I remember that look of desolation on her young face, and how she shrugged it off and reached out to my loneliness instead. Now it's my turn to do the same.

I bend down and pat her knee. 'Come on, Kath. Just think about your wonderful life here. You're healthy, you've got a beautiful daughter and you know so many people.'

'They all hate me. They only invite us anywhere because they like Tom.' She sniffs hard, her head bowing towards my shoulder.

'That's not true. Armelle and Sandrine always ask after you. Anyway, you can pop over and see me if I take up that place in London.' It feels as though I'm talking to Rosa.

Her expression changes, hardens in fact. She sniffs and wipes at her dry eyes. 'Don't go back there. Let's go somewhere else. Like I said, Australia. Before they get back. Leave a note to say we've gone on our road trip.'

Her thoughts are running away with her. She puts a hand on each of my shoulders, like an anchor attached to a chain that wants to drag me down with it, link by link. It's the same touch I felt when she told me about Mrs Holt's death, and I realise she's playing with my emotions again. Just like a cat, she's seeking allegiance. I know she is serious. All it would take is a nod of my head and she'd be rubbing her hands with glee, plotting our elopement. She is more unbalanced than I realised.

Gently I take her hands away. 'Probably not a good idea, Kath. I've got to go and see my father first and tell him I'm retiring from competitive swimming. And I think you should wait to go on a road trip at least until Tom's book is published and the money's rolling in. Come on, the rain's stopped. Let's sit outside and enjoy a nightcap, shall we?'

***

I wake up the following morning to find myself in somebody's living room. My head feels heavy and struggles to work out what I'm doing sleeping on the sofa. That's right. I'm in one of the *gîtes*. Kath had suggested that I move into it for some privacy, since we only needed to keep one free for September's bookings. But why am I on the sofa? My T-shirt feels clammy. There's a mug on the floor beside me. Camomile tea. Then I remember.

A nightmare had shaken me in the early hours, so I'd left my bed. I was swimming in the lake. At first, I was serene and calm, enjoying the gentle stroking of floating reeds as I swam through them. Then I caught sight of something moving, pale in colour, rounded, pulsating rhythmically with the water. As I approached it, I thought it was a fish trapped in a discarded net, so I reached out to free it. But it wasn't a net, it was hair attached to a head. Tom's head. I kicked to get away and screamed out just as I broke the surface of the dream.

I made myself some tea, wrapped myself in a blanket and held the steaming cup to my lips, inhaling the swirling fumes. There were a few claps of thunder outside, but I didn't see any lightning bolts through the shutters, so the storm must have been several miles away.

'Tom, I need you,' I muttered to myself out loud, wishing he was here.

Kath's thoughts are so dark. I don't know what to think. Tom says she's more even-tempered when I'm around, but now I'm not so sure. She seems to be getting more and more unpredictable. I push open the shutters and look over to the house. Kath is standing in the open doorway looking directly at my *gîte*. She doesn't move. Can she see me or is she lost in her thoughts? I can't tell as I wave at her. Her head jolts in recognition, she grins and waves back, then she steps away into the house.

We share an easy morning of cleaning and light gardening. The rose bushes glisten with pearly moisture from the nighttime rain and the silver birch has relinquished some of its branches over the lawn after what was obviously a blustery night. Kath leaves me to run some errands and I take the opportunity to text Armelle and arrange to meet her in Agde for lunch.

The small seaside town is quiet and fills me with a momentary sadness. Summer has started to bid her farewells and will soon leave behind a host of postcard memories of hot days spent at the lake and the beach. In contrast, Armelle is brimming with happiness. It's bursting out of her, from the pink colour in her cheeks to her enhanced cleavage in her low-cut sundress. I embrace her warmly, take in her glowing loveliness, and we sit outside.

I brush away some wind-blown leaves from our table and try to explain why I never told her the truth about Scott. She doesn't judge me, simply sits and listens, and I know she's a true friend. Then I innocently ask her if she has any news. And of course she does. She's ten weeks pregnant. It's early days, but she can't disguise her delight and anxiety all at the same time. I take her hand and promise I won't tell anyone.

'I am so happy for you and Luc.'

'And I've just been promoted, so things are truly looking up for us,' she tells me.

I want to ask her if she and Luc have any news of Tom, but I'm tongue-tied and don't know how to broach the subject.

She reads my mind and studies me carefully. 'Jenny, I know there are things that perhaps you can't tell me. But the other evening, there was something between you and Tom, wasn't there? I could see it in both your eyes when you were dancing. Before Scott arrived.'

Was the feeling between us that obvious? I want to ask, but I don't. My face begins to screw up and I work hard to control my emotions. Armelle reaches over to me and strokes my arm.

'I am here, Jenny. Remember, you have a friend. Whenever you need me.'

I try to recompose myself. 'Thanks, Armelle. And sorry for...' I don't know what to say.

She brushes away my apology. 'You are going to stay for the *vendange*, aren't you, Jenny? It's always a lot of fun.'

'Fun. That would be nice.'

I gaze wistfully out to sea at a sailing boat which has just raised its anchor and is now keeling up and down in the choppy waves, its white sails billowing, filled with high spirits for its next adventure, without a care in the world.

– CHAPTER 24 –

He comes to me at the lake. I am swimming fast and strong, pounding my arms through the water to rid my body of the waves of emotion that haven't stopped pouring out of me since he left. As I turn my head and gasp for air, I think I see him leaning against the cherry tree, despite my best efforts to blot him out. As I swim I imagine the muscular hardness of his chest, those soft locks of hair which nestle in the nape of his neck, damp at the ends where they've absorbed the perspiration from his glowing body. He's a much more physical person now than when I first knew him. Back then he could lounge for hours, reading or writing in his notebook, sometimes just stretched out on his back in the grass looking to the sky for inspiration. But now he is hungry for new experiences, a man who can no longer sit still for long. He needs to smell the earth, cup it in his hands and feel it flowing through his fingers.

At the end of the lake I stop to double-check. The cherry tree stands alone, its branches almost made bare by the autumn winds that have begun to stir and shake its foliage to the ground. My rhythm is lost and I no longer have any desire to carry on swimming. Instead, a longing for Tom rushes through me. It's bone-deep, like a powerful wave crashing onto the rocks. It's his calm reassurance that I need most. He's a bough that doesn't break despite the weight of Kath pushing down on him.

Sapped of all emotional energy, I lie on my back and let my limbs buoy me through the water. The wind has picked up and sends puffs of cloud streaming across the pale-blue sky like a herd of wildebeest. I pull myself up the crumbling bank and reach for the towel in my bicycle basket. A piece of white notepaper flutters to the ground. I pick it up and read it.

'Jen – meet me at Bill's place. It's a 10 minute cycle from here.'

So he was here after all.

There's an address and a sketch of how to find the house. It's on the other side of the village, near the old well. I know the one.

I'm there in five minutes. My dress is clinging to my wet swimsuit, but I don't care. I just want to see him. I ring the brass bell at the imposing gate. I can't imagine that a surf instructor owns this place. It's far too plush, from the outside at least. Tom opens the gate and stands back to let me wheel my bike in. He looks tired, or is he just wary of me? I'm not sure. Closing the gate he takes the bike from me, propping it up against the tall stone wall that surrounds the property. This house must sleep at least ten people.

'Come.' He beckons me to follow him around the side of the house into a back garden which boasts incredible views across the valley and an enormous infinity pool.

'This place is amazing.'

He nods. 'Bill's looking after the house for the owners until the New Year.'

I turn and stand awkwardly to face him. 'Tom, I'm so sorry for not being honest with you. About Scott, I mean.'

He stiffens slightly. 'I take it he's gone.'

'Yes, Scott's gone to hang out with his fiancée.'

A flicker of surprise appears on Tom's face.

'It's a long story. We were never properly in love. Not in the way we... I was with you. It was a stupid–'

'She told me you'd gone too.'

'Who, Kath?'

He nods. 'Rosa and I got back from the airport an hour or so ago. I went upstairs to your room. It was empty.'

'But I've moved into one of the *gîtes*. It was Kath's idea, to give me some privacy. Or maybe it was for her.'

Tom's brows furrow slightly. 'She said she thought that you'd gone back to Australia with Scott, but I didn't believe her, It just didn't feel right that you'd go without saying goodbye. Anyway, I told her I needed to drop Bill's keys back to him, just so I could see if you were at the lake.' There's a tremor of emotion in his voice.

'That seems crazy. Why would she–'

Before I can say any more, his mouth smothers mine and he pulls me towards him. His embrace is suffocating, but I almost crave for him to squeeze my breath out of me if that's what it takes to hold onto this moment.

He pulls back. 'Oh, Jen, I've waited so long for this.' His thumbs smooth down each of my eyelids and move to stroke my cheekbones. 'I think she was testing me to see if I was jealous, and I didn't react, so you don't need to worry. But listen, I'm going to ask Bill if I can stay here while I try to sort out legal matters.'

We cling to each other for a moment, and I can sense that his mind is working overtime.

'We're going to have to take things one step at a time,' he says. His face is solemn. 'Starting with this dress.'

He tugs the garment over my head, then peels back the wet swimsuit from my skin and pushes his hands deep inside to caress my breasts. His hands move down to my buttocks, kneading them softly, stroking the tops of my thighs. I weld with him, dig my nails into his back and run trails along his smooth skin. In that moment, we are transported back to us and what 'us' once meant, and for the first time since I've been here, I truly believe that we can be us again.

He scoops me up and carries me into one of the many bedrooms and drops me onto the bed. Unable to hold out any longer, my hands move down to unbuckle his shorts and reach for him. He responds with a deep groan and gently bites my bottom lip. Together, we tumble onto the cool, crisp linen. But first, he raises his head, and his eyes search mine questioningly.

'Yes,' is the only word I manage to utter before we lose ourselves in one another.

***

She's in the kitchen when I get back. Waiting for me. Tom has gone to the farm to help out with the grape harvest for a few hours and to avoid rousing any suspicion on Kath's part.

She walks towards me, but fortunately I'm saved by an excited Rosa who rushes up to me screaming with delight.

'Jenny, you're here. Mummy said you'd left us.'

'No. I wouldn't leave you without saying goodbye first, would I?' I pick her up and give her a deep embrace, before spinning her round.

'It was only a joke, Rosa.' Kath steps outside, towel-drying her hair. 'Have you seen Tom? Did he come and look for you?'

I'm torn between wanting to interrogate my childhood best friend and needing to keep on good terms with her, at least until the truth about Tom and I comes out. So all I say is: 'No, why?'

I put Rosa down and join Kath on the terrace.

'He said he had to go to Bill's, but he's been gone ages.'

'Did his mum come back with them?' I ask innocently.

'No, but she's coming here in a few months, apparently. Who knows if I'll still be here.'

I choose to ignore this opening gambit and go to play with Rosa, who's full of beans and wants to show me her new skipping rope. It's a good distraction from thinking about Tom and our passionate love-making of earlier in that enormous bed.

I had so many questions to ask him – about his trip, the future, our future – but I didn't want to spoil the moment. My nerves have been pounded from all directions over the last few weeks, so that I have to keep pinching myself to check that this new happiness is for real.

When Tom drives through the gateway at lunchtime, my whole body starts to tremble, perhaps nervous that Kath will pick up on any clues of our illicit meeting of earlier. Rosa runs to greet her daddy and I stand up to give him a welcoming peck on the cheek. Kath remains seated at the table. I sit back down and squeeze my hands together on my lap.

'Just as I was starting to hope – sorry think – that you'd moved out and weren't coming back, dear Thomas.' Kath winks at me and I look away.

Tom sits down and takes a piece of bread out of the basket. 'Well, there was a temptation to get back on a plane and fly out to Canada, Kath, but I know someone who wouldn't have been too happy about that, even if it isn't you, dear wife.' He bounces a happy Rosa up and down on his knee and blows raspberries into her neck. 'Mum says hello to you, Jenny, by the way.'

'How is she?'

'She's great. They were going to come back with us, but Stanley had an urgent bit of business to attend to back home. They're hoping to come at Christmas.'

'I can't wait,' says Kath with a grimace.

Rosa twists round in Tom's lap and starts planting butterfly kisses all over his face. He tickles her playfully and jumps up to swing her round. She's like a baby monkey, all arms and legs. Only Kath has the ability to remain straight-mouthed and unsmiling at their horseplay.

I load the tray with the lunch remains and take it inside, wishing for a moment that Tom and Rosa were my family and not Kath's, dreaming that this is my future and not hers. But I'm the outsider here, aren't I? I'm the fly on the wall observing a family going about its day to day, a family in which I play no part. *Stop it, Jenny.* I'm all over the place. I need to do something, to be busy and keep those dark thoughts at bay. I head off to the utility room to pull the bed linen out of the washing machine and hang it up to dry, counting the pegs one by one as I clip them to the damp cotton sheets. I stand back to inspect my work

252

and enjoy listening to the crisp white geometric shapes flapping in the boisterous breeze.

***

Over the fortnight that follows, Tom and I throw caution to the wind, feeling this urgency to be with each other as much as we can – as though time is running out and our lives depend on it. He has changed as much as me over the summer. An inner strength radiates from him. He's more certain of himself, cuts Kath down when she criticises him, puts her in her place when she's unbearable. Even she has noticed the change, I'm sure. She's more wary around him now, asks his advice as a way of striking up a conversation, rather than just complaining about the odd jobs he needs to do when he gets home from the farm. Any anxiety that I feel about now and the future evaporates when I am with him. We don't talk about what's going to happen after the *vendange*; we just live for the present, secure in our understanding that the future is us.

One morning I come back from the lake and almost collide with her at the entrance to my *gîte*. She says she was looking for some spare batteries. As soon as I enter my bedroom I can tell that she's been nosing around. She's even left some knickers hanging out of my drawers. She wouldn't have found anything. Tom has the letter he wrote to me and I delete my text messages, in case Kath's worked out a way to break into my phone.

Today, while at Bill's, I reveal the extent of Kath's malice to Tom – how she'd convinced my father that Tom had been unfaithful to me.

'I always knew there was something going on,' he says.

'The way he looked at me – especially that time I spoke to him about his plan to take you to Australia.'

'Which was just before our holiday to Turkey?'

'Yes. I didn't tell you because I didn't want to ruin the holiday. I also told your dad that it was your decision to go, not mine, and I wasn't going to be coerced into persuading you to go.'

'You did, though.' I try to keep my tone light. What's the point in trying to push him away now that we've reconciled, even if it is eight years later?

'I did,' he affirms gravely. 'Come here.'

We're outside lounging by the pool. I roll on top of him and push back the hair from his face, his beautiful face.

'I can't say I regret what's happened, Jen, because I can't imagine no Rosa. But, I promise you with all of my heart that we are going to be together very soon. Please believe me.' His breath smells like honey to me. I take my time to linger over his words.

'I believe you, Tom.' My voice is a whisper and I finally understand what it means to trust someone with your life. At this moment, I would hand mine over to him, knowing that he intends to treasure me forever, at whatever cost.

Then I tell him about Kath's visit to her mum over a year ago, and the terrible things Julie had said to her daughter.

His face registers surprise and he turns away to pull a stalk of lavender from the terracotta pot next to us. The air shimmers with scented oil as he rubs the flowers between his fingers. His calm eyes turn to meet mine.

'That makes sense. I just wish she'd told me and we could have talked it through together. Who knows, the outcome might have been different for all of us.'

A feeling of nausea runs through me. Does he mean that things might have worked out between them had she told him? I wasn't expecting that. Surely he means that she could have got help sooner had she been open about the root cause of her depression. I refuse to dwell on what's just been said. We're together now, aren't we? That's what counts.

As we're getting dressed, he reminds me that we need to continue treading lightly with Kath. 'The best way to handle her is to pretend everything is normal. Don't rock the boat or let her know that anything's changed. Then, once you've gone to see your dad in Australia, I'll sort things out with her.'

We still haven't discussed my plans after I've been to Australia. I'm hoping that Tom will ask me to come back to France, then I'll do all I can to find some coaching here. But first he has to deal with Kath. And the thought of that fills me with fear.

**

I feel her eyes boring into me the moment I step into the kitchen and walk to the sink. It's the sense of her silent threats. This nightmare will soon be over. I hope. It's the things she says that take me by surprise regarding events that happened years ago, mulling over them as though she's tasting a new wine. This time the memory is ten years old.

'You know Tom knocked on my door first, don't you Jenny?' she says, while stacking the dishwasher. 'So it wasn't as if I took him from you. He was mine first.'

'Kath, of course I know that. Your name was at the

top of the message, as you'd insisted it should be – alphabetical order of surname as in the school register. We've discussed this so many times.'

'I'm just saying that he was rightfully mine, before he was yours.'

Kath pours too much milk into her cereal bowl and a white stream makes its way along the table. I grab a cloth while Kath continues to crunch her breakfast as if nothing's happened.

Stay calm, Jenny. 'So what time does the *vendange* party start tonight?' I throw the saturated cloth into the sink.

'Sylvie is cooking a pig-roast first, so we need to be there by seven. Rosa's sleeping over in the barn with some of the other children.'

I haven't seen Tom for several days, which has been excruciating, but we're nearly there, I keep reminding myself. With the grapes now in full harvest, he's been up and out of the house by 5 a.m., along with the rest of the village. Spirits are high. Everyone's relieved that the harvest has held up despite the variable weather this year.

I've offered to help Sylvie get the food ready for the evening celebrations. First, Rosa and I drive over to the village winery to take in the full labours of the week. As we arrive, I spot Luc reversing a trailer into the shed. It's filled with crates of claret-coloured grapes still attached to their stalks. Luc waves us over and we join in his whooping as we help empty the crates into a metal machine which Rosa tells me will pull the grapes off the stems to separate them. The activity is very physical and now I wish I'd been more of a part of the picking process. The workers arrive back at the farmhouse just as I'm rinsing some lettuces under the outside tap. They are singing a familiar song, which sounds like 'My Way' in French, arms loosely hung over each other's shoulders, ruddy faces weary yet brimming with excitement for this evening's festivities. Tom is the tallest among them. He looks the most relaxed I've seen him. When we last met at Bill's he told me he's confident about his plan and can finally let himself believe in a better future for all of us, including Rosa. I still have my doubts about how Kath will react to the news that Tom and I are getting back together, but am willing to trust his instincts.

The object of my thoughts pulls up just as the men start to do a conga around the yard, their tanned legs kicking out to the side in unison. Bernard is in front and grabs hold of Kath as soon as she steps out of the car. Normally she would slap him off and refuse to join in, but tonight she's different. She laughs out loud, allows herself to be drawn into the horseplay, her eyes ablaze with... what is it? Lust? Good humour? I can't put my finger on it. Suddenly I feel uneasy.

'Jenny, can you help me?'

Rosa is sawing bread with a knife intended for cutting meat. I race over to the outdoor table to assist her before she chops off a finger, my worries forgotten.

Armelle told me the other week that Eddie has a new girlfriend. She arrives in a swanky black Porsche and is compelled to do the rounds of introductions as I did. Her face is open and friendly, although I can see how awkward it is for her to have to kiss everyone. Difficult to believe that was me once. I look around and it hits me hard, the sudden realisation that I've become part of the local community. Right from the start, they welcomed me with open arms into their tight-knit group. I only hope that I will have a future with them again, once things have settled down.

My reverie is broken by a kiss on the cheek. Kath is positively glowing.

'Penny for them, Jenny?' She reaches over for a piece of bread, tickling Rosa under the arm as she does so.

'Oh you know, just that I'm going to miss everyone when I go.'

'Yes, well don't think about that now. Enjoy this evening first. It might turn out to be full of surprises. Who knows what the future holds.' With that she turns on her heels and walks over to Sylvie, who appears startled to receive such a warm embrace. Bernard wheels over the pig, which has been crackling nicely on the spit, and starts to carve it. Rosa rushes over to help him, oblivious to the fact that this was little Pom-pom the pig who she'd been chasing round the yard several weeks ago. Everyone tucks in heartily, soaking up the copious amounts of alcohol that have already been consumed. I spot Armelle who looks radiant in her pregnancy. She complains that her ankles have swollen to twice their normal size, but only she'd be able to tell the difference. I'm always able to relax when I see her. There's something about her presence that I've always found reassuring. It's that intimacy you find in friendship when you realise that a person would stand by you, protect you, whatever the circumstances. I used to think of Kath in that way once.

Eddie pulls me over to chat to him and Nel, his new girlfriend. They make a striking couple – both very blond and bronzed. She tells me in perfect English that she is a physiotherapist and is hoping to find some work here. Eddie caresses her back as she talks. He takes the opportunity of a small lapse in the conversation to draw me closer.

'Have you seen Kath, Jenny? She is very different today – like a child in front of a Christmas tree, I would say.'

Kath is sitting on Tom's knee, eating hungrily and chatting to some of the other guests. Tom notices us looking over at them and arches an eyebrow. His arms hang loosely to the ground. He turns his palms towards us.

'Tom looks like a man who has a knife in his leg,' says Eddie.

I try not to join in with his and Nel's laughter but he's right. Poor Tom. I wish I could do something for him. He responds to our laughter by tapping Kath's arm and beginning to rise, but this happens so fast that he doesn't manage to save Kath's supper balanced on her lap, which falls on the ground. She laughs off the accident and continues to chat. I'm drawn to the glint of gold coming from Kath's ears. Normally she wears pearl studs, but tonight she has made an effort to dress up. She's wearing a pretty floral long dress and small hooped earrings – just like the ones I saw in that photo the day after I arrived. Earrings that bear a very strong resemblance to the present that Tom gave me years ago to wear to the school prom. They had mysteriously disappeared from my dressing-table at home and I was devastated at the time, looked everywhere for them. I couldn't understand where they'd gone. Kath said I might have accidentally put them in my schoolbag and dropped them when I was taking out my books, but finally I had to accept that they were lost forever. I never told Tom. I was too embarrassed to admit that I'd been so careless with his gift.

I wander over to take a closer look.

'You look gorgeous tonight, Kath. That's a beautiful dress. And those earrings.' I reach out to touch one gently.

'Yes, they're lovely aren't they? One of our Japanese hotel guests gave them to me years ago as a thank you.' She puts her fingers over the earring and draws it away from my curiosity. 'I'm just going to check on Rosa. I'll be back in a moment.'

I watch her move away and realise that it's hopeless to rake up bygones with her. She'd manage to wriggle out of a wormhole if she fell into one.

*****

Night falls and the noise gets more raucous. The children have been ushered to bed so that the adults can party. I can sense everyone's excitement and butterflies soon start to dance around gently in my stomach. A movement behind me makes me turn round and a hand reaches out to grab me and pull me into a dark corner. I am thrust against a face of hard stubble. My mouth reaches up to rub against it.

'Careful Mr Hargreaves, we might give ourselves away.'

'You know, I can't believe we're nearly there, Jen. Freedom wasn't something I'd have allowed myself to think about this time last year.' He squeezes me tightly and I yearn to stay with him for longer. But it's too dangerous. We've come this far. We just need to be patient now.

Bernard and Luc come out of the kitchen carrying a

barrel of beer to take to the barn. Tom steps into the light to help them and I hang back until they have gone, then go into the kitchen to help Sylvie clear up. She waves me away.

'Go and enjoy yourself, Jenny. Tonight is a big celebration for everyone.'

I make my way to the courtyard. There's quite a crowd gathered here. The atmosphere is electric. People are eager for the party to begin. It has been an exhausting few weeks and now they want to let their hair down and have some fun.

Tonight the moon gives us her full attention. She is bulbous and white, casting a brighter than normal glow over the entire farm. The night air is warm and still. I feel slightly on edge, unsure what this *vendange* celebration entails exactly. We have all drunk too much. An underlying feeling of dread settles around my chest and I'm not sure why that is. I still feel as though Tom and I are stumbling into a void, that we've missed something important, some key detail, and a crevasse is going to suddenly appear and swallow us both up. I have a sudden desire to run away, but before I can, an arm grabs hold of me.

'*Viens* Jenny!'

As if sensing my urge to flee, Luc takes my arm and pulls me towards the barn, where two huge stone vats stand waiting for us, both half-filled with swollen purple grapes. He explains that these have been set aside for the celebration and will later become the *vin de maison*, to be consumed by those working or staying at the farm.

Luc peels off his clothes, laughs when he sees my shocked expression, then gestures for me and everyone else to follow suit.

'*Prenez une douche, tout le monde!* Everybody shower!' He sweeps back a dirty nylon curtain to reveal a plastic shower spray and a cracked bar of soap. I giggle nervously.

One by one we quickly get undressed and spray ourselves down. I'm relieved to see that most people are wearing swimsuits. I was worried that I might be the only one.

Luc hands out rubber slippers which we all have to put on so we don't contaminate the grapes, and to protect our feet from the sharp vine stems and tannin stains.

We clamber into the vats. Legs swing. Voices yelp. The mood is merry. I slip as soon as I step down into the deep container and Luc grabs my arm to hold me steady. The sensation under my feet is peculiar, like standing on millions of dead beetles. I half-scream, want to get out and run. I force myself to look down to remind myself that it's only grapes. I laugh out loud at myself and start to relax.

At first, I just hold onto the side, watching the others as they stomp up and down. It's mesmerising. They're like a marching band. Their knees dip down and rise in unison. The squelch and pop of feet on grapes reverberates all around us under the night sky. Soon I understand the rhythm and join in. It's fascinating to look down and watch the plump grapes as they burst open. Exploding juice squirts my legs then trickles down warmly to the bottom of the vat.

Someone puts on some dance music and we modify our rhythm to mimic the faster pace. Linking arms, we shuffle and squelch our feet through the gloopy liquid. Heads are thrown back as the pulsating music sets some people into a trance-like state.

A couple of the seasonal grape pickers are totally inebriated. They laugh hysterically, can contain themselves no longer and fall over into the tar-like mixture. They are hauled up, laughing, now dip-dyed all over in black juice, the whites of their eyes jumping out of their dark faces. I grin and look over to Tom who is bouncing up and down in the other vat, his head bobbing. A wave of euphoria washes over me. The alcohol has kicked in. I feel free, liberated. My chest rises and I lift my head high to the sky to blink up at the stars.

Luc shouts that the job is done and we can all get out. The grapes are now crushed into a thick, dark soupy mixture and it's time to leave it to ferment. We climb out and carry on dancing.

And then Kath comes into the barn with Armelle, arm in arm – an unusual sight. Neither of them has joined in with the grape crushing: Armelle for obvious reasons and Kath said she didn't want to coat herself in the 'vile' liquid. She seems hesitant now, almost unsure of herself. Something bad is on the way, I know. The static starts to rise up from my legs and I can't stop it. She scratches her arm – up and down relentlessly as she scans the place for me between the dancing bodies, and then she smiles. But it isn't a smile. It's a look of victory.

I feel as though I'm watching a film. The actors move around me, the soundtrack plays out loud. I'm the only one on the outside, looking in. Armelle turns to hug Kath and walks over to Luc, pulls him away from the dancing. Somewhere quiet to talk, I can tell. My gaze switches back to Kath. She approaches Tom who's on the far side of the barn and pulls him round to face her. He bends down so she can shout into his ear over the music. I walk towards them slowly, weaving between the dancers towards Kath, the ticking time-bomb. But I don't reach them. Tom stands up straight and runs his hand through his hair wearily. His long arm drops to his side with frustration. He looks over to me. Our eyes connect. He shakes his head and strides out of the barn.

– CHAPTER 25 –

Streaks of rain splatter hard onto the windscreen, making visibility almost impossible. The wipers swish back and forth on full power, like two puppets swinging frantically to a ragtime tune. Their work is futile, however: as soon as they rake away the water, another foggy splash appears. My shoulders are tensed up high, so I take deep breaths, try to sing something happy to distract my sorrow, but it cuts through and a horrible strangling noise fills the void instead. The car shudders into a deep pothole, catching me off-guard. I wrench at the steering wheel sharply, too sharply, and swerve to a stop.

Suddenly, an arm slaps against the window. My high-pitched scream pierces the air, but it's only a tree branch impaled by the wind against the side of the vehicle.

For goodness' sake, Jenny, pull yourself together.

Tears stream down my face, drop off my nose and run down my neck. I had to get away from that place as soon as I could. I woke up at 4 a.m. with a throbbing head and a heavy feeling in my stomach. I made it to the loo just in time to vomit. The thought of seeing Kath again so soon after she announced she was pregnant made me vomit once more before I crept into the main house and took the car keys. I scribbled a note, telling them I had a burning desire to see Carcassonne at sunrise. Who knows if they'll believe me. At this point, I really don't care.

I sit and wait for a let up in the storm, totally immersed in a chamber orchestra of rain: there's no let up. My shaking fingers grapple with the dial to find a station that'll distract me, but the radio mocks me by spouting out a fuzz of white noise instead.

And that's when the realisation finally hits me and I drop my head onto the steering wheel. I've come to the end of the road. The journey I embarked upon more than ten weeks ago has finally derailed. Whatever my purpose was for coming has failed and I now have to accept my fate and leave. Kath's right. She'll always win. Whether it's with me or Tom. Whatever it takes.

Exhausted, I turn the car around and head back, picking my way through the remnants of the now-passing storm. After a blistering hot summer, it's startling to see the devastating impact that autumnal weather can bring. Dustbins are strewn across the road, an early riser out with her Labrador struggles to walk in a straight line, blocked drains are spewing rainwater across the main road.

I drive through the quiet village aimlessly like a somnambulist. Shutters are still closed, even at the *boulangerie*. People have an excuse to sleep in now that they have picked all of the grapes and their bellies are filled with last night's celebratory drink.

I'm not surprised to see that the public car park is empty as I pull into it. The lake looks like the contents of a witch's cauldron: a murky brown liquid, filled with twigs, leaves and other wind-swept debris. I shut off the engine and get out, reaching to wrap the car blanket tightly around me. The cherry tree is now bare: its sodden leaves are spread underneath it like a golden eagle's wing. And soon they'll turn to mulch.

I tiptoe cautiously down the muddy path in my impractical light pumps. The wind has dropped, leaving behind a misty curtain of drizzle. A twig snaps close by. That's when I see him, sitting on one of the boulders. He's holding a fallen branch, breaking it up and throwing bits into the water. He doesn't notice me at first, wrapped up in his thoughts, probably, like me, trying to work out how the hell we ended up like this. When I get closer I see that he's completely drenched. His grey T-shirt clings transparently to his chest, he shakes his head as though trying to rid it of a nest of wriggling snakes.

The squelch of my feet alerts him to my arrival. He comes over and tries to draw me close, but I resist. I have to, for my own sanity.

'Jen, I've been worried sick. Why did you take off like that?'

'Tom, I'm leaving today. Can you take me to the station once I'm packed?' I refuse to look at him. It'll break me.

'Listen, Jen, please don't rush this. Let's wait for the scan to see if she's telling the truth. I know she isn't. She just wants to be in control. She's desperate.'

He reaches out to touch me but I take a step back. I try to keep my voice calm and measured, but it sounds more like a desperate shout.

'Tom! I can't do this anymore. I'm finished here. Rosa needs you more than ever now. You have to try and work things out with Kath, at least for your children's sake.'

'Please, Jen, just let me try to work something out for all of us. Just wait a few days.'

'No, Tom, I can't. I'm sorry, but I've made up my mind. I've got to go.'

I walk away, my pumps now two sodden clodhoppers on my feet. The tears start to stream again but I won't let him see them. I can't.

***

I stand at the hob, frying onions. They spit and sizzle in the hot oil. Perfectly formed golden rings piled haphazardly on top of each other. I'll never challenge Kath about those gold-hooped earrings she was wearing at the *vendange*, but she knows that I know they're mine. How could she have been so dishonest? We spent an entire day searching for them and she knew all along that she had them. What was it that rankled with her? The look of love on my face when Tom gave them to me? The careful way that I handled each twinkling treasure whenever I took them out of the box?

A car door slams. I poke at the onions, which are now almost black and crispy-looking, thanks to my obsessing. I'm sure no one will notice once I've added the tomatoes. I turn up the extractor to blast away the acrid smell.

I've been held prisoner here for the last week. It wasn't my choice to stay, but as soon as I got back to the house after seeing Tom at the lake, I broke out into a cold sweat and fainted on the terrace. Tom shouted my name and came to save me. My knight in shining armour. But he was too late to take me away to our fairytale castle. Instead, he carried me into the house and bellowed for the wicked witch.

The doctor came and told me I had a throat infection

and was suffering from a fever and needed to stay in bed for a couple of days. Kath and Rosa relished playing at nursemaids, taking it in turns to read me stories and feed me soup, while I moved in and out of sleep. Kath said that she hadn't told Rosa about the baby yet, but wanted to wait until she could show her the scan picture. Tom popped his head round the door several times, but Kath wouldn't leave me alone with him. His eyes have lost their sparkle and he's losing weight too. His collarbone juts through his T-shirt and his jeans are beginning to slip over his hips.

The kitchen door shudders open and Kath enters laden with shopping bags. She struggles to close the door with her foot. Her face is flushed. I rush to help her.

'Hey let me take those. You shouldn't be carrying anything heavy.'

She refuses to hand over the shopping bags. 'Nor should you, Jenny. And I wish you weren't leaving so soon either. You've only just got out of bed! And what's that smell? Where's Tom and Rosa? Aren't they back yet?'

'Burnt onions. No, Tom rang to say that Rosa was having a costume fitting for next month's school show.'

'A shame you won't be here to see her.'

I feel my shoulders tense as Kath ambles over to the hob. Her screwed up nose tells me what she really thinks. She twists her head to smirk at me.

'Your dad's going to be pleased to see you, mind you. Hopefully he'll drum some sense into you and persuade you to carry on competing.'

I go back to onion stirring and ignore her.

She turns to her shopping and takes out large rustling bags of crisps and peanuts, one by one, like a magician pulling a string of handkerchiefs out of a top hat.

'Thought I'd stock up on some nibbles for your leaving party.'

'What party?' The penny drops. 'Listen, Kath, it's very sweet of you but I'd rather just leave without a fuss. Anyway, I'm sure to visit again once the baby arrives.'

She opens the fridge door to load small containers into it – olives, bright-red salsa and a multitude of dips. I remember my dinner and switch the kettle on for the couscous.

'Too late, I've already invited everyone round on Friday evening, so you'll just have to grin and bear it, Jenny. You're good at that.'

That 100 per cent smile is plastered over her face. I don't know what it is – the glinting teeth, the tone of her voice or just the way she expects me to accept what she's said with my usual graciousness – that unsettles me first. The kettle is boiling, the steam rising slowly like fog, and that's when 'little Jenny Parker' undergoes a metamorphosis. I don't want a party. The thought of having to be cheerful at what will be more like a wake than a celebration is loathsome. All of that anger, frustration and revulsion starts to swell up inside me like a balloon. I realise my hand is wrapped tightly around the kettle handle and my nails are digging into my palm.

Kath shuffles over to me. 'Oh, Jenny, come on, it'll be fine. You'll be fine.'

I feel her hot breath on my ear, her hand on my back. My spine stiffens from top to bottom, like a line of soldiers preparing for battle, and a sound breaks through the silence – there is a crack, a gasp, and a sharp intake of breath. I look down at my burning hand, back to Kath. Her cheek is red, her bottom lip is trembling.

Kath shakes her head. The mark on her cheek looks angry. 'Jenny, you must be out of your mind.'

'You know it's taken me a long time to work you out, Kath. Years in fact. All those times that I forgave you for your bad behaviour, your jealousy, your lies – don't you dare treat me like an idiot!'

I take a step towards her. She's backed into the corner.

'My father told me what you'd been up to, just before I left Australia. I was willing to give you the benefit of the doubt. I always trusted you, you see. But these last few weeks I've had my eyes wide open and the reality stinks.'

Kath folds her arms, starts to speak. I hold up my palm.

'I can just imagine how you used to sit there in my kitchen, egging my father on to take me away from Tom, how he wasn't good enough for me, how he was unfaithful. How could you possibly lie about that? Then you goaded Tom, encouraged him to release me, telling him I needed to make a success of my swimming career for my dead mother's sake.' I struggle to hold back the tears, but I succeed – somehow. 'But what upsets me more than anything is that you knew that I didn't want to leave the UK. You knew it would break my heart. You even knew that competing didn't mean that much to me, that I only did it for my father. But you carried on twisting and turning the knife until you had everyone on your side.'

'Jenny that's just not fair. I had your best interests at heart.'

'Blow my best interests! If you'd cared about me as a friend, you'd have supported me and persuaded my father to keep me where I was at home. With Tom. With you, even.'

Now Kath's expression begins to harden. She starts advancing towards me. 'I needed to get you away, Jenny. Couldn't you see? All those years that I dedicated myself to you, watching and listening to all of those people sucking up to you. My mum more than anyone. She couldn't get enough of you – and you her.'

'Kath, that's not true. I–'

She thrusts out her arm, rigid as a spear. 'Then when Tom came along and swept you off your feet, you didn't just think I'd stand by and let that happen, did you? You were mine first, not his. But it wasn't supposed to end that way. Your dad messed that up.'

I put a hand out to keep some distance between us. 'What do you mean, I was yours first? So when you couldn't come to Australia you thought you'd take Tom instead?'

Kath looks at me with a glimmer of contempt. 'Of course not. I was going to come to Perth once I'd saved up enough to apply for a working visa. But you weren't interested, were you? You emailed to say you were coming back for *him*. For my mum, too, I expect, seeing as she loved you and she didn't love me. And that's when I knew I had to put a stop to it once and for all.'

She turns her back on me and starts to move towards the kitchen door. I follow her, my face contorted with anger. 'So you did get my email. I knew it. I thought you cared about me Kath? I trusted you.'

'I trusted *you*! You said we would be together forever, remember?' She points at me.

'Kath, we were young.'

'I believed you, Jenny. You broke my heart.'

'So you thought you'd break mine too. Was that it?'

Her mouth twists into a snarl while she considers my words. 'Not really. It just fell into my lap somehow. When Tom dropped into the hotel, it didn't take much to get the lovesick dog into bed after a few drinks. Promised I'd help get you two get back together, but I fell pregnant. And he chose to do the right thing and marry me. You always said he was a man of honour, didn't you?'

'Yes, well not this time.'

We both spin round to see Tom in the hallway, holding a sleeping Rosa in his arms. I think the sight of her kills the anger in me straightaway. He goes into the lounge to put her down.

When he returns, Kath jumps in first with her excuses.

'Listen, Tom, none of what you heard is true,' she says. 'I'm just angry, I don't mean any of it.'

He turns his back on her to deal with the extractor fan. 'Of course it's true. You and me were a one-night stand that went wrong. OK, it worked for a while, but let's face it, we've only stayed together for Rosa's sake. Why don't you admit it?'

He moves to close the hallway door quietly.

Now Kath stands between us both, scratching at her arm. 'Tom, you know that's rubbish. The last few years have often been great. Rosa has simply been the icing on the cake.'

'Bullshit and you know it. Now's the time for us both to grow up and move on.'

'But we're having a baby. You have to stand by me.'

Her hands stroke her belly. I can't see how Tom's going to ignore this fact.

'We're having a baby?' Tom steps towards her. 'I've just come back from Luc's. He's completely beside himself. He finally broke down and confessed. It seems that you two have been having an affair for the past six months and you've told him that the baby is his. So which is it to be, Kath?'

I hear my sharp intake of breath, not quite believing what I am hearing. Yet at the same time, I know it's true. It all makes sense. The affair, Luc and Kath arguing that day. How could I have missed the signs? Kath, though, looks entirely unrepentant. She crosses her arms.

'He said that he wanted to patch things up with Armelle, without a thought for me, so I let him have it. He deserved it.'

'You're unbelievable,' growls Tom. He reaches for a chair and sits down to unlace his trainers.

I'm in the middle of this, but feel on the edge as though I'm watching a play unfold before me. As if hearing my thoughts, Kath turns my way to bring me into the drama.

'It's no different from the two of you going at it behind my back. Don't think I haven't worked out what you two have been up to these past few weeks. And before that, you were wandering around after Tom or any other man who showed an interest like a dog on heat, Jenny. Why do you think I encouraged Scott to come here?'

Before I can reply, Rosa opens the door and walks in yawning, still half asleep.

'What's for dinner, Mummy?'

***

I leave through the back door, jump on the nearest bike and pedal fast towards the lake. There's a truck in the distance, parked on the side of the lane. Its shape looks familiar. I pedal harder. Luc is sitting on the bonnet smoking.

'*Salut!*' He raises his hand and looks down, but not before I notice the tears in his eyes.

I let my bike drop to the ground and move to console him. He allows me to embrace him while his arms remain loose at his sides.

'Listen, Luc, I've just heard about you and Kath – and the baby.'

He looks up, surprised. 'I am frightened to tell Armelle.'

'I think you should tell her in case Kath tells her first. Armelle is a good person and I think she will forgive you eventually if you are truthful.'

'I love her so much.'

'I know, I know.'

'I don't know why I was so stupid.'

As he weeps on my shoulder, I silently wonder what Kath is going to do next.

***

After cycling around in the dark for hours, I turn into *Les Olivades* and creep across the front as quietly as I can. Tom is sitting at the outside table. He gets up and takes my bike from me, propping it against the wall. We clasp each other tight.

'Jen, I'm leaving her, whether she's pregnant or not, so please don't encourage me to stay for Rosa's sake. She won't want to grow up in the middle of mutual antipathy.'

I nod and just hold onto him.

'I can't deny that I'm not concerned about Kath's

weird behaviour, so I won't be able to leave here until I can be sure that Rosa is safe. Tomorrow, I'm going to talk to a solicitor.'

There's nothing more to say. He kisses my hair and I close my eyes and wish hard.

***

I wake up in a sweat. I feel as though I've been tossing and turning all night, fighting demons. The clock shows 03.00. Hours to go. I try to relax back on my pillow, but sense a presence in the room. Looking over to the chair I jump. It's Kath, wrapped in my spare blanket, watching me. I fight to hold back the fright that races through my veins.

'Jesus, what is it?' I sit up fast and turn on the bedside lamp.

'I just wanted to watch you for a while, like I used to when we were young. You still make those gurgling noises in your sleep, you know.' Her face is expressionless.

I lie back, waiting.

The voice that cuts through the silence is neither harsh nor gentle, but I feel it like a lash. 'Why didn't you own up to killing Pilot? I know it was a mistake, but you still did it.'

The fear takes a grip of my heart.

'I don't know what you're talking about. I didn't kill him.' I sit up, bite my lip and lean back on the headboard.

'Come on, Jenny. I know it was an accident, which is why I never said anything. The light-bulb needed changing in the garage. You accidentally mixed rat poison into his food, instead of biscuits, didn't you?'

I feel her eyes on me, waiting for a response. She must be right. I can't deny it. A week after we buried Pilot I went back into the garage to look for the gaffer tape. By then Tom had replaced the bulb and I could clearly see the two bags sitting side by side on the shelf, the dog biscuits and the rat poison. I wondered then if I'd made a terrible mistake, but I was too scared of Tom's reaction to admit it, so I just pushed it to the back of my mind. Pilot was his best friend, after all.

But if Kath didn't kill the dog, then I must have done. I feel the blood draining from my face.

'Why didn't you tell Tom?' I whisper.

She looks at me so calmly. 'Because I'm a good friend, Jenny. You may have marked me for a bad apple, but as I said to you once before, I've always had your best interests at heart.'

I feel a pulse beating in my throat, uncertain what she'll say next. The bed mattress sinks as she sits down next to me.

'And I know you don't believe me, but I didn't kill Mrs Holt. That was an accident. And the reason I encouraged your dad to try and get you to go to Australia in the first place was to get you away from my *mother* who never stopped going on about your bloody amazing achievements.' Her voice is jagged. I sense the root of her anger.

'Oh Kath, not this again.' I bring my knees up to my chest.

'I really hoped that with you gone for a while, she might come to her senses and show me some love. But that never happened. Then I told her that I was planning on leaving Somerset too and do you know what she said?'

Her voice wobbles with emotion. I shake my head.

'"Good riddance!" My own mother. Can you believe it?'

I try to remain untouched, but it's impossible. There's a part of me that feels sorry for Kath. All she ever wanted was to be loved. I can see that so clearly now. I wonder if that's why she's avoided getting too close to her friends here. She's afraid they'll reject her, in the same way that her mum did. Our friendship was different. Two lost souls who found strength together. 'Sole survivors on planet Earth' as we used to say.

If only she knew what kind of friend I really am.

I wish morning were here so that I could throw open the shutters and get rid of the darkness which is seeping through the walls and penetrating the room.

'Let's talk some more in the morning, Kath. We can go for a walk and clear the air.'

'OK.'

I pat her leg to reassure her. She moves closer to me.

'Can I sleep here tonight, Jenny, for old times' sake?'

I nod, turn over and switch out the light. We lie there in the dark, two spoons, side by side, not touching, in silence. It could be another time. We could be eleven years old again. Each with our own set of dreams for the future. Who could have imagined we'd end up here?

– CHAPTER 26 –

The sound of car doors slamming shut rouses me. Kath's already up – she must be taking Rosa to her ballet rehearsal. I remember her saying that it was an early start as they were running through the first act. I slide out of bed and reach for my robe on the back of the door. Perhaps I can surprise Tom and climb into bed with him, if he's having a lie-in.

In the house, it looks as though someone's been having a food fight. Cupboard doors are open, there are tealeaves scattered all over the worktop, a milk carton lies on its side. The pestle and mortar is out on the draining board. Then I see the empty packet discarded in the sink. Kath's medication. A thud upstairs tells me that something's wrong.

'Tom?' I run up the stairs two at a time, into Kath and Tom's bedroom. 'Tom, where are you?'

I race to the bathroom. He's half collapsed over the toilet bowl, his fingers forcing their way down his throat. He retches and vomits into the bowl.

'Shit, Tom, what's happened? What's going on?'

His eyelids are half-closed and his body is crumpled up on the floor.

'Come on, let's get you in the shower.'

It takes all of my strength, but I manage to put him under the shower head and turn it on. He drinks readily, coughs and almost chokes on the spray.

'I think she must have put something in my tea,' he says, leaning on me.

'Are you sure it's not food poisoning?'

He shakes his head. 'I feel... chemically poisoned, like somebody's drugged me.'

'Her meds are downstairs. The packet's empty, though.'

I push his hair back off his face and study his face.

'She must have crushed her pills into my tea.' He wipes water from his eyes. 'She must really hate me.'

'How much did you drink?'

'Just a couple of sips. I knew it didn't taste right.' He struggles to stand up, so I prop him up and walk him to the bedroom.

'Tom, I'm going to call an ambulance.'

'No, I'll manage. We need to find out where she's gone. She'll have taken Rosa. That's the point. We need to find them.'

I try to put myself in Kath's head. She woke up this morning and saw me lying there asleep. Something made her decide to kill Tom – or at least try to harm him – and then what? Perhaps she has just taken Rosa to ballet and then she's going to come back for me. But does she intend to hurt me? I start pacing up and down the room, trying to work it through.

'Why the hell did I say those things to her last night?' he says. 'I knew she was unstable. It's all been building up to this. I should have made moves to protect Rosa long before I had it out with Kath. I'm a fool.'

'Listen, Tom, I'm to blame if anyone. I just couldn't hold it in any longer and it all came pouring out of me like some sort of volcanic explosion.'

A ringing breaks the silence. It's a phone. My phone. I run downstairs to the kitchen and grab it from the sideboard, scared it's going to ring off.

'Hello! Kath, is that you?'

I walk back upstairs to be close to Tom.

'Where are you, Jenny?' says Kath.

I try to keep my voice level. 'Still in bed, why?'

'Rosa and I are waiting for you at the lake. We're ready for our road trip.'

I put my fingers to my lips. Tom nods from the bed, as he struggles to prop himself up.

'OK,' I tell her casually, trying to hide my fear from Tom. 'Just give me five minutes and I'll be there.' I hang up.

'And?' His eyes look wild.

'She's at the lake with Rosa.'

His eyes widen in horror. 'She might have got hold of one of the farm's rifles.'

'Tom she won't hurt me, I'm sure of it. She just wants me to go and reassure her that everything is fine. I don't know what she intended to do by giving you her medication – if she did. We don't know that for sure yet.'

Tom gets to his feet and lets me lead him downstairs, leaning on the wall for extra support. 'I'll follow on my bike and stay hidden. I've got to be sure Rosa is safe. That's the most important thing.'

'Here, have a sugar hit.' I throw him a cereal bar.

I make my way to the truck. Tom's legs have started to come back to life as adrenalin kicks in and he follows me out unsteadily.

'Just be careful,' he says. 'And don't let her fool you.'

I nod and climb into the truck. No longer will I trust that woman, whatever she throws at me. After last night's revelation, I truly thought that we were going to be able to work through this.

The two-kilometre drive to the lake feels like the longest journey of my life. My throat feels tight and my stomach is jittering. I almost have a head-on collision with a tractor but manage to pull over just in time to let it pass. I turn into the lake car park but can't see Kath's car anywhere. Then my phone rings next to me on the passenger seat. I turn off the engine and pick it up.

'Jenny, I need you to tell me that you're coming with us,' says Kath immediately.

I look around the lake. It's deserted.

'Kath, where are you? Of course I'm coming. I'm here, aren't I?'

'I woke up this morning and looked at your beautiful, peaceful face. And I realised what I needed to do. I had to get rid of Tom,' she says mechanically. 'The only way we can have a future, you, me and Rosa, is if he's gone.'

'Of course you're right, Kath. You, me, Rosa and your baby on our road trip. Best friends forever. Remember?'

I look round frantically, and suddenly see her car appear on the opposite side of the lake – the very deep part, which is out of bounds to swimmers. A child in the passenger seat is waving at me. Kath gets out and leans against her car door. There's no way to get to her quickly. I'd have to drive back through the village and take the main road to loop back. Or swim. But there's no time.

'Is that Rosa with you?'

Kath ignores the question. 'When you said you were

coming to visit, I genuinely hoped that it really was me you wanted to see. But as soon as you saw Tom, I knew.'

I know she's looking at me from the other side of the lake, her free hand waving around as she speaks. How the hell am I going to get her to calm down?

'Kath, please come over here and let's talk face to face. Or shall I swim over to you? What about Rosa? And your baby, we have to think about him or her, don't we?'

'There is no baby,' she says in a monotone. 'I was lying.'

At that moment there's a rustle behind me and Tom appears. Shit. She'll see him.

'What's he doing here? I trusted you, Jenny.'

Kath takes the phone away from her mouth and watches us for a few moments. I have a strange sense of time standing still and then stretching, getting longer and longer. Without warning, Kath throws her phone into the lake.

'What's she doing? What the bloody hell is going on?' says Tom.

Slowly, Kath makes her way back to her car. Tom and I start hollering at her, watching in despair as she starts up the engine and Rosa waves at us. I feel hope when I see she is reversing the car all the way back to the very end of the lane.

'She's coming over to us,' I tell Tom, but he shakes his head and gets on his bike.

And then it clicks. I know exactly what she's about to do, but it's already too late to do anything about it.

Her engine starts to roar loudly, and at great speed she suddenly launches it forward towards the lake. The car dives off the edge, into the water. It falters and nose dives, hits the surface with a huge smack, big gurgles of water churning all around it.

'Kath! Rosa!' I hear myself scream.

I seem to be rooted to the spot in shock, my hands on my head. This cannot be real. Tom shakes me out of my stupor by diving into the water. I come to my senses and follow him, soon outflanking him as I swim the hardest I've ever swum in my life.

I get to the scene first. The car is beginning to sink. Taking a deep breath I dive under and swim down. I catch sight of Rosa sitting in the car just staring out at me, crying. There's still air in the car and she can breathe. I motion for her to undo her seatbelt and wind down her window by hand. She doesn't move. Then she sees Tom behind me and that makes her react. I've run out of air, so quickly resurface and take a few big gulps before diving down again. Now Rosa has wound the window halfway down and carries on turning the handle. Her face bobs in and out of the rising water, but I can see she's determined. She's her mother's daughter in so many ways. I swim to the front of the car and there is Kath in the driver's seat with her eyes shut. Her body is submerged already and her door refuses to budge. I turn to see Tom dragging Rosa out through the half-open window, so I help them up to the surface.

All three of us splutter and gasp for air when we get to the top. Rosa starts to panic and flail her arms around.

'Where's Mummy?'

'Tom, take her back to shore,' I order, and dive down once more.

The car is totally submerged now and is sinking at an angle. The water is so deep here that there isn't much time before the car is going to disappear out of sight. I test Kath's door. The pressure inside must have equalised as the water level has risen inside the car, and it opens. Kath isn't conscious, although her arms are gracefully bobbing about in the water. She's strapped in but luckily the belt releases when I press down on it. I drag Kath out. She is a dead weight. My lungs are burning. I kick upwards dragging one of her arms – still she doesn't move. We reach the surface and the sudden exposure to air seems to revive her. She gasps frantically to breathe in as much air as she has lost.

'Kath come on, lie still and let me get you out of here.'

I'm struggling to hold her upright. I can see Tom on the bank leaning over Rosa, who is coughing hard.

Still she says nothing. Then all of a sudden, without even a glance at me, she pulls me hard, down beneath the lake surface. Down further and further away from life, away from my future. I battle to break hold of her grasp but she clings on tight. This is not going to happen. I haven't come all of this way to let her take me down with her. I want to live. I want my freedom. I have to get away from her.

So I fight and wriggle with all my might but now she grabs both of my legs as I try to swim away. I punch down at her head but the water pressure gives me no strength. Then I force a foot down onto one of her hands, urging her to release me. Finally, I free up one leg and I know that this is my last chance. I feel dizzy, my lungs ache, won't hold out much longer. I summon one final kick out of my weary legs and manage to break away from her grip, while her fingers frantically try to grasp me again.

Too late.

I swim away, up towards the surface, leaving Kath to make her own choice: life or death.

– CHAPTER 27 –

The plane ascends slowly, a big bird straining to gain height. I look at the beautiful coastline below, picking out the geographical features of this diverse region that I will soon be calling home: the crazy paving of the Camargue and its marshland; the straight narrow channel of the Canal du Midi perpendicular to the coast, almost nudging into it; the Mediterranean banded in different stripes of blue, turquoise and green; and the one blot on the landscape, the wind turbines, like an army of aliens from another planet.

Even though I'm returning to France in four weeks, the separation already feels almost impossible to bear after all we've been through this past month. It'll be good for Tom and Rosa to spend time alone together, to try and readjust, while I'm in London and they're sorting through Kath's affairs. It'll also give Tom the space to tell his friends and colleagues about us. There are sure to be a few raised eyebrows. However, Tom assures me that his only concern is that Rosa is happy. He's right. Of course, Armelle and Luc know already, and I'm sure Eddie and even Sylvie have an inkling, so it will just bring things out into the open, and settle any overhanging suspicions, so that we can all begin to move on.

We've had what's felt like an army of visitors at *Les Olivades* these past few weeks. Kath's family came over as soon as they heard the news and we decided to press ahead with a memorial service as quickly as we could. We've been told it could take time before the water gives up Kath's body. She deliberately chose the deep side of the lake because she knew it would be near impossible to save her and Rosa. A part of me quietly admires her for the strength of character she showed in throwing herself into the thing she was most afraid of – water. Fortunately, in that spur of the moment decision, she under-estimated the determination of her own daughter to get out of the car.

Kath's mother, Julie, stayed on for a few days longer than the rest of her family.

'So how were things with you and Kath, Jenny, after all this time? I have to say, I've always admired you. Kath can't have been an easy friend. I know she wasn't an easy daughter.'

She turned her head away so I couldn't see her tears as we sat outside at the back of the house, watching Rosa on the swing.

'Actually, It was good to spend time with her again, in spite of everything that happened. I just wish I could have saved her.' My eyes well up.

'Jenny, you were a good friend to Kath, so don't you beat yourself up about that.' She pulled me close for a hug. 'And I just want to say thank you for thinking of me over all those years and sending me Mother's Day cards. That meant a lot. Kath never sent me a single one.'

Julie withdrew from me and squinted at Rosa in the autumnal sun, the softness gone in an instant. Like mother, like daughter perhaps.

'But you were always so good to me.' I smiled at Julie. 'And I'm glad you never told Kath – about the cards, I mean. She wouldn't have understood.'

Rosa shouted at us at that point, so we stood up to watch her with the 100 per cent smiles we'd learned to master so well over the years.

'Rosa is a wonderful child. She has all of Kath's best bits – her sense of spirit and adventure, her wilfulness and curiosity. I'll constantly remind her of that. There was a lot to be proud of in her mother.'

'Thank you,' says Julie softly, and I realised then that I'll never really know what happened between them.

My main hope is that the events of that fateful day will become a blur for Rosa. She asked Tom if her mum tried to kill her. He said Kath accidentally went forward instead of reversing out of the lane at the lake. She's accepted that story, but I wonder if she will work out the truth for herself one day. Of course, she never will know the whole truth. No one will. No one except me.

You see, something else happened in the lake. At least I think it did, although I'm starting to doubt my own version of events. The lack of air in my lungs sent me into a dreamlike state, so that when I finally reached the shore I felt as though I'd been moving between life and death myself. I'm certain that I plunged back down into the lake to try and rescue Kath. At that point, Tom was swimming back to shore with Rosa. And, as I said before, Kath dragged me down into the bowels of the lake. Her strength was extraordinary. She pulled and pulled me down among the waving reeds towards darkness and death. I struggled and fought my way out and broke my way to the surface. Kath didn't follow me.

That's where the account I gave the police parts company with the truth.

I treaded water for what felt like ages, fighting to get my breath back, wondering where she was. I was worried, I was confused, I was so angry. I dived back down and that's when I saw her. Somehow she had become trapped in the reeds. Her foot had become tangled up in them and she was struggling to free herself. She reached out to me to save her. I swam down to her foot to try and release it. That's when she grabbed hold of my hair, pulled on it as if to say, 'Whatever happens to me, you're coming too.'

And that's when I made my decision. She was going to hold onto me like this forever, wasn't she? She was never going to let me be free. And most of all, she'd never let me have Tom. I would spend the rest of my life looking over my shoulder, wondering if she was watching me, waiting to hatch a new plan. That's when I pulled my hair forcefully out of her grasp. She clung on very hard, and some of it came away at the roots and remained in her hand, but I didn't care. I kicked up towards the surface. Away from her. Towards a future with Tom and Rosa. A future that didn't include her.

No, I didn't leave Kath to make a choice. I made a choice on her behalf: life or death. And I chose death.

– POSTSCRIPT –

Two months later

After everything that's happened these past few months, Tom hasn't noticed that his daughter has shot up several centimetres and desperately needs some new garments that don't look as though they've shrunk in the wash. Now, as we sort through Rosa's clothes, making a list of all the items she's outgrown, dancing about in front of me – tall and slender like a sunflower with her long curtain of dark hair, sun-kissed at the ends – Rosa struggles to push her head through her gym top.

'You look like a headless monster.'

I tickle her under the arms, which are trapped by the fabric. She collapses to the floor wriggling and giggling. It's so great to see her enjoying life. Sometimes she forgets all about her mum for a few minutes or even hours at a time. That's when she smiles.

Tom's been working at the farm this week, trimming back the vines and ploughing the soil to cover and protect them from the fierce winter cold, which will soon arrive. He's finished his novel and the manuscript is sitting with his agent, bound and ready to send out to publishers. The only blot on the horizon is Kath.

A team of divers came to the lake last month to try

and retrieve her body, but the water was too murky and deep for them to get any proper visibility. They told Tom that her corpse should float to the surface with time, once enough gas builds up in the body to make it buoyant, but Tom is impatient for closure. I too feel a strong need to put things to rest. To put Kath to rest.

Finally, today, the authorities are returning with more equipment – an electronic device that should be able to find Kath via soundwaves, and some sort of towing apparatus to pull out the car, which, they say, might have pinned Kath's body to the lake bed. Tom has gone to watch the operation.

'I need to see her for myself – to be sure. I know it won't be a pretty sight, Jen, but it will mean that we can be at peace. All of us.'

We still haven't told Rosa about our relationship. I want to wait until we've buried Kath. I've moved back into my old room and Tom creeps into my bed every night as soon as Rosa's fallen asleep. We've nearly been caught out a few times when she's woken up crying in the middle of the night, convinced that she's seen Kath standing over her bed.

The afternoon darkens early and a bitter wind begins to blow outside, sending clouds tearing across the sky. Rosa and I had planned to play hide and seek in the garden, but we decide to play indoors instead. She runs upstairs while I start counting, periodically glancing out of the window for Tom, hoping that everything will be resolved very soon.

I realise that I've already gone way past fifty counts and make my way upstairs to look for Rosa.

'Coming, ready or not!' I shout.

I can hear her moving around in her bedroom, but take my time looking in all of the other rooms, to make her believe that I'm at a loss to find her.

Something's banging outside. Must be a door blowing about on its hinges. I run downstairs and out through the kitchen, surprised by the force of the windstorm that's brewing. There's an ominous greyness in the sky. The chill in the air bites at my face.

The banging is coming from one of the *gîtes*. Tom must have gone in there this morning to retrieve his ladder. I stick my head into the *gîte's* living area to check that all's well. Everything looks fine.

There's a rumble of thunder above.

'Jenny!'

Rosa is screaming.

I slam the *gîte* door shut and run back to the house. Rosa is waiting for me in the kitchen, her expression distraught.

'Where did you go, Jenny? I was hiding under my bed waiting for you to find me and then I saw a moving shadow. I thought it was you but when I came out it was gone. I called and called and you didn't come. Then I got scared.' She winds her arms closely round my legs.

'Sorry, sweetie, but a door was banging away outside, and it's about to pour with rain I think. You go and hide and I'll start counting again.'

I can feel Rosa relax in my arms. I pat her back and she gives me a smile. 'OK, Jenny. You can start counting!'

She runs away into the living room. I walk upstairs into my bedroom and begin counting again while I'm putting away some of my clothes.

I stop abruptly.

There's a box in the middle of my dressing-table. A blue velvet box with the familiar jewellers' logo embossed in gold on the lid. A box once given to me by Tom. *My earrings.*

Panic starts to rise in my throat. I move towards the box and open the lid. They sit nestled in the soft cushion, glinting at me like a warning.

How the hell did they get here?

My phone rings. Tom.

'Hello, Jen?'

'Hello?' I can barely reply, my mouth is so dry.

'Jen? Are you all right? Listen, it's not great news I'm afraid. We've got the car, pulled it out, but there was no sign of Kath nearby. Her body's disappeared. She's gone.'

There's a sound outside. The engine of a car, revving away.

'Is Rosa OK, Jen?' says Tom, as if reading my mind. 'Can I talk to her?'

Rosa.

I look to the window, but see nothing outside except a grey rain starting to hammer on the glass.

'Rosa! Come out, wherever you are, Daddy wants to speak to you.'

I run downstairs two steps at a time, clinging onto the phone, frantic now, running from one room to another.

'Rosa, where are you?'

The back door swings open and the wind tears past me into the house. I can still make out the sound of a car engine, but now it's moving away down the lane.

The *gîte* door starts up again, banging on its hinges. But I know I shut it.

There's a piercing scream.

Mine.

I run out into the rain as the sound of the engine gets fainter and fainter, and I sprint as fast as I can. Until I know it's too late.

– ACKNOWLEDGEMENTS –

I first discovered the South of France as a teenager. My best friend, Kate, and I took the Magic Bus to St Tropez and found seasonal jobs selling sarongs on the beach. We had a summer filled with so many adventures that I have since held this part of the world close to my heart. The Languedoc (now part of L'Occitanie) is a beautiful region of southern France and I never tire of driving along its narrow roads, passing through picturesque villages set amongst vineyards.

For me, this story is about the power of friendship and I would like to salute all of my friends who inspired me and urged me to write, including those who read my manuscript at its early stages. Love and thanks to Kate (best friends forever!), Rachel, Sophie, Clara, Karen, Suzanne, Tracy, Aimi and Gill, plus my mum and dad who gave me the memories that I drew upon to write about – huddling round the TV as a child to watch the Olympic Games, a love of France and endless days spent at the outdoor swimming pool in Somerset, where I grew up.

Many thanks to the amazing editing and publishing team at RedDoor who believed in me and my story. And, most of all, my love to John, Cora, Isaac and Lucas who put up with me writing at the kitchen table most weekends while trying to keep an eye on the dinner.

Although I have tried to keep the story as real as possible, all mistakes, intentional or not, are my own.

– ABOUT THE AUTHOR –

Since completing a degree in French, *Jo Baldwin* has spent a large proportion of her life in France, first in Paris where she worked in magazine publishing, and later in the Languedoc where she has a holiday home. Jo now lives in Oxford with her husband and three children and works in educational publishing.

Find out more about
RedDoor Publishing and
sign up to our newsletter
to hear about our latest
releases, **author** events,
exciting **competitions**
and more at

reddoorpublishing.com

YOU CAN ALSO FOLLOW US:

  @RedDoorBooks

  RedDoorPublishing

  @RedDoorBooks